I0645903

A CONFLICT
OF INTEREST

By the Author

View from the Top

A Conflict of Interest

Visit us at www.boldstrokesbooks.com

A CONFLICT OF INTEREST

by

Morgan Adams

2025

A CONFLICT OF INTEREST

© 2025 By Morgan Adams. All Rights Reserved.

ISBN 13: 978-1-63679-870-7

This Trade Paperback Original Is Published By
Bold Strokes Books, Inc.
P.O. Box 249
Valley Falls, NY 12185

First Edition: June 2025

This is a work of fiction. Names, characters, places, and incidents are the product of the author's imagination or are used fictitiously. Any resemblance to actual persons, living or dead, business establishments, events, or locales is entirely coincidental.

This book, or parts thereof, may not be reproduced in any form without permission.

Credits

Editors: Jenny Harmon and Stacia Seaman
Production Design: Stacia Seaman
Cover Design by Tammy Seidick

Acknowledgments

Thank you to my amazing wife, who is my dearest friend, forevermore. I would be nowhere in this life without her. Thank you to my biggest fan, Roshine. Thank you to my loyal Instagram followers who have become my virtual pen pals: Cass, Heather, Eleni, Victoria, Cat, Lau, Nori, Sarah, Armi, and so many more. Thank you to everyone who has been with me since my first book, *View from the Top*. Thank you to my amazing editor, Jennifer Harmon, who provided so much essential insight and advice for this book. Thank you to Sandy Lowe, Ruth Sternglantz, and the entire Bold Strokes Books team for allowing our voices to be heard. Thank you to everyone who continues to support me on this journey as an author. I hope to keep providing you with sapphic entertainment and happily ever afters for years to come!

To my wife, who supports me in all that I do.

CHAPTER ONE

A na Mendez opened the email within seconds of its arrival. "Firm-Wide Announcement," the subject line read. The sender, Frank Bauman, was the CEO of the law firm where she worked, so she knew it must be important.

> *Byron & Browning congratulates Simon Bellinger on becoming a new managing partner at the New York City office. Simon has been with the firm for the last ten years. During that time he has...*

Ana stopped reading. She didn't need to review the accolades of another white, male attorney who had just wined and dined his way to the top. Besides, everyone knew Simon was next in line to make partner, even though he was a subpar attorney at best. He played golf with two judges and was godfather to one of the other managing partners' children. What she cared about was what the email *didn't* say. If Simon was now a managing partner, that meant...

She leaned out of her small, dark internal office and peeked at the row of offices that lined the windows to the unobstructed view of the Manhattan skyline.

There's an empty of counsel position.

Ana had been working her ass off ever since she started as a junior associate at Byron & Browning over five years ago. She thought for sure she'd have this place whipped as quickly as she had Con Law back in law school. Alas, the good old boys' club was alive and well at Byron & Browning, even in a city as progressive as New York. Year after year, Ana had watched her less experienced and less intelligent male colleagues get promoted around her.

That's why last year she had decided to become a mentor. Taking on a leadership role would certainly get her noticed, right? Wrong. All it did was get her more work, more responsibility, and absolutely no additional pay. Oh, and a little heartbreak for good measure, when she inadvertently developed a major crush on one of her mentees, a fresh out of law school junior associate, who proceeded to reject her advances and throw her over for one of the managing partners. But that was a story for another day.

Ana wouldn't be overlooked again. Not this time. This time she had the ace up her sleeve. There was an open of counsel position and Ana knew just how she was going to get it.

This will make them proud.

She thought of her family back home, or more specifically her mother. No matter how far Ana seemed to climb in her career, it was never enough to get a "well done" or a "good job" from that woman. She had graduated top of her class at Columbia Law School, a school which she had attended on a full academic ride, mind you, and still all she heard at graduation was a "ready for the real world now, mija?"

Maybe it was her mother's stubbornness still clinging to her Cuban roots. She came from the old "I walked uphill to school both ways with no shoes. You kids don't know how lucky you have it here in America" way of living. Thank God her family lived all the way in Miami while Ana was safe here in Manhattan.

She opened a new tab on her screen and clicked to the file that read, "*Estate of Mark Solomon v. Mount Sinai Hospital, et al.*"

This was the one. This was the case that was going to get her that promotion at last.

Byron & Browning was, for all intents and purposes, a civil defense firm. Situated on the top floors of a high rise in Midtown, it was one of the most elite, selective, and demanding firms in the country. Ana remembered her first time walking through the double glass doors, the embossed "B&B" parting as she had pushed her way inside. Back then, she thought this was the place where her dreams would come true. But that was five years ago. She was fresh out of law school at Columbia and the world was her oyster. Or so she had thought. Ana had since learned that Byron & Browning was where dreams went to die and hours turned to years in the blink of an eye. She typically spent her days, and often nights, reviewing construction contracts, sending letters filled with case law and legalese to opposing parties, or defending landowners and other professionals who had been accused of not keeping their property in a safe condition or not designing a building up to code.

But when one of the insurance adjusters you work with tells you that a close family friend died on the operating room table during what should have been a routine cardiac procedure, you magically become a plaintiff's medical malpractice attorney overnight. And so that is how Ana had come to find herself representing the estate of Mark Solomon.

The case wasn't overly complicated. Mark Solomon had been fifty-six years old when he went in for a cardiac ablation at Mount Sinai Hospital and ended up dead on the operating table. He left behind a wife, three children, a massive estate out in the Hamptons, and a summer home in Naples, Italy. What had gone wrong? Well, that was Ana's job to find out. She had spent the last two years meeting with experts, deposing almost every person who had been involved in the surgery and doing research on the procedure, and the best she had been able to come up with was that the operating surgeon, Dr. Joseph Schumacher, had possibly been negligent in his actions. A vague and nondescript answer to account for a man's death.

Negligent was fine—it would technically meet her burden of proof—but negligent didn't answer all of the questions Ana still had about the case. Negligent wouldn't sway a jury to award millions of dollars to a grieving widow who was already richer than God. She needed a finite reason for this man's death. How could a doctor make such a horrendous mistake? There was more to the story, she knew it. Her gut had been telling her so for years. But so far everyone had essentially testified the same way.

"There was nothing unusual about the procedure. The vitals were good. The doctor followed the standard of care." Blah, blah, blah. Ana knew coached testimony when she heard it.

But she only had one deposition left, and it was a non-party doctor who was a surgical resident at the time of the operation. It was pretty unlikely he or she even remembered much about the case, let alone something that could help Ana win the big money she would be asking for from the jury. To make matters worse, her boss had decided to file the lawsuit out on Long Island, where Mr. Solomon had lived. That was bad for Ana. Long Island liked their doctors and hated people who sued them. She knew she would have a hard time making her case before a jury of Dr. Schumacher's peers.

If she could pull this off, if she could win this trial or even get a big settlement from it, she knew it would be her golden ticket to advancing her career.

"Knock knock," a low voice said at her door. Stella Torres, Ana's self-declared work wife, stuck her head inside.

Ana waved her in quickly. "Oh my God, did you hear about Simon making partner?"

Stella came fully into the office and took a seat across from Ana's desk, propping one foot up on the corner and leaning back. She wore a navy blue three-piece suit and tie. A tapered fade traced the top part of her ears where it ran into a controlled mess of wavy black curls, and her brown leather oxford shoes matched the exact brown shade of her belt. Ana always said that Stella was the most handsome person in the firm, bar none, and Stella always not-so-humbly agreed.

"Um, duh, why do you think I came in here so fast?"

"Who do you think is in line for the open of counsel spot?" Ana tapped her chin.

Stella let out a hearty laugh. "Oh please, don't you mean, who's your competition?"

Ana blushed. She had been friends with Stella since Stella had started working at Byron & Browning about two years ago. They took a stab at dating once, but like so many queer relationships, ended up mutually friend-zoning one another after a few dates. She was a senior associate, like Ana, but Stella had a much longer way to go before promotion since her experience before coming to the firm was in mergers and acquisitions, not civil litigation. Stella didn't seem to mind. She had no ambition to become a partner like Ana. She was content to collect her paycheck and go home at a somewhat human hour every night. Life, according to Stella, didn't revolve around work—a concept that remained foreign to Ana.

"You know me too well," Ana remarked with a smile.

Stella shook her head, and her short hair tossed back and forth. "Oh, I know you *way* too well." Stella flashed a quick wink across the table. "In the biblical sense."

"All right, all right, but seriously, who do you think they're considering?"

Stella leaned forward, pretending to contemplate the question. "Hmm…I think we should probably talk about it over drinks tonight." She kept her face serious and pensive.

Ana started to open her mouth but was immediately cut off.

"Oh, come on, workaholic. It's Pride month! At least come to

Cubby with me? Tiana will be there. I'm just saying." Stella wiggled her dark, thick eyebrows.

Ana rolled her eyes. Stella's favorite pastime, when she wasn't trying to find herself a new beautiful woman to hook up with, was trying to find Ana new, beautiful women to hook up with.

"I don't need help hooking up, thank you very much," Ana said, crossing her arms.

"I know you don't, that's the craziest part. You're like, so good at flirting when you put your mind to it. So why you choose to spend your nights wasting away in this dark little office is beyond me."

Ana tilted her head, considering the offer. "I am a pretty good flirt, aren't I?"

Stella nodded. "Hey, you got me into bed."

"Oh please, like *that* was a challenge."

Stella bellowed a laugh and feigned offense. "Excuse me, I'll have you know I have a very refined palate when it comes to women."

"Oh sure, if by *refined* you mean you like women. Any women. Anywhere. Any time."

"I am offended that you think so little of me, Ms. Mendez."

Ana rolled her eyes and quickly clicked around on her calendar. She actually didn't have any more meetings or calls for the rest of the day. Maybe a drink and some harmless flirting with strangers would do her good. It had been a while since she got laid, and it might be nice to loosen some of that tension before her final deposition in the *Solomon* case on Monday.

"Fine, one drink. But I'm not traipsing all the way down to the Village for it. We can grab one here, at the Junction."

"The Junction?" Stella shrieked. "God, could you pick a more hetero bar? Gag. Okay fine, I will make this sacrifice for you. But it better be a very strong drink." Stella removed her legs from the desk and stood up. "See you at six?"

Ana nodded and returned her attention to her computer. She had received fourteen emails in the few minutes Stella had been in there, all of which required her immediate attention before she could leave for the day.

"Better make it seven." Ana grimaced.

Stella gave her a quick salute and walked away.

Ana really hoped that her medical malpractice case panned out well. She was sick of looking at white walls for twelve hours a day.

CHAPTER TWO

Rachel Cohen checked her phone for the tenth time that hour. She couldn't help it. She wasn't on call, but she wanted to check in and see how her patient from Tuesday's surgery was doing. She scanned the notes quickly on the online portal and breathed easily as she glanced over the latest note from the rounding hospitalist.

> *Pt is day 3 post op. Sutures healing well, is now on full solid, low-cal diet. Is asking for chocolate pudding.*

Rachel smiled at the last part. She could picture Mr. Wentz now, smiling and happy, asking for pudding and ice cream and candy. Some men never grew up, even when they had a quadruple bypass and the surgeon told them they should be eating salads instead of sugar.

She set down her phone, feeling calmer. She couldn't help but be an overly caring surgeon. She had seen firsthand what happened when a surgeon made a mistake. When something went wrong on the operating room table. When surgeons didn't take responsibility for their own actions. And that memory haunted her more now than ever.

She pulled the drink closer to her. She had no idea how she had ended up in Midtown of all places on a Friday night. After her shift ended, she just couldn't face going home to her empty apartment, even with her cat waiting for her. Not with Monday looming over her. Not with what she was going to have to *do* on Monday.

So, after leaving a long day of work at Mount Sinai Hospital, Rachel had hopped on the 6 train at 96th Street and headed south before getting off at 33rd Street and wandering around. She came across this bar, the Junction, on a whim and decided she could use a drink.

"Another?" the bartender asked kindly.

She looked down at her nearly empty martini glass. She really shouldn't. She wanted to be up early to go for a long run in the morning. The weather was supposed to be nice, and nothing cleared her head quite like a long run around Central Park with the sun shining down on her. Maybe she could even swing by her parents' house and bring her mother some fresh challah from Silver Moon Bakery at 105th Street.

"Next one's on me," a low voice rumbled over Rachel's shoulder. A tall, blond-haired, blue-eyed man loomed over her, a charming smile plastered across his flawless face.

"Name's Preston. I work—"

"Let me guess," Rachel said, slowly eyeing the man up and down. "You work in finance?"

The man's smile faded. "Well…yeah, actually I do."

Rachel continued. "And you stopped here on your way home from work? You almost never come to places like this alone, so it must have been fate that you saw me sitting here all alone too, right?"

His smile was now completely gone, and the sound of snickers came from a table full of similarly dressed men seated across the room. Finance clones, from the looks of it.

"And let me take another guess and say that those gentlemen laughing at your expense are your colleagues? I bet it went something like this, 'Yo, you see that redhead over there at the bar? You think the carpet matches the drapes?'"

The man's face was now bent into an angry frown, and his face grew red.

"Fuck you," he said under his breath as he turned away. His friends hooted and laughed at him as he slunk back to the table in defeat.

"No thanks, you're not my type," Rachel said as she raised her glass to his friends, who waved and applauded her from across the room.

She returned her attention to the bartender, who was wiping down the counter, laughing beneath his breath.

Rachel tossed back the last remains of the martini and set the glass gently on the bar. She hated coming to places like this for that exact reason. There was always a Preston. Always some slimy straight man assuming that just because she was wearing a dress and had long hair, she must be straight. Even when she went to gay bars, she still sometimes got accused of being queer bait. Short of her fucking a girl right there on the bar, she was pretty sure no one would believe she was gay at first glance. The tortured fate of a femme lipstick lesbian living in Manhattan.

Rachel shook her head and reached for her wallet. She didn't know why she had even come here. It wasn't distracting her from Monday and it wasn't making her feel any better. She needed to get home and rest so she could go on her run in the morning. She needed to—

"Hi," a soft voice said, barely louder than a whisper.

Rachel turned her attention to her right to take in who owned the sultry voice. Her glare was met by a woman with long, thick, wavy black hair and dark, olive skin. Her eyes were brown with flecks of gold in them. Beneath a set of full red lips was a body composed of soft curves that made Rachel's eyes linger a little longer than what was probably acceptable. Her royal blue dress had a slim black belt around the waist, and her black velvet pumps brought her ample chest directly to Rachel's eyeline.

"So, I guess offering to buy you a drink is the wrong move right now?" the woman said as a confident smile spread across her face.

"That depends." Rachel turned toward the woman. "Do you have a gaggle of idiots hiding somewhere in the bar? Or did you make a bet that you'd nail me before you came over to talk to me?"

The woman laughed softly. "I wouldn't call it a gaggle, but I am here with one idiot, yes. My friend, Stella right over there." The woman pointed to another person across the bar who waved goofily and raised a beer in their direction. "And as far as making any bets, well, let's just say I'm not the gambling type. I'm only interested in something if it's a sure thing."

Rachel felt a rush of blood spread to her chest at the realization of what was happening. This woman—this stunning woman—was hitting on her, here, in this bar full of straight people.

Intrigued by the woman's confidence, Rachel continued the game.

"And what makes you think I'm a sure thing?" She propped her head on her hand.

"I think you just answered that yourself," the woman said, inching closer.

Rachel laughed. "What's your name anyway?"

"Ana," the woman said, extending a delicate, perfectly manicured hand. "I'm Ana."

CHAPTER THREE

Ana dropped her keys on the floor of her apartment, not caring whether she ever found them again or not. She felt two hands reaching around her waist in the dark and the smell of gin coming toward her. Suddenly, a pair of plush, warm lips pressed against hers, and Ana fought to catch her breath.

God, she was glad she had finally gotten her own place last year. Having roommates would be the absolute worst scenario in what was currently playing out to be a pretty amazing evening.

She and the beautiful redhead at the bar had hit it off quickly, and after a few very strong drinks, courtesy of a kind bartender and Stella, Ana had suggested they come back to her place. Rachel—the woman's name was Rachel, she was pretty sure—had agreed. A short cab ride from Midtown to Long Island City, and thirty minutes later, here they were.

"Should we move to the bedroom?" Rachel whispered in her ear. Her voice was soft and playful. Goose bumps lit up Ana's arms and she grabbed a fist full of hair.

"Why? It's just us here," Ana replied, turning around and pressing Rachel against the wall.

"So, you like people watching you, then?" Rachel retorted, taking another nibble at her ear and tilting her head to the other side of the room.

Ana glanced over to the tall row of windows facing out over the water. The apartment was once an old factory that they had chopped up and turned into tiny apartments. It had one bedroom barely large enough for a queen-sized mattress, a bathroom with a standup shower that could fit two really skinny people or one normal-sized person, and a kitchen that her mother would describe as "one ass only." But wow, what a view.

"I'm more of a voyeur, personally," Ana replied. She gently grabbed Rachel's face and pulled her close once again. "I like to watch."

Quickly, they moved into Ana's room, while clutching desperately at one another, trying to remove any and all space between them. Ana stopped kissing her long enough to turn her around and unzip the pinstriped dress she was wearing.

Rachel let out a slight gasp as her dress slid down around her feet. Ana turned her back around and drew her in her close. She was just able to make out the outline of tight, firm abs in the glow of the streetlight, and she wished they had stayed in the living room where it was brighter so she could admire her physique more closely. She could also make out a white lace bra and matching set of lace underwear, which she *really* wished she could admire a bit more.

But there was no time for that. Rachel was getting greedy now, and Ana felt the zipper of her own dress being undone behind her back as Rachel pressed quick, wet kisses down her neck and collarbone.

Ana undid the small belt around the waist of her dress before letting it fall completely to the floor. She looked down quickly to confirm that she was wearing one of her sexier bras and stepped out of her black heels. The look on Rachel's face all but confirmed that she was in fact wearing her cute underwear.

"Wow," Rachel said, as she took a step back and admired Ana.

Rachel took Ana's bottom lip in her mouth before taking both of Ana's breasts in her hands. She gently pinched one of Ana's nipples through the thin black fabric of her bra, and Ana let out a hiss through her teeth at the sensation.

"Is that okay?" Rachel asked and Ana nodded breathlessly in reply.

Soon, they were tumbling back toward Ana's bed, her soft, navy blue duvet catching them as they landed with a thud. Splashes of black and white lace painted across a dark navy canvas as the two women rolled back and forth across the bed, bodies pressed against each other.

Ana pulled down the strap of Rachel's bra and kissed her shoulder before moving lower, until finally her mouth landed on what it had been searching for. Rachel's nipple perked up instantly as she began sucking on it gently.

"Oh God," Rachel said. She arched her back and grabbed the back of Ana's head to pull her closer.

"Is *that* okay?" Ana asked. She stopped momentarily and looked up at Rachel with a grin.

Rachel's face flushed red as she grabbed Ana's face, pushing her back down onto her breast.

"How about we stop asking each other that? If I don't like something, you'll know," Rachel said brusquely.

Ana nodded slowly, her mouth still on Rachel's breast, and let her hands explore the lean tone of her body, trying to enjoy with her hands everything she was unable to see.

Line after line of muscle was displayed beneath her as Ana moved her hands from Rachel's stomach down to her legs and eventually up around her backside. There wasn't an ounce of excess fat on the woman, a stark contrast to Ana's own more curvy features, courtesy of her good genes and her mother's fantastic cooking.

But if the differences in their figures were any concern to Rachel, she certainly didn't show it. In fact, it seemed like she couldn't get enough of Ana's body as she grabbed her ass, her breasts, her waist, and every inch of Ana that she could get her hands on.

Ana's fingers found their way to the small curve of Rachel's hips and finally to the outline of her underwear. She pulled the thin layer of lace to the side, pressing her fingers against the warm, beating pulse waiting for her.

"Is this—" Ana began, but before she could finish her sentence Rachel's hand was covering her mouth.

"Didn't we just agree to stop asking that?" Rachel pled, her voice raspy and quivering.

Ana decided not to prolong her suffering and moved two fingers down Rachel's slit before slowly sliding inside the warm, wet folds.

Rachel let out a loud groan beneath her as she started to move two fingers deep inside, curled in just the right way to make Rachel writhe with pleasure.

"Fuck, you feel good," Ana groaned into Rachel's ear as she moved on top of her.

Rachel responded by digging her nails into Ana's back and pulling her closer.

Ana could feel Rachel begin to tighten around her fingers, and she quickened her pace to match her growing need. Sweat began to form on the curve of her spine, and she could feel a smooth moisture between their bare stomachs now, but she didn't dare slow down.

"I'm getting close," Rachel whispered into Ana's ear, and the encouragement sent Ana into a frenzy, working harder but still taking her time to ensure that the woman beneath her got the full experience. She wanted to make her come more than anything right now, but she didn't want to rush it. She wanted to savor every moment she could. She wanted to give her a night she would never forget.

But within seconds, it was clear that Ana had no choice in the matter, and after a few more curls of her fingers, Rachel collapsed over the edge. A string of profanities flew into the space around them, and Rachel's firm grip on Ana's back released as her orgasm unfolded into Ana's hand.

Ana rolled off to the side, wiping a trickle of sweat that had formed on her forehead. Rachel lay beside her, legs still spread, breathing heavily. Ana leaned up on her elbow to get a better look at the woman she had just satisfied.

"Wow," Rachel said. She rolled onto her side and looked up at Ana with the goofy afterglow of good sex swirling around her freckled, porcelain face.

"Wow," Ana said back. She reached down and brushed a strand of scarlet hair out of the way.

Even in the dim glow of the streetlight, Ana could see how stunning this woman was. This woman she had just brought home that she barely knew. She knew her name was Rachel—God, she really hoped her name was Rachel—and she knew she worked at a hospital. Other than that, they had skipped the small talk. But now, looking down at her lying in her bed, it was like all Ana *did* want to know was more about Rachel.

"So, what is it you do for work again?" Ana asked.

Rachel shook her head. "Uh-uh, no way." She grabbed Ana's face, pulling her down before pressing her lips against hers.

"Oh, come on," Ana said as she pulled back gently. "At least tell me a little something about you before the night is over."

"Get down here," Rachel whispered between kisses, tugging at Ana's bra strap. "The night hasn't even started yet."

Chapter Four

The light from the street poured in through the cracked-open window, and Rachel looked around the unfamiliar room. The smell of sex still hung heavy in the air, and she grabbed her head from the throbbing ache of too much gin.

It was a small room, barely big enough to fit the bed she was lying in, and she saw her dress crumpled up on the floor by the open door. She shifted her weight and began to slide out of bed when she heard a faint moan from the person lying beside her.

There she was. The beautiful woman from the bar last night. Her skin was smooth and shiny against the streetlight as she inhaled slow, deep breaths. She was sprawled out on her stomach, the sheet barely covering her naked body. Rachel found herself tempted to lie back down. To curl up in this stranger's arms and fall asleep.

But then what? They'd wake up tomorrow and go all U-Haul lesbian and spend the day frolicking around Central Park together? Get real. That type of thing only happened in cheesy movies. Real life wasn't like that. Real life was waking up in the morning and the woman's wife—or husband—walking in the door. Or them forgetting your name, or giving them your number but never hearing from them ever again. No, Rachel had plenty of those memories, thank you very much. She was going to keep control in this situation. She'd be the one to leave and spare both of them the awkward morning conversation leading to the obligatory taxi ride home.

Speaking of taxi rides home, where the hell was she exactly? She remembered going across a bridge in the car last night and she was pretty sure they were heading east, so that must mean Brooklyn or Queens. Man, she really hoped she wasn't way out on Long Island right now.

She reached for her phone on the nightstand and checked the clock: 4:52 a.m. She flipped open the rideshare app and found her exact location.

She was relieved to see she was still in Queens—Long Island City, to be precise. It was actually a convenient ride for her on the 7 train. Under normal circumstances, she could be here in twenty minutes or less from her apartment on the Upper East Side. But these were not normal circumstances, and no force in heaven or earth would get her on the subway at this time in the morning.

Ana shifted her weight again and stretched out her hand, her long, jet black hair tumbling over her face as she did. Rachel fought the urge to reach over and smooth out her wild mane and place a soft kiss on her forehead.

Instead, she slid off the end of the bed, grabbed her dress and shoes from the floor, and prepared to leave. Taking one last look over her shoulder, she felt sad at the idea of walking away from this beautiful woman forever. She found herself wishing there was a way they could see each other again.

It's for the best, Rachel told herself as she met her ride downstairs a few moments later. *It would never have worked out anyway.*

CHAPTER FIVE

So, wait, she just left?" Stella asked as she sat across from Ana's desk on Monday morning.

Ana tried not to bristle at the inquisition following her night of amazing, mind-blowing, earth-shattering sex with a stranger. She was annoyed enough that yes, Rachel—she was sure her name was Rachel—had in fact left in the middle of the night before she could get her number or social media or even her last name. Now she was doubly annoyed that Stella was pestering her about it.

"You know I have a deposition at ten, right?" Ana said.

Stella checked her smartwatch. "Dude, it's nine thirty. You've got plenty of time."

Ana rolled her eyes. "Not all of us walk into court at ten thirty for a nine o'clock calendar call."

"Oh, come on. It's the Boogie Down Bronx, you know anyone who shows up on time there is just begging to sit around and wait."

"Sure, but what about the bike ride you go on every day before court while everyone else is sitting and waiting for your ass?"

Stella shrugged and flashed a coy smile. "What can I say? La Colombe is the best coffee around, and I don't want to take the subway to get it."

"Regardless, some of us like to be early to things."

"Oh please, you're just using this depo to get rid of me and avoid talking about the little mermaid you took home Friday night." Stella crossed her arms.

Ana lifted an eyebrow.

"You know, because the red hair."

Ana let out a laugh. "Oh my God, you are an actual twelve-year-old boy."

"Fourteen. I've definitely hit puberty."

Ana threw a rubber band across the desk at her. "Will you get the hell out of here so I can finish prepping?"

"Relax. What do you even have to prep for with this case anyway? You know it like the back of your hand. Haven't you deposed like ten people already?"

Ana nodded. "Six, but yes, I do know it. I can basically quote the operative note. But I still want to home in on any reference to this resident. The record doesn't mention him very much. Just that he scrubbed in with the rest of the staff and then there's a brief mention of him speaking with the family after…well, you know."

"After the dude dies on the table," Stella said.

"Have some decorum, Stella, dios mío."

Stella shrugged. "What? The dude died. That's why we have a case, isn't it? You want me to go grab flowers or something?"

Ana shook her head. "You really are a twelve-year-old boy."

"Fourteen," Stella corrected, before finally leaving Ana alone in silence.

Ana skimmed over the notes she had read dozens of times now.

PGY-6. Scrub in time: 22:03

That was it. That was the extent of this person's involvement in the operating room as far as Ana knew. She assumed this deposition would be short, but she still needed to be thorough. She had to be sure she had a clear picture of exactly what happened on the night Mark Solomon died. She wanted every scalpel and lap pad accounted for.

She scanned the document again, trying to focus on the task at hand.

Without permission, her mind floated back to Rachel and the incredible night they'd had together. God, what she would give to see her again. To even get her last name or learn basically anything about her.

She didn't know why Rachel had left in the middle of the night like that. Sure, they were both drunk, but not so drunk that neither of them knew what was happening. Not so drunk that there was any question of consent. Ana couldn't fathom what had gone wrong to make her sneak out in the middle of the night like that.

Oh well. Some women were only looking for one night, and that was okay. She could let sleeping dogs lie. Or so she told herself as she finished gathering up her binder and exhibits and made her way down the long hall toward the conference room.

Her thoughts shifted back to her deposition as she walked, passing office after office, all walled by clear glass windows that allowed the bright Manhattan skyline to pour into the otherwise dark office. That was what she was working for today. An unobstructed view from the top of this big, beautiful building she worked in. That was why this case, this deposition, was so crucial. And that was why it was imperative that absolutely everything go according to plan today. The last thing she needed was any surprises.

Ana turned to enter the conference room, shooting a passing glance at the corner office where Simon Bellinger would soon be moving in. The words "Darcy Hammond, Managing Partner" were still engraved on the nameplate outside the door, even though she had been gone for months now.

Good riddance, Ana thought. Darcy Hammond had been the only female managing partner of the firm before her abrupt departure. But when you sleep with one of the associates that you're on trial with, things are bound to fall apart. Ana had initially been sad to lose a person she had once looked up to, but eventually the sadness had turned to joy when the junior associate she had slept with left shortly thereafter. Apparently, they were living together in Brooklyn now, or so the firm gossip mill whispered.

"Good morning, Miss Mendez," Ana's favorite court reporter said as she entered the room.

They were the only two in the room, which wasn't surprising. Ana was always early, and she liked to make sure that the reporter had all the exhibits pre-marked and any pleadings they needed. She also liked to be in the room when the other party arrived. An old power trick she'd learned from one of her continuing legal education courses.

"Good morning, Carol. Can I get you a cup of coffee?" Ana asked politely.

She would normally have a secretary do such a menial task, but for Carol she would always make an exception.

"Oh, no, none for me, hon, I'm cutting back on all the caffeine." Her thick Long Island accent clung to every word.

Ana nodded and sat down. She handed the exhibits to Carol one by one and told her how each should be marked. Then she quickly slid them back into her binder to keep them from opposing counsel's eyes until the last possible second.

"Counselor."

Ana looked up to see David Blackstone, defense counsel for the hospital in the lawsuit. That meant he represented the nurses and the residents who were present at the operation. The individual doctors who were named in the lawsuit were all represented by separate counsel since they were technically independent contractors and not employed by the hospital.

"Good morning, David." She nodded briefly before returning her attention to the exhibits.

"I believe we are just waiting on my client and counsel for the named doctors," David said.

"I'm here," a voice said from the door to the conference room.

The hairs on Ana's arms and neck instantly stood up. She knew that voice. She could never forget that voice. She'd heard that voice moaning in her ear just the other night. But no, it wasn't possible...

Slowly, Ana looked up from the conference room table. And who should be staring down at her but the little freaking mermaid herself.

Chapter Six

D r. Cohen, this is the plaintiff's attorney, Ana Mendez."
Rachel heard the words her attorney spoke, but she was frozen in place. Paralyzed.

This isn't happening.

This can't be happening.

How is this happening?

Ana stood slowly. She appeared to be in a similar state of shock and disbelief.

"It's uh...nice to meet you." Ana extended a hand but quickly withdrew it. "I mean, not nice under these circumstances, obviously." Ana looked down at her papers and began shuffling them around aimlessly. "Um, David, just give me a minute, will you? I think I left something back in my office."

Ana walked quickly out of the room, her heels making a deep clacking sound against the tiled floor as she moved with haste.

Rachel looked over at her attorney with a blank stare.

"Nothing to fear, Doc." He rested a large hand on her back. "It's just like we practiced on Friday afternoon. You answer only the question that's asked of you. No free information. And remember your five golden answers. Yes. No. I don't know. I don't remember. I don't understand your question. And don't forget, there was nothing unusual about this procedure. You didn't notice anything strange about Dr. Schumacher's behavior. Everything was kosher, so to speak." He gave her a reassuring smile and a nod.

But all Rachel could hear was Ana's voice whispering in her ear the other night. All she could see was the look she had given her when they first met at the bar. Calm, cool, collected, confident. Ana had looked anything but calm or collected when Rachel saw her a second ago. The natural color had drained from Ana's face and she looked as if she had seen a ghost.

How could she have let this happen? How could she have been so stupid? So reckless? So unprofessional? She wasn't the wild risky girl who went home with a stranger she met at a bar. She didn't even date anymore, let alone go home with someone she had just met. But she had been so upset and stressed about today that she had acted out of character. The one time in her neat, collected, tidy life she had decided to live on the edge, and look at what it got her. A whomping regret so big it could ruin her entire career.

She wanted to scream or run away or crawl out of her skin, if that was even humanly possible. But instead Rachel just nodded. She had been dreading this day ever since she was served with the subpoena three months ago. Being forced to talk about one of the most traumatic experiences of her life was going to be bad enough. Being forced to *not* talk about it was going to be even harder. She had made herself sick with worry over what to do. She couldn't have imagined then that things could have gotten any worse, but somehow, they just had.

"I actually need to use the restroom before we begin," Rachel said. She looked helplessly at the court reporter, who offered her a friendly smile.

"It's down the hall to your left, Doctor. If you hit the lobby, you've gone too far."

Rachel nodded politely and tried to control her pace as she exited the conference room and rounded the corner heading left. Once she was sure she was out of eyesight, she allowed the full panic of the situation to hit her.

Her palms began to sweat and her stomach started to do somersaults. As she neared the bathroom, she could hear her heart pounding louder in her ears. She had never had a panic attack before, but she was pretty sure this was what it felt like.

Once safely inside the bathroom, she walked to the nearest sink and turned on the faucet. Leaning over and splashing the cold water on her face, she was grateful she never wore much makeup. The last thing she needed was streaks of mascara running down her face. She focused on breathing. Taking in slow, small breaths at first and then long, deep ones that filled her chest cavity. After about thirty seconds she opened her eyes.

"Okay," she told the reflection staring back at her. "You can do this. This doesn't change anything. This is just a minor inconvenience. Like that time you missed your final exam in college because you got the day of the week wrong. It's going to be fine. This is just a bad coincidence."

Or is it...

Rachel tried to fight the inner voice that started to whisper in her ear, but she raised an eyebrow at her reflection.

This was a coincidence, right? How would Ana have even known what she looked like, let alone where she would be Friday night? There was no way she had planned all of this just to throw her off.

It's the twenty-first century. Anyone can be found online.

Rachel shook her head. It was impossible. Rachel hadn't planned on going to that stupid bar. She hadn't even told her sister or her best friend she was going there. Plus, there was no way Ana would do that. She couldn't have faked what had happened between then. She had been way too into Rachel. Ana had approached her. She—

Rachel thought back to their first meeting at the bar. She had been there with a friend. How long had they been there? Were they just waiting for her to show up all along? Was this all part of her master plan? Get Rachel in bed hoping she would talk about the case? Or maybe just throw her off her game today? Oh wow, she was really spiraling now.

"Keep it together, Cohen. This is why your mother thinks you've been living alone for too long."

After silencing her paranoia, Rachel tossed another splash of water on her face and took a final deep, long breath.

"You can do this."

She adjusted the simple white top she was wearing and ran her hands across the top of her black suit pants, ironing out the few wrinkles from where she had been sitting in the cab on the way over. After a few more seconds of pep talk, she exited the bathroom and made a beeline for the conference room, not stopping to look over her shoulder or at any of the offices that she passed. She didn't know which one belonged to Ana and she didn't want to know. In fact, she wanted to avoid as much eye contact with Ana as possible today. She hoped this would be a short deposition. How long could it really be? She was only a resident back then, and she had very little involvement in the operation at all.

Except what you saw before the operation. Except what you haven't told anyone about.

"Dr. Cohen," her attorney said as she reentered the conference room. "All good?" he asked in a way that reminded her of her basketball coach back in high school, hyping her up before game time.

"Great," Rachel lied.

She took her seat and began tapping her fingers on the glass table, nothing but the sound of the clock and her short nails hitting the table to pass the time.

"Long trip in?" the court reporter asked, clearly trying to make some form of conversation.

Before Rachel could answer, Ana was back. She tried to ignore the sweet, soft smell of Ana's perfume that seemed to surround her as she walked to the opposite side of the table. She tried to ignore the memories that came flooding back as she took her seat. Memories of her lips pressed against Ana's neck. Memories of the glisten of Ana's sweat as it dripped down her soft, bare stomach. Memories of the strong smell of sex mingled with eucalyptus that hung heavily in the air of her small apartment as they drifted off to sleep together.

Suddenly, her attorney's phone began to ring loudly, shaking Rachel from her reverie.

"Excuse me a moment," he said. "Don't start without me," he added and smiled at Ana, who just stared blankly back at him and then looked down at her still-closed binder.

As soon as he left, Rachel missed him. At least with him there she had some form of shield between Ana and herself. Now it was just them and the court reporter alone in the conference room.

Rachel looked down and began to pick at her nails, desperately trying to avoid looking anywhere but at the set of dark eyes waiting for her across the table. She could still smell Ana's perfume floating around the room like a specter hanging over her head, waiting to descend upon her senses. Rachel had never smoked, but she suddenly wished she did just so she had an excuse to get the hell out of that room.

She didn't know how long the silence lasted—it felt like hours—but finally, her attorney returned, and she exhaled audibly at the relief.

"I've just received a call from Sheryl Peterson, the attorney for the doctors. It seems she's been in a car accident this morning and she is unable to make it. She's asked that we adjourn the deposition." His voice rang with concern and his eyebrows were creased into a deep frown.

Ana jumped up almost instantly. "Oh no, a car accident? Gosh, I hope she's okay. Well, we can't go on without her, now can we?

Another day it is. I'll have my secretary reach out with new dates and we'll work something out. Nice to see you, David." She reached out and briskly shook the man's hand. "Carol, I'll text you." She smiled down at the court reporter quickly. "Doctor," she said, and nodded at Rachel before leaving the room. Her large binder and pen still sat on the table, and a few seconds later, Ana reappeared, grabbed her binder, spun on her heels, and left again.

The court reporter shook her head, seeming as confused as Rachel was.

"I've never seen her move so fast." The court reporter chuckled as she began to pack up her things.

"You must have scared her, Doc. Big feat! Ana can be quite the steely one," her attorney said. He patted her gently on the back and laughed.

"So, what happens now? Is it over, or…?" She knew it was wishful thinking.

"Not quite," her attorney responded. "We will need to pick a time that works for all of our schedules and come back so you can give testimony. But don't worry, we'll make sure it fits your busy schedule, I assure you."

Something told Rachel there would be no assuring her in this situation.

CHAPTER SEVEN

Y ou up for a drink after work?" Ana tapped her finger impatiently on the doorway to Stella's office.

"I'm gonna have to call you back," Stella said, and hung up the phone call she was on. "I'm sorry, you must be confused. You look a lot like my friend, Ana Mendez, but she would never be caught dead having a drink on a school night."

"How's five at the Ainsworth?"

Stella reeled back in shock. "Okay, now I know you've fallen and hit your head or something. You? Finish a workday at five?"

"Stella!" Ana said. She clenched her teeth together in a way that she knew must make her look exactly like her mother.

Stella looked slightly terrified in response. "Five o'clock. The Ainsworth. You got it, boss."

Ana walked back to her office and sat down at her desk as she attempted to process everything that had just happened. Rachel Cohen. Her name was Rachel Cohen and she was the third-year resident in the operating room when Mark Solomon died. She was the last witness to the case that was going to bring her some well-deserved recognition at this firm. She was the one person standing in Ana's way to success. And she was the one person Ana had fucked only two nights ago.

She dropped her head into her hands and ran her fingers through her hair. She began to rub her temples slowly. It's what her mother had always done when she was little and got hurt, or upset, or in trouble.

Ana wished she could call her mother right now. She wished she could cry and tell her that she possibly just blew the biggest promotion of her career and that if anyone found out about her sleeping with a witness in one of her lawsuits, she would be fired on the spot. But after thirty-one years of life, she knew better. Rosa Mendez had been one of the best mothers in the world when Ana was little. She was constantly encouraging her to strive for greatness, to not limit herself, to not tie her fate to anyone else. Her mother was great when it came to pushing Ana. But her mother was not someone you admitted mistakes to. She was not someone you called and cried to and said that you just literally fucked up your only chance at being made partner one day. She wasn't even someone you said the words "fucked up" to. Ana knew all a phone call would bring her was condemnation and chastisement.

She was daydreaming about being back home in her small town just outside of Miami. She was imagining the smell of pastelitos wafting down the hall alerting her that dinner was almost ready, when her phone buzzed loudly.

> **Antonio:** Yo, lil sis! Papi told me you were up for some big gig at work. That's dope.

Perfect timing as always. Her little brother, Antonio, was twenty-six years old but had the emotional capacity of a teaspoon. His biggest thrill in life was getting new Nikes for Christmas every year even though Ana knew her parents couldn't really afford them, and he spent his free time fixing up an old sports car with their father and playing video games out of his parents' house where he still lived. But that didn't matter. He was the boy, and as such, even if he was a car salesman at a local dealership, his successes would always trump hers, even if she did make partner one day. And likewise, his failures would always be minimal compared to hers.

> **Ana:** Yup

She didn't want to be so short with him, but the last thing she wanted to talk about was her job right now, especially with him.

> **Antonio:** Don't fuck it up, kid. Papi will be pissed.

He added a winky face at the end to imply that he was joking, and she knew he was. Manuel Mendez was perhaps the most docile and soft-spoken man she had ever met. When she came out as bisexual a few years ago, it was his opinion that she was most afraid of. He was, after all, Cuban, Catholic, and a self-proclaimed Republican after meeting Reagan for two seconds back in the '80s. But shockingly, he had simply smiled and kissed her cheek and said, "Whatever makes you happy, mija." Both of her parents had been supportive in that regard. "The pope is okay with it, I am okay with it," her mother had said, before wiping her hands in the air as if she were Pontius Pilate absolving herself of any sin. Her parents had their shortcomings, for sure, but she was grateful for their love and acceptance when it came to her sexual orientation.

She set the phone down and tried to distract herself with work. Five o'clock could not get there soon enough. Why hadn't she just told Stella they were getting a liquid lunch? Since they billed their time, there were no set office hours for attorneys at Byron & Browning. She could technically leave anytime she wanted.

But the loud sound of an incoming email reminded her exactly why that had been wishful thinking.

The next time Ana checked the clock on her computer, she was glad to see it was 4:50 p.m. One perk of having one of the busiest careers in the country was that your days always seemed to fly by. The bad part? Well, your days always seemed to fly by.

Ana tossed her bag over her shoulder, dropping her work phone in it as she made her way to the elevator. Stella was waiting for her in the lobby, her blazer tossed over her arm with the sleeves of her shirt rolled up.

"Ms. Torres, you know displaying tattoos is against firm policy," Ana said quietly, motioning to Stella's full sleeve that was now on partial display.

Stella rolled her eyes. "You could sue me, but you'd lose."

Ana smiled, grateful for their familiar banter as they entered the elevator. Once they were safely inside, Stella turned toward Ana.

"So, you gonna tell me what's going on?"

Ana continued to look forward at her silvery reflection in the elevator doors.

"Not here," she whispered.

"All right, all right, but this better be good. I haven't gotten shit done all day today because I've been too distracted by whatever it is you're not telling me."

Ana cocked her head sideways. "How can you be distracted by something you don't even know?"

Stella shook her head. "Tell me you *don't* have ADHD without telling me."

A few moments later Stella was holding the door open for her as they entered the Ainsworth. It was risky choosing this place. The Ainsworth was the unofficial bar of Byron & Browning, and a lot of associates and of counsels went there for happy hour after work. Lucky for her, it was still too early for most of her colleagues to be done with work, and after a quick glance around the room, she confirmed the coast was clear.

"A Pacifico for me and a mojito for her," Stella said to the bartender as they nestled into two seats at the end of the empty bar.

Ana waited while the bartender mixed her drink. She knew she needed to have a little bit of a buzz going before she started this story. Stella, seeming to know her intentions, waited, tapping her fingers anxiously and staring at the Yankees game being played at the screen above their heads.

When their glasses finally clinked together in cheers, Ana could tell Stella's patience had run its course.

"You remember the woman from the other night? Rachel?"

Stella nodded. "I don't think I ever got her real name, but sure, I remember Ariel." Stella took a deep swig of her beer.

"Okay, well, she's kind of the doctor I was supposed to depose today."

A shower of beer rained down over Ana and the bar.

"Shit, I'm sorry, but…shit! Are you fucking kidding me?" Stella began to wipe down the bar as Ana dabbed a napkin across her face.

"Nope, actually not kidding at all."

"I think I'm actually speechless."

"Well, that would be a first." Ana set the napkin down on the bar. "How do you think I felt when I walked into the damn conference room today and there she was?"

Stella's mouth dropped open again. "You *saw* her in the office today? Holy shit, Ana, what the hell did you even do?"

"Yes, I saw her in the office! I was supposed to depose her all day. God, I was just sitting there talking to Carol, organizing my exhibits, and then I look up and bam! There she is. Long, perfect, flowing red hair and the bluest eyes you've ever seen."

Stella hesitated a moment. "So, you're saying she looked good?" A sly grin spread across her face.

"Oh, you cannot be serious right now."

"What? I'm just saying, sometimes the whiskey goggles can mislead someone. It's nice to know you bagged a true hottie."

"Bagged? I didn't bag anything other than a big heap of trouble. What the hell am I going to do now? I mean, I have to tell Paul, he's the partner on this case, this is a clear conflict of interest. No way I get the of counsel job now, and my mother, God, I already know what she's going to say—"

"Whoa, whoa, whoa, let's just slow down here." Stella placed her hands on Ana's shoulders, and Ana steadied herself before taking another sip of her drink. "Before we go falling on our sword, let's just take a step back and assess the situation."

Ana knew this tone. Stella had a knack for minimizing problems and talking her way out of trouble. She was a Jedi Master of bullshit. It was one of the things that had instantly turned her off about Stella in a romantic sense, but one of the things she loved about her as a close friend.

"Oh, God, do I even want to ask what you're thinking right now?"

Stella smiled coyly and stroked her chin. "I'm just saying why don't we look at the facts. Just the facts. You met a woman at a bar. You had no knowledge of who this woman was prior to sleeping with her, correct?"

Ana crossed her arms. "Cross-examining me, Counsel?"

Stella shot her a look of reproach. "Bear with me."

"All right, fine. That's correct."

"And you didn't exchange numbers or have any contact with her after said hookup and before seeing her today, correct?" Stella continued.

Ana nodded. "Still correct. I didn't even know her last name until today."

"And you, in fact, have still not deposed her in the *Solomon* case, correct?"

"Yes, that's correct. The attorney for the hospital adjourned it right before we started today. Car accident or something. Oh, God, I should have called her office and checked on her. Poor Sheryl." Ana bit down on her thumbnail.

"Oh, Jesus, send some flowers tomorrow, Mendez. Stay with me here."

Ana refocused her attention onto Stella.

"So, the way I see it, no knowledge of any preexisting situation. And no deposition taken. No conflict of interest!" Stella tossed her hands in the air and took another sip of beer, seemingly satisfied with her foregone conclusion.

Ana contemplated what she had just said for a moment. "Wait, so you're telling me to just brush this whole thing off and pretend it never happened?"

Stella shrugged. "Pretend what never happened?"

"Very funny. But what happens when I do actually have to depose her?"

Stella took another swig and continued. "Have a junior associate cover it for you. She was just a resident, right? What more information could she possibly have about this case that you haven't gotten from the other witnesses already? That way, worst case scenario, something comes out one day, you can say you weren't even the one involved in her deposition. It's foolproof."

Ana bit her thumbnail again and considered everything Stella had said. She was technically right; there was really no sense in shooting herself in the foot since nothing had actually happened today. And it would be easy to get a junior up to speed on the case. She could just lie and say she had a court conference or something on whatever day the deposition was rescheduled for. Plus, this meant she never had to see Rachel Cohen again. Ana ignored the twinge of pain that shot through her heart at the thought.

Ana lifted her martini glass. "Stella, you're a freaking genius."

CHAPTER EIGHT

Y ou what?"

Rachel flinched as she waited for her sister, Noa, to finish reacting. It was exactly the response she had expected when she told her about having sex with the attorney who had been making her life miserable for the last three months. Well, not her directly, but her law firm had brought the suit and issued the subpoena. It was the reason Rachel had lost so much sleep lately and had taken to running long distances six days a week.

"I know, I know." Rachel dropped her head into her hands as Noa finished drying the dish she had been scrubbing for the last two minutes.

"Mommy, Mommy!" Noa's daughter came running into the room.

Noa squatted down to pick her up. "Yes, Estie, light of my life, what is it?" The little girl's curly, dark hair bounced up and down and her brown eyes danced with mischief as she looked at her mother.

"Is Auntie Rachel staying for dinner?"

Noa looked over at Rachel, silently inviting her to join them.

"I will if I get to sit next to you!" She reached over and tickled the little girl's belly. Estie threw her head back and squealed as Rachel wiggled her fingers.

Noa set her down gently on the floor. "All right, now go play with your brother for another ten minutes. It's almost ready." Estie ran into the other room. "And wash your hands!"

Rachel shook her head. It was still hard for her to believe that her sister was a few years younger than her and already had two children. Estie, who had just run off into the other room, was five, and Benjamin was two and a half. She could hear him making train sounds in the other room while Estie talked a million miles a minute reading to herself.

"You're a cardiac surgeon, Rachel," her sister always told her when Rachel was feeling down about being almost thirty-five and still painfully single. "You cut people's hearts open while I'm over here changing diapers and making Shabbat dinners." But it only helped so much. Thirty-four was essentially eighty in Jewish years, and as far as their Upper West Side mother was concerned, she might as well be a full-blown spinster.

"Okay, so wait," Noa said once Estie was out of earshot. "What the hell happens now?"

Rachel shrugged. "I don't know, I mean, I still have to go through with my deposition. It got canceled literally as we were standing in the conference room about to get started."

"By who? By her?" Noa asked.

Rachel shook her head. "No, one of the attorneys got in a car accident or something. Not that I would ever wish harm on anyone, but praise God for that small miracle. I don't know what I would have done if I had to sit through hours of looking into those golden brown eyes."

Noa lifted an eyebrow. "Golden brown, you say?"

"Did someone say gold?" Noa's husband, Jacob, walked in and dropped his bag in the chair next to Rachel before kissing her on the top of the head.

"Hey, Jake," Rachel said, as he crossed the kitchen and kissed Noa on the cheek.

"Rachel was just filling me in on her latest romantic rendezvous, and boy is it a doozie."

Rachel hid her face. "Oy vey, Noa, do you have to tell the whole world?"

Noa looked around the room. "The whole world? What world? I told Jake. He's family. Doesn't count."

Rachel turned ten shades of red and shook her head. "Yeah, well, Mamala is family too, and you better not plan on telling her, or your little ones are going to be without a mom pretty quick."

"Oh my, threats of murder on such a lovely night!" Jacob laughed at Rachel before he walked over to the refrigerator and pulled out a bottle of white wine.

"Relax, princess, I won't tell our mother that you totally banged the attorney that's suing you."

Jacob's face went pale as he finished pouring a glass. "You did not," he said, sounding like a little girl in middle school.

"I like, totally did, Jacob," Rachel replied in a fake Valley Girl accent. "And technically she's not suing me directly. She's suing my hospital. I just got subpoenaed."

Jacob winced. "Sounds like you'll be needing this, then." He slid a full glass of wine over to her. "I'll leave you two to gossip, but I expect to be debriefed in bed later." He wiggled his eyebrows at Noa, and she smiled and gave him an exaggerated wink in return.

Their marriage was exactly the type of relationship Rachel wanted for herself. Jacob was kind and supportive, a loving, doting father, and he worshipped the ground Noa walked on. She loved watching them interact. They laughed together over silly inside jokes and reality TV. They'd wept together when Noa miscarried their first child, a girl they had named Ruth. They lifted each other up when one was having a rough day. And they challenged each other when one was being bullheaded or stubborn on a topic. Jacob really was the perfect partner, in Rachel's eyes. Well, except for the fact that he was a man, of course. Rachel had learned way back in middle school that she wasn't interested in men, unless it was to play sports with.

"Okay, but really, what are you gonna do, Rach?" Noa asked, as she pulled a hot pan of rosemary chicken out of the oven.

"I really don't know. I mean, should I tell my attorney? What if it makes me look even worse in the lawsuit? What if it hurts the hospital in some way? Or worse, what if I get fired for a breach of ethics or something?"

Noa set the pan down on the stove and placed her hands on her hips. She looked just like their mother when she did that. In fact, she looked like their mother most of the time. Noa had inherited their mother's dark hair and brown eyes, which she had since passed down to Estie and Benjamin. Rachel, on the other hand, was the only redheaded member of the family. Red hair was common amongst Ashkenazi Jews like them. Her great-grandfather had red hair, or so she had always been told. Once in elementary school, her father had shown Rachel an old photo of him and her great-grandmother standing at Ellis Island from sometime in the early 1940s shortly after they immigrated from Austria, having escaped Poland just in time to avoid the camps. Everything they owned had been shoved into a single steam trunk.

"You carry his strength and resilience with each strand," her father had said, tenderly touching her hair and rubbing her back. "Be proud of it."

And most of the time, that worked. Rachel *was* proud of her heritage. She was proud of her family who came here with nothing and made a future for their family. She loved being Jewish about as much as she loved being a lesbian.

But man, had it been tough growing up with a sister as beautiful as Noa. Where Rachel had been the scrawny, nerdy tomboy of the family, Noa had been the class president, the cheerleader, the prom queen, and the teacher's pet all rolled into one. That was probably why Rachel had dedicated herself to her studies and sports in high school. They were the only areas she had bested her sister in, even now.

"I never understood why you were all in a twist over this deposition anyways. You were a resident, for crying out loud. What could you possibly have seen go wrong?" Noa chimed in.

Rachel felt her stomach clench at the mention of the Solomon surgery.

"I don't want to talk about it," Rachel said coldly.

"So you've said a hundred times, but I think maybe you're overreacting," Noa said, pulling out five plates. "I mean, you had a one-time thing and you maybe have to see her again for this deposition, but other than that, it's done, right?"

Rachel nodded. "I guess. I mean, yes, it's totally done."

"She hasn't mentioned wanting to see you again?"

"No. I left before we even exchanged numbers that night, and we barely spoke today."

Noa nodded, beginning to place pieces of chicken on each plate. "Then I say let bygones be bygones. Be professional. Be polite. Answer her questions, and that's the end of it, you know? It's not like you have feelings for her or anything."

The words dug like a knife into Rachel and she fought hard to control her reaction. "No, yeah, totally. Definitely not."

Her lies either worked or Noa was too busy counting out an equal amount of broccoli onto each kid's plate to notice the quiver in her voice as she spoke.

"Great. So just chalk it up to more life lessons, as Mamala would say. Oh, speaking of which, are you going to Shabbat dinner this week? You know she's going to ask me when she calls tomorrow for the tenth time this week."

Rachel shook her head. She had missed dinner last Friday night, and look how that had turned out. She *should* learn her lesson like Noa said and go to her parents' house for dinner like a nice Jewish girl. But for once, Rachel actually had plans.

"Can't. It's Pride this weekend, and I promised Charlotte we'd go out in the Village."

Noa tsked under her breath, doing a spot-on impersonation of their mother. "Hashem, forgive me, I have raised a disgrace of a daughter. Skipping Shabbat to go to bars!" Her face grew into a wide smile as she finished the sentence.

"If she only knew," Rachel said, and soon the two sisters were laughing together in unison.

Chapter Nine

"Oh, come on. It's Pride! Lighten up a bit, will you?" Stella elbowed Ana in the ribs as they forced their way into the crowded bar.

Cubbyhole, or just Cubby as the locals called it, was one of the two lesbian bars remaining in Manhattan, and it was approximately the size of a large walk-in closet—no pun intended. It was busy on a normal Friday night, but during Pride week the lines wrapped around the block as women from every walk of life inched in for cheap beer and watered-down well drinks.

Ana had chosen a simple but sultry outfit for the evening. A slim-fitting black T-shirt tucked into high-waisted denim shorts with holes and rips that showed off a good portion of her thighs. She had let her long hair stay down, flowing behind her in perfect waves, and put on a full face of makeup, of course. She wore her black P.F. Flyers to give her a more tomboy-femme aesthetic, but also, she just really loved these shoes. They reminded her of her favorite movie growing up, *The Sandlot*, which let's be real, was the only reason anyone would ever wear P.F. Flyers this side of 1955.

Stella wore a hot pink short-sleeved button-down with little pineapples printed all over it, black jeans, and her black and white Nike Pandas. How she wasn't burning up in those pants was beyond Ana. It must have been a hundred degrees in the bar between the heat from outside and the number of bodies that were crammed inside it.

"That's exactly why I don't want to be here. It's so busy I can barely breathe, let alone make my way to the bar for a freaking drink." Ana wiped her arm as a particularly sweaty woman rubbed against her on her way to the bathroom.

"Oh, relax, who are you, Ellen-ezer Scrooge?" Stella made a dorky face at her own joke.

Ana shot her a blank stare.

"Get it? Ellen-ezer like Ebenezer, but Ellen because...because gay?"

"Brilliant," Ana said, her voice monotone. Stella elbowed her once again in the ribs and Ana smacked at her. "Fine, fine, you're witty as ever, Stella Torres. Your cup runneth over with puns and humor."

Stella grinned. "That's more like it."

Ana looked around the crowded room again. They had waited almost an hour to get inside. She didn't even want to think about how long it was going to take them to actually get a drink. And even then it would be so sugary there was no chance of her getting drunk within the next two hours.

"How are we even going to get up there?"

"Here, follow me." Stella took Ana by the arm and began wiggling her way through the crowd, schmoozing and flirting as they walked.

"Excuse me, beautiful, thanks, gorgeous, mind if I just squeeze behind you there, babe?"

Ana chuckled as she watched Stella charm her way right up to the bar.

"Ta da!" Stella said when they finally arrived, a grin of success plastered across her face.

Ana slow clapped in astonishment. "Impressive. Most impressive."

Stella laughed. "All right, don't start talking *Star Wars* on me now. We're here to hook up, not hook up with each other."

Ana ignored her and looked down the bar. Their next challenge had just presented itself. There were only two bartenders working, and dozens of hands waved bills in the air to try to get their attention. The bar was cash only, so even holding up a credit card would do Ana no good.

"Hi there," Stella said, turning her back to Ana within seconds of their arrival at the bar.

Ana leaned around Stella's shoulder to see a petite brunette with a pixie cut and icy green eyes staring up at her. Ana could tell by the look on the woman's face that Stella was just her type.

"Well, hi," the woman replied, her eyes unmoved from Stella.

"I'm Stella, but you can call me anything you like." Stella leaned down and gave the woman a kiss on the cheek. A bold move, but that was Stella's style. She was anything but subtle.

"Charlotte," the woman said in reply. "You can call me Charlotte."

Feisty, Ana thought, snickering to herself.

"Mind if I buy you a drink, Charlotte? My friend and I were just trying to flag the bartender down." Stella turned her body, allowing Ana to enter the woman's view.

"Ana," she said, politely extending her hand.

"Hi, I'm—"

"Charlotte," Ana said cutting her off. "Yeah, I got that part."

Charlotte gave her a quick up-down before returning her attention to Stella. Instinctively, Ana pulled out her phone and began to swipe quickly on the only dating app she still had. She knew it was weird to be virtually looking for a date when she was literally surrounded by women interested in women, but somehow it felt easier to her than all of this. Ana was great at flirting, sure. But she was more of a one-on-one kinda girl. She preferred to select her target and focus only on that for the night. Crowds this big just overwhelmed her and brought out her rarely seen introverted side.

Left, left, left. Ana was swiping almost as fast as the women could appear on her screen. Hair too long, hair too short, eyes too dark, eyes too light. Too tall, not tall enough. Not into sports, way too into sports. Ana was picky, she knew that much about herself, but she was fooling herself if she thought there was anything actually wrong with the women she was sliding past. The truth was there was only one woman she had been picturing in her mind all this past week. And of course, it was the one woman she wasn't allowed to be picturing. Dr. Rachel—*perfect hair, perfect smile, perfect face*—Cohen. Growing annoyed with the onslaught of unsuitable women who didn't hold a candle to Rachel, Ana began slowing down, trying to give the potential suitors a chance.

Charlotte's voice tickled Ana's eardrum as she swiped. "I was just telling my friend that Pride is such a special time of year. She didn't want to come out, but I told her that she had to. Well, she's already *out*, but you know what I mean. Like, come out here. Like tonight."

Ana listened as Charlotte and Stella chatted more while she continued to scroll in a desperate attempting to disconnect from the crowded room. She heard someone clear their throat over her shoulder and she looked behind her to see a person with teal and pink hair staring at her. The implication was clear. Order a drink or move.

Ana shot them a dirty look but set her phone down on the bar and once again started vying for the bartender's attention.

"So, where is your friend, then?" Stella asked Charlotte, her back still turned to Ana.

"Bartender!" Ana shouted, waving her hand in the air.

A woman with short brown hair wearing a dirty white crop top nodded her acknowledgment and held up one finger. A few seconds later, and success had been achieved.

"Vodka and cranberry for me. Any beer will do for her." Ana tilted her head to Stella, who was still too caught up in Charlotte's emerald eyes to even hear Ana ordering for them. Ana considered asking Charlotte what she wanted to drink but decided against it. That was Stella's job, not hers.

The bartender sloppily made her drink, cranberry juice and bottom shelf vodka spilling all over the bar, but she didn't seem to notice or care. She slammed the drinks down on the bar and yelled that it would be eleven bucks for both of them.

Maybe it was worth the wait with drinks this cheap.

"Here," Ana said, sliding the bottle of beer to Stella.

"Oh, thanks! But hey, we gotta get something for my girl Charlotte here and her friend who is…joining us?"

Charlotte looked around the room briefly and then glanced down at her phone. "She said she just walked in. She should be…oh! There she is!" Charlotte began waving her arms in the air and calling out for someone across the room.

Ana took a deep sip of her drink and lifted up her phone. Not to swipe, but more so she would have something to be doing while Stella flirted with Charlotte and whoever was about to appear. It was her security blanket.

"Stella," Charlotte said, extending her arm into the crowd. "This is my best friend, Rachel. Rachel, this is Stella and—"

"Ana." The soft voice echoed in Ana's ears, and she lifted her face from her phone long enough to see the perfectly framed face of Dr. Rachel Cohen.

"Oh, you have got to be fucking kidding me," Ana said, sharper than she intended.

"Ho-ly shit," Stella said, taking a deep drink of her beer and suddenly pretending to be mute.

"Wow, you really are stalking me, aren't you?" Rachel snipped.

"Yup, you guessed it. On top of handling a full caseload and suing scumbag doctors, I also stalk you in my free time."

Ana felt her blood begin to boil. She was annoyed. She had agreed to come out with Stella as a means to forget this person, and there she was once again in her face. A beautiful, flawless reminder of one of the biggest mistakes of her legal career.

"Scumbag doctors? Well, that's rich. I saved two lives today, what about you? How do you spend your days, Counselor?"

"Wait a minute, this isn't—" Charlotte began. Her face showed that she was just now putting the pieces together.

"Ana Mendez." Ana nodded to Charlotte. "I'm the attorney suing your good buddy here."

Rachel's face grew so red it matched her hair, and she looked around the bar in apparent embarrassment. "More like the attorney making my life a living hell," Rachel quipped back. "And she's not suing me, she served me with a stupid subpoena so I'd have to come testify in her stupid lawsuit."

Ana narrowed her eyes. "Careful, Doctor. The statute of limitations hasn't expired, you know. There's still plenty of time to bring you into this thing permanently."

Ana saw Stella's eyes grow wide from her periphery, but she didn't care. She was overstimulated and hungry and hot, and now she was face-to-face with the single most distractingly, frustratingly beautiful woman she'd ever met. And she was pissed about it.

"Oh, yeah, because naming someone in a lawsuit will fix all your problems, won't it?" Rachel's face continued to grow red, and Ana assumed it meant she was just as pissed off by this interaction as she was.

Good.

"You know what, don't let me take up any more of your valuable brain space. You've got lives to save, after all." Ana took a long gulp of her drink, nearly draining the glass before slamming it down on the bar and turning around to shove her way out of the bar.

Stella lingered behind for a moment. "Guess this is a bad time to ask for your number?" she said in the direction of Charlotte.

"Stella!" Ana shouted over her shoulder before elbowing her way through the crowd. Stella followed her.

Once they both were outside, Ana smelled the warm breeze mixed with the aroma of hot garbage that seemed to permanently stain the air during summertime in New York, and she started to feel nauseous. She couldn't believe that had just happened. She was so freaking angry. Why was she so angry?

"Of all the gin joints in the world, am I right?" Stella asked, running her fingers through her short, sweaty hair.

Ana rolled her eyes. "Let's just get the hell out of here."

CHAPTER TEN

D r. Cohen, Dr. Cohen, line one." A voice over the intercom echoed loudly above Rachel's head.

Rachel shifted her focus from the mug of coffee she had been staring at all morning. The break room at Mount Sinai Hospital was large enough that she didn't have to make small talk with other doctors she knew. But it also meant no one knew where to find her when she wasn't on the floor. Luckily, she wasn't hungover. They hadn't stuck around at Cubby long enough for her to be hungover. After Ana had stormed out of the bar last night, Charlotte had tried to convince her to forget about her and have a drink.

"Look around you. You're a doctor surrounded by beautiful women. Live a little!" Charlotte had said.

But Rachel just wanted to go home. It was so busy she could barely breathe, and crowds like that just triggered her anxiety. She hated feeling people breathing down her neck, touching her without her permission, rubbing their sweaty bodies against her. It made her claustrophobic to just think about it.

Much to her chagrin, they had stayed for another half hour, mostly to ensure that there was no risk of running into Ana and her friend out in the street somewhere, but then, finally, Rachel had gone home to the loving, needy arms of her cat, Elijah.

A ridiculous name for a cat, most would say, especially considering the fact that the cat was a girl, but the name made sense if you knew her origin story. A few years ago, Rachel had been celebrating Passover at her parents' house. In Rachel's family, part of their tradition included the children ending the Seder by opening the door for the prophet Elijah. Usually, the children left the Seder disappointed, because of course an undead prophet from thousands of years ago does not walk through the open door. This particular year, however, when little Estie had swung open the door, she was met with something even greater than a prophet. She was met with a small calico kitten staring up at her, meowing as loud as its tiny lungs would let it.

"Can we keep him?" she had squealed in the direction of her parents.

The look on Noa's face had been enough to make the real Elijah come back to earth. She was still pregnant with Benjamin at the time, and the idea of having a kitten, a two-year-old, and a newborn all under one two-bedroom roof in Brooklyn was clearly too much for her. Rachel had seen Jacob also try to form words that would let Estie down easy.

"What if I keep her and you can come visit?" Rachel had said instantly without even thinking.

She still didn't know how the damn thing had gotten inside the building, let alone up to the fifth floor where her parents lived. But just like that, Dr. Rachel Cohen, esteemed cardiac surgeon at Mount Sinai Hospital, had become a total cat mom.

And so, last night, after leaving the overcrowded bar, she had been more than happy to get home at a semi-decent hour, pop a cup of instant noodles into her microwave, and cuddle up with Elijah on the couch, while an episode of *Friends* played in the background.

She had fallen asleep on the couch to the sound of Ross Gellar yelling about being on a break. But she had been thinking about the stunning woman with long, wavy black hair who smelled like some kind of sweet candy. Then she had woken up at five a.m. to the sound of Elijah purring loudly in her face.

"Dr. Cohen, Dr. Cohen, line one."

Rachel snapped her attention back to the break room as the announcement played a second time. She picked up her phone and dialed the line.

"This is Dr. Cohen."

"Hi, Dr. Cohen, your patient in 402 is asking for you. I tried to tell her you were with other patients and to talk to the PA, but she refused."

Rachel signed. "Mrs. Moriarty? Yeah, she can be a bit testy. I'll swing by on my way to see Mr. Weston in 410 in a few."

"Thanks, Dr. Cohen, you're the best," the nurse said.

"No problem," Rachel responded and hung up.

She knew she could have told her just to send the PA anyway, or a hospitalist for that matter, to check on the patient. That's what her colleagues would do. She was really under no obligation to race around answering questions any RN could answer, but Rachel didn't operate that way. If a patient needed her, she was there. She was constantly giving out her personal cell phone number to the family members of her patients, telling them to call her day or night with concerns or questions. And they did. Rachel's mother said it was the reason for her complete lack of any serious relationships.

"You've made that hospital your spouse," she would say, but Rachel couldn't help it. She had seen good surgeons and bad surgeons over the years, and she refused to be one of the bad ones. In fact, she wanted to be one of the great ones. It was why she had decided to pursue this career in the first place. To make an actual difference in people's lives.

She took another sip of her coffee, dumped the rest down the sink, and headed to the elevator bank. Rachel pushed the up button and waited for the world's slowest elevators to arrive. She pulled the phone from her pocket after feeling a low buzz vibrate against her thigh.

Charlotte: where r u?

Charlotte was in her thirties and a nurse, for heaven's sake. The fact that she still texted like a teenager instead of spelling out words annoyed Rachel more than anything, but she ignored it on account of Charlotte also being the most outspokenly loyal friend she had ever known.

Rachel: Elevator, heading up to 4th floor. Why?

Charlotte: omw

After what felt like ages, the elevator door dinged open and Rachel stepped inside, pushing the button for the fourth floor. She was only on it for a single floor before the silver doors opened again.

"Hi!" Charlotte blurted, stepping into the elevator.

"Jesus, what the—"

"Language, Doctor." Charlotte smiled as the doors slid closed.

"How the hell did you find me that fast?"

Charlotte waved her off. "Oh please, you're the most predictable person I know. Let me guess, you were hiding in the break room downstairs, sulking over a cup of black coffee?"

Rachel averted her eyes. "No."

Charlotte stared, unblinking.

"I was not sulking."

"Sure, Rach. Whatever you say," Charlotte retorted.

The elevator opened onto the fourth floor, and Rachel stepped out.

"Wait!" Charlotte said, grabbing her by the arm and dragging her into the nurses' station.

Rachel looked around, embarrassed at the scene her best friend was causing at work.

"What on earth is so important it can't wait until I see a patient?" Rachel said through gritted teeth.

It didn't faze Charlotte. Nothing did. That was probably why they had stayed best friends for so long. Rachel would get into one of her introverted, brooding moods and Charlotte would always be there to pull her out of bed and force her back out into society. No matter what the reason, whether it was from the inevitable failure of her latest romantic fling or from news that one of her patients had passed away, Rachel was the "let's stay home and watch *Little House on the Prairie* reruns" one, and Charlotte was the "let's fly to Florida so we can learn how to scuba dive" one.

Charlotte continued, "Gee, I don't know, maybe it's about an extremely sexy attorney we bumped into last night before you clammed up and made me leave the bar?"

Rachel rolled her eyes. "We are so not talking about this right now."

Charlotte stepped closer and lowered her voice. "Oh, come on, you totally flaked on me and haven't said two words about it since. I gave you time to digest everything last night, but now it's time to spill."

Rachel checked her watch. She had arrived faster than expected to the floor, even with Charlotte's little detour. She could spare a few minutes, but God, she really did not want to talk about this right now, especially in the nurses' station a few feet away from her patients.

"What do you want me to say, Char? It was freaky seeing her after our hook-up the first time. It was even freakier seeing her a second time. Seriously, if I bump into her a third time, I may call the cops for stalking or something."

Charlotte chuckled. "Okay, well, we both know how tiny the lesbian community is here. I mean, you and I have fucked each other by two degrees of separation on several counts."

Rachel looked around to confirm no one was listening to their conversation.

"Yet another reason why I don't like going to bars."

Charlotte pressed on. "I don't know. If you think about it, the last two times you've been to a bar, you've met a really hot woman. Granted, it was the same woman both times, but still, those are good odds."

Rachel pinched the bridge of her nose. "Is this really all you wanted to talk about? Or can I please go check on my patient now?"

Charlotte waved her hands. "Go, go, but don't think this conversation is over."

Rachel shook her head and started in the direction of Room 402.

"Oh, Rach, just tell me one thing."

Rachel turned around and crossed her arms, knowing that Charlotte wouldn't wait for her consent before continuing to talk.

"What did you think of her friend, Stella? Pretty hot, right?"

Rachel shook her head. "You're incorrigible."

"What? I'm just saying!" Charlotte shouted after her as she walked down the hall.

CHAPTER ELEVEN

W hat up, sis?" Ana's brother said. He held the phone too close to his face and blew on the screen like he was cleaning his sunglasses.

"Hi, Antonio, I don't have too long, I just wanted to say hi."

Antonio made a face that looked like he was in pain. "Bro, don't tell me you're still at the office right now. It's like, dark, outside." He squinted into the screen, clearly trying to see her background.

Ana looked around her office. There wasn't much to see. Just a small desk, where she currently sat, with two massive computer screens on it and a bookshelf filled with folders and Redweld files for active cases she was working on. On her desk was a single photo of her family all standing on the beach back home. Her brother had his arm draped around her in the same way he had since he was finally taller than her, which had happened when he was about twelve years old. Their father was wearing a wide-brimmed straw fedora, his smile gleaming in the sunlight as he held up a tiny fish he had caught off the pier. Their mother had both arms wrapped around Antonio, of course, and her face welled with pride just to be standing with them.

Ana missed her family, even if they did drive her absolutely bonkers at times. And yes, on nights like this, when she was here alone in a dark, cold office and knew all she had to go home to was a cup of soup from a can and the blinding city lights, she missed being back home.

She missed palm trees and sunshine and good Cuban food. She missed live music in Hialeah and going to see a movie with her friends from high school. She missed driving around downtown Miami in her dad's old Camaro that he had fixed up when he was Antonio's age. She missed chasing the ice cream truck with her brother when they heard it in their neighborhood.

But those days, that life, it was all behind her now. This was her life. This was her chance to really make something of herself. To really make her family feel like all their hard work and sacrifice was worth it. To prove that you could be raised in a poor, immigrant family in some no-name town on the outskirts of Miami and still become a successful bigwig attorney in Manhattan.

"Yes, I'm at work, but it's fine. There are a bunch of people still here." Ana tried to soothe her misery at still being at the office past eight on a Tuesday. "How's the car coming along?" she asked, trying to shift the topic back to Antonio's favorite topic—himself.

"It's looking so sick, let me show you." He jumped up from his bed and left his bedroom, then walked down the steps of their childhood home.

It was weird to think of Antonio still sleeping in the same bed he had once peed in as a kid. At first, she thought it was temporary, but over time it became apparent that he had no intention of going to college or trade school, or moving out at all. They couldn't be more opposite if they tried. Where Antonio had no drive in his life, Ana had enough for the both of them. The day she graduated from the University of Miami, she had informed her parents that she was moving to New York for law school at Columbia. She could still hear her mother sobbing at the realization that Ana would no longer be a twenty-minute drive away.

Antonio opened the garage door and flipped the camera around to display a candy apple red 1967 Mustang. The wheels were a shiny black and there were two black racing stripes along the hood. The last time Ana had seen the car, it had been black and covered with rust stains. She was impressed by the changes in such a short amount of time.

"Bonita, wow, Antonio. It looks amazing. Papi been doing most of the heavy lifting, I assume?"

Antonio wrinkled his eyebrows. "No way, he basically sits in his chair over there and *supervises* me these days. I've done all the engine work myself, plus I designed the details of the interior and the paint job."

Ana smiled. "The colors remind me of papi's old Camaro. Remember when we were in middle school and he would drive us around in that thing? We thought we were so fancy."

Antonio laughed. "Speak for yourself. I *was* fancy."

Ana smiled. She hadn't heard her brother this excited about something in a really long time. When they were little, Antonio was always the one who preferred to play with his Hot Wheels or stay inside and play *FIFA* on whatever gaming console he had at the time. She had been the outgoing, social one between the two of them. It was a natural fit now, thinking of him hiding under the hood of an old car, her father pointing his finger from across the room, giving instructions.

"What are you gonna do with it when it's finished?"

"*She* is going on the market. Well, after I show her off at a few car shows, that is." Antonio gave her a wide grin.

An email notification came up on her computer screen, but she ignored it. She had maybe exaggerated the number of people in the office with her at the moment. There were a few junior associates huddled together in the conference room organizing exhibits for an upcoming trial, and the custodial team had started to vacuum down the hall. Truth be told, it was creepy as hell being there when it was so empty, but Ana knew once she logged off for the day, she would only be met with more work the next day.

"What's her name?" Ana asked, choosing to focus on her brother's passion rather than her lack thereof.

"Sally Ride."

Ana raised an eyebrow. "Like the first American woman in space?"

Antonio shook his head. "No, you know, like the song...ride, Sally, ride." He started laughing.

Ana laughed back and felt a weight begin to lift as she enjoyed the moment with her brother.

"Maybe you should take it for a road trip up to see me," Ana joked.

Antonio shook his head. "No way, man, you're not getting me in that cold-ass place."

"It's July, estúpido, it's like a hundred degrees here right now."

He shrugged. "Whatever, man, not gonna happen."

Ana gave up. Her brother would never leave Miami, she knew that. She just hoped eventually her mother would be satisfied having one child—her favorite child—literally under her roof so she would stop trying to pressure Ana to move back home.

"So, how's life up there? Got ladies lined up around the block, I bet," he said playfully.

Ana let out a loud sigh. "Yeah, right. Oh, actually, that reminds me, I've got a line waiting outside my office right now." Ana leaned over and looked at her door.

"Well, you could! If you weren't all huddled up in that dark-ass office of yours."

Ana feigned offense. "Excuse me, I worked my butt off for this office. And you're one to talk, hiding in that dark-ass room over there."

Antonio nodded. "You right, you right. But hey, I got something in the works."

Ana raised an eyebrow. "Oh, really, got a lady I need to know about? Oh, God, it's not Camilla from down the street, is it? Tell me you're not dating Camilla."

"Not saying a word," Antonio said, holding back laughter. "But no, I'm not dating Camilla."

Ana exhaled dramatically and wiped fake sweat off her brow. Another notification came in her emails, and she checked the time. If she had any hope of leaving before nine, she had to get back to work.

"I gotta go, but text me later?"

"Yeah, yeah, just do yourself a favor and see some sunlight soon. You're starting to look like a gringa tourist. You know, the ones who wear socks with their sandals."

"How dare you."

"Peace out!" Antonio yelled before abruptly hanging up.

He was right, she really should get out and enjoy the good weather soon. She'd been cooped up so long she had almost forgotten it was summer until she had mentioned it to Antonio just now. She made a mental note to take a day off the next time it was warm and sunny on a weekend. For now, she just wanted to finish responding to these emails and get the hell out of the office.

Chapter Twelve

Rachel finished blending a kale and celery smoothie and wiped her forehead. She had just finished a ten-mile run around Central Park, and there was nothing better than a fresh, healthy snack during her cool-down time. She poured the green liquid into a glass and watched as it reached almost exactly to the top.

"Perfection," Rachel said to Elijah, who sat at her feet, clearly confusing the sound of a blender full of vegetables with a can of tuna.

"You don't like kale, silly girl," Rachel said, patting Elijah on her head and walking into her living room.

She sat down on the simple navy blue sofa and propped her feet up on her coffee table. Aside from a short, wide mid-century modern style bookshelf that doubled as her TV stand, that was the entirety of her furniture for the largest room in the place, which wasn't saying much. The apartment also had a bedroom, a bathroom, and a washer and dryer that were next to the dishwasher in the kitchen. The landlord had told her she was welcome to paint the walls if she liked, but Rachel had never taken the time to do it. There was no point really. She wasn't home much, and when she was, she was reading, or watching TV to decompress, or playing with Elijah, who luckily was as introverted as she was.

Rachel had school photos of her niece and nephew on her TV stand/bookshelf combo and a photo of her family at the Passover Seder last year. Then there was a photo of her and Charlotte on their mutual graduation day, Rachel in her baby blue Columbia robes, hunter green hood, and rounded hat, and Charlotte with her royal purple NYU robes and black squared hat. She loved that fate had intervened and allowed her to graduate a second time with her best friend from high school, even if it had been from different schools.

The apartment was small, but it was more than enough space for one woman who was rarely there and a cat whose favorite hobbies included eating and bird watching from a hammock hanging in the window.

Growing up in New York, Rachel was used to living in small spaces. She couldn't imagine growing up somewhere without the sounds of ambulances or car horns playing in the background. Too much silence in her surroundings terrified Rachel, and nothing caused her more anxiety than the idea of being off in the woods in a cabin somewhere with just the sounds of crickets and tree frogs to lull her to sleep. She needed the chaos and noise of the city. It made her feel safe.

When she had moved into the apartment a few years ago, it was the first time in her entire life Rachel had lived alone. When she was little, there had been Noa and of course her parents. Then throughout college she had a new roommate every year. Immediately after medical school, she and Charlotte had shared a place until Rachel finally earned enough to afford her own place and Charlotte moved in with some friends from nursing school in Harlem.

Now, after a few years of calling the small apartment on the Upper East Side home, Rachel realized that she liked living alone. It suited her. Plus, her apartment was a perfect location for work. At the corner of 82nd and York, her commute consisted of a quick walk to the 6 train for a single stop, or a nice long walk of about twenty blocks. All in all, it usually took her half an hour to get to the hospital most days. If she wanted to see her parents, she just went for a run through the park and up a few blocks and she was on the Upper West Side. If she wanted to see Noa and the kids, she hopped on the M train out to Williamsburg and she was there in 45 minutes max. It was a great setup.

But even with the perfect combination of logistics and introversion in place, Rachel still felt lonely sometimes. She had considered buying a plant or maybe even a goldfish to make it homier, but the plant would die with lack of water and Elijah would probably eat the fish. This was all she needed, she reminded herself in the moments of emptiness. This was sufficient.

Sometimes Rachel felt guilty, sitting there in her nice, clean apartment when there were so many who lived with nothing in this city. Rachel pacified her imposter syndrome/superhero complex by doing as much volunteer work as possible, but still, it never felt like enough. She had become a surgeon because she wanted to impact people's lives, to leave the world a better place than the world she was born into, but some days she felt like Sisyphus, pushing a boulder up an endless hill.

After she finished her smoothie and stretched, Rachel took a hot shower and returned to the living room wrapped in her towel, only to find Elijah curled up in the exact spot she had been sitting on the couch.

Of course.

"Excuse me, that is my seat," she said, lifting the animal and moving her to her lap.

She picked up her phone and checked the time. This was absolutely one of those rare days when Rachel would love to veg out on the couch and binge an entire season of a TV show, but she had committed to doing volunteer work downtown, and if Rachel was anything, it was committed.

After a few more moments of relaxing with Elijah purring on her lap, Rachel let out a big sigh and stood up, willing herself to get dressed.

She picked up her phone to check the time again and was met with a text from Charlotte.

Charlotte: Can't wait for tomorrow night! You're my hero.

CHAPTER THIRTEEN

"Coming!" Ana said in response to the knock at her door as she scuffled her bare feet across the hardwood floor.

She was in the process of putting in an earring, and her dress was so tight at the knees she couldn't move faster than a shuffle at the moment. Thank God for Spanx.

Stella was on the other side of the door when she opened it. She let out a wolf whistle and followed it up with a catcall.

"Not too shabby yourself." Ana eyed Stella up and down quickly before putting in her next earring.

Stella adjusted her cufflinks and ran a hand through her gelled-back hair. "Oh, this old thing?" She pointed to her crisp black tuxedo. "I only wear it when I don't care who I see."

"Yeah, yeah, I'm sure we all have tuxedos just hanging in our closets."

"Well, you're one to talk. I mean that dress is...wow." Stella clutched her chest and looked her up and down.

Ana slipped on her heels and studied herself in the full-length mirror that took up a good portion of her small living room. Her dress was black and floor length, appropriate for the black-tie affair they were heading to, with a slit that started at mid-thigh and ran all the way down her left leg. Her pointy-toed black stilettos only served to accentuate the length of her legs in a way that made her feel tall for once. Ana tucked a strand of hair behind her ear before applying a little more hair spray to ensure one half was tucked back while the other half fell down her chest in thick curls and waves. The top of the dress was a halter top, which made her already C cup boobs look like they could fill out a solid D. Ana had to admit, she looked sexy AF. Maybe she'd luck out and meet someone who could fuck her brains out and help her forget the annoying redhead who had consumed her thoughts and dreams since their frustrating encounter at Cubby a few nights ago.

It was like every chance life got, the universe was there to put Rachel Cohen in her brain. While she was sitting on the subway that morning, there was a sign for Mount Sinai Hospital over her head. While she was waiting in line at Gregory's yesterday, someone named Rachel ordered coffee right in front of her. Every redhead she passed on the street made her do a double take. It was maddening.

"Think I'll get any action in this thing?" Ana asked, pulling her boobs up higher in the dress and putting on ruby red lipstick.

"I'd basically guarantee it. But don't forget, you agreed to let me crash here tonight. Don't be a dick and make me take a hundred-dollar taxi all the way up to Washington Heights at two a.m.," Stella added.

"Don't be ridiculous." Ana smacked her lips together and looked at Stella in the reflection. "The subway still runs at two a.m."

"Very funny, Mendez." Stella gave a fake laugh and stood up from the couch. "Ready to rock this thing?"

Ana slid her phone and wallet into the tiny purse she was carrying. "Let's do it."

The Center Dinner was hosted every year during Pride by the Lesbian, Gay, Bisexual & Transgender Community Center, more commonly known as the Center. The event was held as a way to honor trailblazers and people of impact in the LGBTQ+ New York City community. It was a major deal to be nominated for an award and an even bigger deal to win one. But Ana and Stella weren't going for that. They were going because Byron & Browning was a premier sponsor at the event, meaning they paid a shit ton of money to put their name on flyers and banners and promotions, all in the name of diversity, equity, and inclusion.

Usually the firm sent Darcy Hammond, but since her abrupt departure from the firm, there was a serious shortage of queer representation—an opportunity Ana saw and took advantage of immediately.

Not only was it her subtle way of telling the managing partners that yes, she—the high heel and lipstick wearing senior associate—was bisexual, but also to take yet another one of those leadership roles she so desperately craved.

The firm was more than happy to send her with her *date*, Stella, and Stella was more than happy to scoop up as many free drinks, hors d'oeuvres, and hopefully attention from beautiful women as possible in one evening. It was really a win for everyone involved.

"Okay, don't forget we have to get photos on the red carpet for the firm newsletter. I want the diversity points and I want the Los Angeles office people to know my name," Ana said as they pulled up to Cipriani on Wall Street, where the event was being held. A line had already started forming out front, and Ana felt herself getting nervous.

"You got it, boss," Stella said. She gave Ana a calm, reassuring smile.

Stella was always cool and collected in situations like this. She might as well be a lion walking into a den of lambs for all she was concerned. She had no concept of intimidation or social anxiety. Ana did, she just hid it exceptionally well under a veil of extroversion and relatability. She inwardly decided they would snag a drink as soon as they got inside and get a little liquid courage flowing before mingling and networking.

They waited their turn for photos as couple after couple lined the carpet outside the venue. When it was their turn, they meshed so well into their designated positions that most probably assumed they were actually a couple. Ana rested her hand on her hip, shifting her leg forward to reveal itself from beneath the high slit. Stella kept one hand in her pocket and the other on the lowest part of Ana's fully exposed back. To an onlooker, she was making a pass, but Ana knew it was just her way of reassuring Ana in the moment. Letting her know she was there beside her, holding her up.

When they were finally inside, Ana stopped to collect herself. "I bet I blinked through every shot," she said fixing her hair again.

"No way. Your eyes are beautiful, your dress is beautiful, you're beautiful, I'm beautiful, now let's go get a drink." Stella grabbed Ana gently by the elbow and ushered her toward the bar.

Cipriani Wall Street, the venue for the dinner, was steeped in classic New York City opulence and history. It was once the location for the New York Stock Exchange and the United States Customs House, and it had served as the headquarters of the National City Bank. Okay, she might have done some googling before the event.

It had a high domed ceiling and a balcony overlooking the main room where hundreds of circular tables were placed. Each table had a tall centerpiece bursting with various types of white flowers. The room was illuminated with dimmed, rainbow-colored lights and there were three large bars. Circular tables filled the center of the room, and a balcony overlooked the space where a DJ stood playing posh loft music. Ana had never seen so many people all dressed to the nines in one place. She felt like she had stepped into a modern Gilded Age event and she was waiting for a valet to come and offer her some cigars and brandy. Instead, she opted to get her own drink and headed toward the first available bar to the left of the massive room.

"Mint mojito," Ana said to the bartender, dropping a twenty in the tip jar.

Tip them early and get heavy pours all night, a lesson she had learned early on in her going out days.

A few moments later the bartender, a cute person with a fauxhawk and a nose ring, slid her the drink and added a flirtatious smile for good measure. Ana raised her glass to them and smiled wide.

"Gracias," she said, using the ultimate tool in her arsenal—her fluency in Spanish—to gain a slight blush from the bartender.

"Oh, damn, already pulling out the Spanish. You are working for it tonight, girl." Stella took a sip of her beer and chuckled.

"Well, whatever works, right?"

Whatever it takes to get Rachel freaking Cohen off my mind, that is.

CHAPTER FOURTEEN

Rachel adjusted her bespoke baby blue tuxedo jacket and wiped her hands on her matching pants. Charlotte had convinced her to order a custom tux for the event, even though it was ridiculously overpriced.

"It brings out your eyes, and you look so damn sexy in it," she had said at her final fitting at the tailor's shop two weeks ago.

The jacket was double-breasted with large gold buttons and a peak lapel. The pants were slim cut, and she wore nude high heels, which made her already long legs look even longer. The boxy cut of the jacket was a perfect fit for her slender frame. Her hair was slicked back into a low, tight bun and her dark eye shadow, also courtesy of Charlotte, gave her eyes a smoky, sultry appeal that made their natural blue color shine out from the darkness.

Rachel felt slightly underdressed, looking at the white dinner jacket and black tuxedos and evening gowns that filled the room, but soon she started to see a steady flow of cocktail dresses and suits, and her nerves relaxed a bit. The room was packed—there must have been over five hundred people present—which was doing nothing for her nerves.

"Stop doing that," Charlotte said, coming up beside her and handing her a glass of champagne.

"Doing what?"

"Comparing yourself to everyone in this room. You're here to accept an amazing award. They should be comparing themselves to you."

Rachel sighed. Charlotte was right. Rachel had won a few academic accolades before, but nothing this significant had ever happened to her. When she got the email telling her she had been nominated for the Hometown Hero award from the Center this year, she had been too shocked to speak. When she got the second email telling her she had won the thing, she quite literally almost passed out. Noa physically had to hold her upright in her seat as she read the email out loud to her and Jake.

Rachel knew she had chosen a special career when she elected to be a cardiac surgeon, but she didn't realize that she could also have such an impact on the LGBTQ+ community in addition to that special profession. After all, what do triple bypasses and gender rights have to do with one another? Well apparently, not that much, but when you're a cardiac surgeon who volunteers at places like the Bowery Mission and Trinity Place on your few days off, the community takes notice. When you single-handedly convince the hospital you work at to donate over a hundred thousand dollars to those places, the community takes notice and gives you an award for it at a fancy dinner. On top of that, Mount Sinai Hospital had been a sponsor of the dinner for over ten years now, so while it was surprising to Rachel that she had been given the award, she suspected it also had something to do with who was donating the big chunk of change to the event. Noa had told her that was just her inner saboteur trying to convince her that she wasn't worthy of the thing, but Rachel had ignored her.

"Come on, let's go snag our seats, the ceremony's about to start," Charlotte said as they walked to the front of the room where other award recipients and VIPs were seated.

After about an hour of listening to other individuals receive various awards for their impact in the community, Rachel was feeling less worthy than ever. The little voice in her head that was constantly whispering that she wasn't good enough was no longer whispering, it was screaming.

Rachel felt her hands getting cold and clammy. "I'm gonna go grab some water."

"No way, your award is up next!" Charlotte whispered.

Rachel swallowed hard and her throat suddenly felt drier than the Gobi Desert. "Just go accept it for me, will you?" Rachel made a move to stand up and Charlotte jerked her back down into her seat.

"No way. You are going to get up on that stage and you are going to accept that award because, Rachel Cohen, you fucking deserve it. Now, turn off your brain, hold your shoulders back, and take another sip of this." She slid a glass of champagne to Rachel, who gratefully drained the rest of the glass.

"Our next award is the Hometown Hero award," the host announced from the stage.

"Oh, God," Rachel said out loud, wishing she hadn't already finished her drink.

"This award is designed to honor local New Yorkers who have dedicated their time, energy, talents, and skills to the New York City LGBTQ+ community. It is awarded to the person we feel has most embodied the definition of a hometown hero."

I am worthy. I am worthy. I am worthy.

Rachel began repeating mantras in her head and focusing on her breathing.

"Our recipient this year is nothing short of extraordinary. Raised on the Upper West Side, she is a cardiac surgeon at Mount Sinai Hospital, where she spends her days and nights performing complex procedures that have saved countless lives. In her limited free time, she volunteers at local shelters for LGBTQ+ youth, and last year she was responsible for convincing Mount Sinai Hospital to donate over one hundred thousand dollars to several of those shelters."

A round of applause echoed around the room, and the host paused and smiled while Rachel closed her eyes and pretended to be invisible.

"Because of her tireless efforts, thousands of members of the LGBTQ+ community who suffer from housing insecurity now have a safe and affirming place to lay their heads at night. At these shelters they receive free food, free counseling services, career services, and even hands-on job training whenever possible."

Just breathe. Just breathe. Just breathe.

Charlotte reached out and rested her hand in Rachel's, and Rachel opened her eyes to look at her. A reassuring smile was plastered across her face and she gave Rachel a confident head nod before looking back to the stage.

"It is my honor to present this year's Hometown Hero award to none other than Dr. Rachel Cohen!"

The entire room erupted in applause as Rachel sat frozen for what felt like and eternity. Charlotte nudged her and mouthed "Go" as Rachel convinced her legs and the rest of her body to slowly stand up from her chair and move.

She ignored the shaking in her knees as she walked up each step toward the tall man holding out a silver engraved plaque to her. Rachel smiled and gave the man a quick side hug.

"Thank you," she said into the microphone trying to hide the tremble in her voice. "This really is such an honor." She looked out into the crowd but could only see the bright lights shining down on her. Trying to remember the words she had recited in her head a hundred times, she looked down and cleared her throat. "I don't really know what else to say other than how proud I am to be part of such a supportive and empowering community. I am truly humbled by this award. Thank you."

Rachel lifted up the plaque a little and smiled as the room applauded and she stepped down off the stage.

Thank God that was over. Now she could finally relax.

CHAPTER FIFTEEN

S hit, I missed the Hometown Hero award?" Ana said, returning from an emergency run to the bathroom. Wearing a tight dress was a killer move as far as looks went, but her Spanx made her feel like she had to pee all the time, and it took several extra steps of caution to actually use the restroom.

Stella looked like she'd just seen a ghost as Ana sat down at their table in the back of the room.

"All good?"

Stella just sat with her mouth hanging open staring in the direction of the stage.

"I don't...I don't even know what to say."

Ana adjusted herself in the seat and scooted closer.

"Okay, you're kinda freaking me out. I was only gone for like fifteen minutes. What could have possibly happened?"

Silently, Stella lifted her hand and pointed a finger at a woman walking along the wall of the room heading toward the bar. She had a baby blue tuxedo, an incredible body, and...and a thick head of red hair.

"You have got to be shitting me," Ana said, loud enough for several people at their table to shoot her a dirty look.

"I swear to God, dude, the universe is either playing a dirty game on you or is being the ultimate matchmaker. This shit should be in a lesbian Hallmark movie or something," Stella whispered.

"What the hell is she even doing here?" Ana asked, annoyance immediately present in her voice. "God, doesn't she have a life? And she calls me the stalker."

Stella shook her head. "No, dude, you don't understand. She just...I mean...*she's* the Hometown Hero."

"Shut the fuck up." Ana's mouth dropped open.

Ana reached across the table. "Mind if I borrow this?" she said to a blond woman who looked annoyed at their chatter.

She knew she should have grabbed a program when they first got there, but her focus had been on the free alcohol, and by the time she had gotten around to looking for one they were all gone.

Ana flipped through it. There it was in a full page of color, complete with a photo and everything. "Hometown Hero: Dr. Rachel Cohen," the program read. "When Dr. Cohen isn't performing complex cardiac surgeries at Mount Sinai Hospital, she can be found volunteering at local LGBTQ+ shelters for unhoused youth such as New Alternatives, the Bowery Mission, and Trinity Place. Dr. Cohen grew up on the Upper West Side with her mother, father, and sister. A lifetime member of her local synagogue, Dr. Cohen claims she owes her success to her supportive Jewish community and her family. 'My family is,' according to Dr. Cohen, 'the best part of me.'"

Ana stopped reading and stared at the photo for a moment. *She really is a beautiful woman*, Ana thought, as Rachel's soft, blue eyes stared back at her from the page. Ana flushed a little thinking about how quick those eyes could turn from soft to sultry and from sultry to fiery. She looked back to the paragraph where Rachel talked about her family. Ana couldn't have described anything in better terms herself.

My family is the best part of me too.

Ana looked over her shoulder. There she was, standing at the bar all alone, in a perfectly tailored tuxedo. It was funny, but from where Ana stood, Rachel didn't look like the doctor who had walked into her office. Or the snarky woman she had bumped into at Cubby. Right now, she looked like the woman Ana had approached in the bar that first night, then taken home. She was leaned over chatting with the same bartender that Ana had flirted with earlier. Was she flirting with them too? Ana couldn't be sure, but she could be sure of one thing—Rachel Cohen looked incredible in blue. The tailored pants hugged her long legs in all the right places, and the cut of the blazer gave her an air of dominance that made Ana's heart race a little as she watched her shift her weight in her high heels from left to right.

Oh, fuck it.

"I'll be right back," Ana whispered to Stella and, without thinking, stood up from the table.

"Wait, are you serious?"

"What?" Ana answered. "I'm just thirsty." She glanced over her shoulder and walked directly to the bar where the woman with the red hair and eyes that matched her tuxedo stood, not knowing what was coming for her.

CHAPTER SIXTEEN

I liked your speech," the bartender said, and flashed a charming smile at Rachel.

Rachel looked down at her drink and smiled. She hadn't planned on flirting with anyone tonight. In fact, she hadn't planned on even talking to anyone but Charlotte, she was so nervous, but now she was feeling slightly tipsy after chugging a few glasses of champagne. Not to mention she had a major buzz from just finishing her speech in front of hundreds of people. What harm could a little flirting do?

"Thanks, I just spoke from the heart," Rachel responded. She tucked a rogue strand of hair behind her ear and did her best attempt at batting her eyelashes without looking like the woman from *Misery*.

Judging by the cute bartender's reaction, the mission was a success. They leaned in closer, a single dimple appearing on their left cheek.

"So, you're a surgeon. That's pretty cool," they said, flashing a row of perfect white teeth.

Rachel looked down at their sleeve and was just about to ask what one of their tattoos meant when—

"Well, well, well, who's stalking who now?"

Rachel turned slowly. *You have got to be kidding me.* Standing less than a foot away from her in the most stunning black dress Rachel had ever seen was Ana Mendez.

"Wow," Rachel said, both from the utter shock of seeing Ana and the undeniable radiance she was emitting.

"Don't be too surprised, Doc, the lesbian community is basically the size of a peanut shell."

"Queer community," the bartender chimed in, still leaning over the bar.

Ana nodded. "You're right, the queer community is basically the size of a peanut shell, thank you."

The bartender smiled and looked back and forth between the two of them. Rachel just stood there, unable to take her eyes off Ana, and watched while Ana crossed her arms, accentuating her already plump breasts in her revealing, low cut dress.

"Can I get you a drink?" the bartender asked.

"That depends, am I interrupting something?"

"Other than this entire event? No, you're not interrupting," Rachel managed to say, a hint of spite mingled with flirtatiousness in her voice.

Ana raised an eyebrow. "In that case, I'll have a mojito. I'm sorry, I didn't catch your name earlier..." Ana paused while she waited for the bartender's response.

"Jax," they responded and reached across the bar to shake Ana's hand.

"I'm Ana. I'll have a mojito, Jax. Actually, make it two, one for me and one for our hometown hero over here."

Ana flashed Rachel a deadly smile that said "come here" and "I hate you" all at once.

Rachel tried to wrap her head around what the fuck was actually happening. By the time she had processed that this was real life, that Ana Mendez, the attorney single-handedly trying to ruin her life (aka Ana Mendez, the best sex she'd ever had), was at the same dinner where she had just accepted an award for changing people's lives, their drinks were ready.

Ana slid the glass over to Rachel, who hesitantly lifted it from the bar.

"To the Hippocratic oath," Ana said, a flash of mischief behind her dark eyes. "First, do no harm," she said, before taking a sip of her drink.

Rachel narrowed her eyes. "I didn't think bloodsucking lawyers like you believed in not doing harm," she quipped. "Seems like the only thing you *are* good at is harming people, actually."

Ana tossed her head back and let out a low, soft laugh. Rachel couldn't help but stare at her elongated neck as her throat bounced up and down. Even if she was laughing at her expense, she looked beautiful doing it. Rachel resisted the urge to wrap her hand around Ana's neck and press her mouth against her full lips. Instead, she took a sip of her drink to force herself to stop looking at Ana.

As if she sensed the spike in Rachel's libido, Ana took another small step closer and invaded the last inch of personal space left between the two of them. Rachel felt her heart drop into her stomach as Ana leaned in. Her lips grazed the top of her earlobe and the heat from her mouth sent tingles down Rachel's spine as she whispered, "I think we both know that isn't the only thing I'm good at."

Rachel tried to mask her reaction. She tried to hide the blush that immediately crept up her chest and onto her cheeks at Ana's proximity and the implication she had just made, but she knew it was no use. Her fair skin always betrayed her, and she was certain she matched the shade of her hair right now. Ana took a step back and tossed her hair over her shoulder, a smug look of satisfaction spread across her painted red lips. Rachel bit down on her cheek to try to hide the frustration—both sexual and otherwise—growing inside her.

Seemingly sensing the tension between the two women, Jax took the opportunity to help a woman at the other end of the bar choose a wine.

Rachel set the drink down on the bar, determined to keep her wits about her.

"What do you want, Counselor? What are you even doing here?"

"So formal," Ana said taking another slow, intentional sip of her drink. "I'd like to apologize for my behavior at the bar the other night. I was surprised to see you, to say the least, and you didn't exactly catch me in my element. I was overstimulated and grumpy and I might have maybe taken that out a little on you." Ana flashed a smile of innocence, a single dimple popping up in her left cheek. Rachel stood unabashed with her arms crossed. "Anyway, my firm is a premier sponsor of this event. No need to ask what you're doing here," Ana said, motioning to the silver plaque lying on the bar.

"I guess you heard my speech," Rachel said, her cheeks once again burning with embarrassment.

Ana shifted her weight and leaned against the bar. Rachel pretended not to notice how she stuck her ass out with the movement or how she bent over just enough to allow more cleavage to pour out of her dress.

"Sad to say, I missed it," Ana said. "Care to share the details?"

"It was for my work fundraising and volunteering at local shelters for unhoused queer youth."

She noticed a shift in Ana at that. A bit of the fire behind her eyes seemed to dim and simmer, like someone had poured flour over on a kitchen fire. Maybe she wasn't expecting a genuine answer? Or maybe she didn't expect Rachel to be involved in charity work?

"That's…" Ana began. She cleared her throat. "That's actually admirable of you."

Taken aback by the response, Rachel picked up her drink again to fill the silence. "Thank you?"

Ana took another slow slip, averting her eyes toward the bar, as if trying to decide what to say next. Rachel took the opportunity to stare openly at Ana's body for the first time and, God, she was glad she did. She knew she was gorgeous—after all, Rachel rarely went home with women she wasn't dating, let alone one she met at a random bar in Midtown. Only a true beauty would have convinced her to go out on such a limb. But that had been after work, with drinks flowing and the smell of the subway lingering on their clothes. When they had had sex, the lights were out and Rachel had only really gotten to observe her body through the glow of the streetlight. But now, standing before her in a floor length evening gown that hugged her generous curves in all the right ways, Rachel was starting to see what had drawn her in in the first place. Ana Mendez was stunning.

"What?" Ana said, setting her drink down on the bar. Her mouth curved up into a half smile and Rachel looked down, avoiding eye contact.

"Nothing." She checked the gold watch on her wrist and looked around. The speeches were finishing now and people were beginning to mill about the room. It wouldn't be long before the bar would be brimming with people and their brief interlude would be over. She wondered if Charlotte would come looking for her soon. Did she want her to come and find her? Did she want to be dragged away?

"Tell me more," Ana said, stepping a little closer to Rachel again.

Rachel inhaled the sweet smell of her perfume and ignored the dizzying effect it had on her inhibitions.

"More about what?" Rachel asked.

"This." Ana reached her arm around Rachel and let her index finger gently stroke the plaque on the bar. "Tell me more about how you earned it."

Rachel looked down at Ana's hand and followed the line of her arm up to her neck and eventually her lips.

She inhaled slowly, steadying herself as she shifted her attention to Ana's eyes.

"I told you," she said, unable to hide the quiver in her voice. "I raised money and volunteered at homeless shelters for queer youth."

"I doubt that's all it was," Ana said, seeming genuinely interested in the conversation. "This is the Hometown Hero award. They only give this thing to someone who's made a real impact in the community."

Rachel averted her eyes and reached for her drink. She was feeling tipsier and knew she needed to stop, but it was either be drunk on the mojito or be drunk on Ana, and one felt way more dangerous than the other right now.

"Why would I tell you anything about myself?" she managed to say, her voice as sharp and cutting as her weak reserve would allow in the moment.

Ana furrowed her brows and gave Rachel a slow, lingering look that started at Rachel's pointy stilettos and worked its way up to her chest, her neck, her lips, and finally her eyes.

"I guess you wouldn't." Disappointment echoed at the end of her sentence, before the flame behind her eyes illuminated again. "If you ever change your mind," she leaned over and slid a hand into Rachel's jacket pocket, leaving something inside, "I'd love to hear more. Off the record, of course," she said with a wink.

Ana drained the rest of her drink, turned, and left. Rachel stood, dumbfounded, watching and waiting to see if she would look behind her.

She didn't.

When Ana was finally out of eyesight, Rachel reached into her pocket and pulled out a business card.

Ana M. Mendez, Esq. Senior Associate, Byron & Browning.

Rachel flipped the card over. A phone number was handwritten on the back.

CHAPTER SEVENTEEN

W hat's going on with the *Notashi* case?" Ana snapped her attention back to the meeting she was in.

She met with her supervising partner, Paul, biweekly to review cases and make sure they were on the same page with where the cases were heading. At least, that's what Paul said the meetings were for. In reality, they usually ended with her walking away with a list of assignments longer than she could count, on top of the ones she still hadn't finished from their last meeting.

That was the thing about partners. All they had to do was rattle off the tasks to do, they didn't actually have to sit down and do them. It took Paul five seconds to say, "Draft a response to their demand for indemnification and defense," whereas it took Ana three hours to get it done.

The attenuation of time between Paul assigning the work and Ana actually doing the work constantly led to tasks needing to be done faster and faster. Sometimes she felt like she was battling a Hydra, chopping off one head just to have two more grow back in its place. Alas, that was the life of a lawyer at a big firm in New York.

This was the life she wanted, the life she chose for herself, or so she reminded herself at least once a week as she slurped ramen from a Styrofoam cup hunched over the dim glow of her computer screen at nine p.m.

"Discovery is done, the note of issue is being filed at the next status conference, and then our motions will be due ninety days after that," Ana rattled off, completely from memory.

She had a high caseload, over fifty cases, all in litigation, but she took pride in knowing them better than anyone else at the office.

"Great. Go ahead and get started on our expert affirmation, we don't want to be behind the ball."

Ana nodded as she scribbled down the note to herself. Because why shouldn't she start working on a motion that wasn't due for months when she had things literally due next week?

"And the *Solomon* case?" Paul asked.

The mention of the name caused Ana to stiffen up in her seat.

"It's on track," she said vaguely, not wanting to be pressed further about the adjourned and not yet rescheduled deposition of a certain cardiac surgeon.

"How many depositions are left?" he asked.

Ana shifted her weight in the seat. "Just one."

Paul nodded. "Good. Stay on top of that last doctor. I want that thing wrapped up as soon as possible. I hate those med mal cases. They take so much time and almost always go to trial."

Oh, I'll stay on top of her.

Ana clicked her pen anxiously, hoping to change the topic. "Anything else?"

Paul paused for a moment and checked the clock. It was four forty-five; their time had already gone over.

"Nope, that'll do it for today."

Ana flipped the used pages of her legal pad back into place and clicked her pen a few more times for good measure. "Sounds good, I'll just get back to work then."

"Oh, Ana, I've been meaning to ask you one thing."

Ana stopped near the door.

"I heard you went to a charity event at some, um…at a place this week?"

Ana cringed slightly at his effort to broach the topic of her sexuality. "Yes?"

"That's good, I uh…I'm glad to hear those type of events interest you." He shifted in his seat and folded his hands. "What I mean to say is, at Byron and Browning, we value diversity, and I'm just glad to see you're taking part in all we have to offer. You know, as a member of that, um…community."

Ana considered letting him keep going. It was possible he would talk himself straight into a discrimination lawsuit and she wouldn't have to worry about working for any promotion. But of all the partners at the firm, Paul was probably the least awful, and she couldn't let him hang himself any longer.

"Thank you, it's nice to work at a firm that values diversity." She almost gagged as soon as the words left her mouth.

She was many things, but a suck-up was not one of them. But this was all part of the game. She had never learned to golf, and her tennis serve needed work, so the diversity card was probably her best way to the top at this boys' club.

Ana left and walked toward her office, stopping in the kitchenette on the way. She grabbed a random hunter green mug from the cabinet that said *Stetson Law* in all white letters and poured a cup of now-burned coffee, letting the aroma reinvigorate her.

After she sat down at her desk, she checked her cell phone. Nothing but a few texts from her brother showing photos of the progress he and their father were making with the car restoration and a text from Stella asking for a template of an expert witness disclosure.

She set down her phone, ignoring the texts. Who was she kidding? She wasn't checking because she cared if her brother or her best friend texted her. She was checking to see if the incredibly sexy surgeon she had slipped her number to last week had reached out.

Ana shook her head. *What the hell was I even thinking? Giving my cell phone number to a doctor I am literally about to depose?* She rubbed her temples, trying to be gentle with herself. *It's no big deal. You were tipsy, she was tipsy. She probably threw the thing away as soon as you left. She was clearly hitting on the bartender anyway.*

"Oh, my God, Ana, stop caring who she was hitting on. Stop caring that she didn't text you. Stop, stop, stop!" Ana chastised herself out loud and slapped her cheeks. "Focus. You got this."

With that, she pulled up her email and forwarded yet another template of an expert witness disclosure to Stella. She told herself she wouldn't check her phone until she left the office that night. A resolve that lasted a grand total of five minutes.

"Heyo," Stella said, swinging into her office about an hour later.

"Hey, Stell, I already emailed you that template," Ana said. She kept her attention on her computer.

"Oh, yeah, thanks." She paused briefly. "So…are we gonna talk about the red-haired elephant in the room or are you just gonna keep ignoring me?"

Ana turned to Stella. "I'm not ignoring you, it's just been a busy day."

Stella raised an eyebrow. "Ana. I've known you for like literally years now. I know when you're avoiding something because you don't want to talk about it, and I totally respect that. But this is the third time you've run into this woman in three weeks. I don't believe in God, but after this, I may need to convert to something. What's a religion that accepts gay people?"

Ana laughed. "A lot of them. And yeah, okay, fine, it's weird. Unbelievable even, but...I don't know, I just don't want to talk about it, okay?"

Stella leaned over her desk. "You know I'm a lawyer too, right? I can smell bullshit just like you can. Something happened at the event. I know it."

"Easy, Perry Mason. Nothing happened, we just talked."

Stella stood up and crossed her arms. "Talked? About what? Her award?"

"A little, yeah."

"Well, I can't blame you there. I mean, the woman is truly incredible. The way she spends her free time volunteering, the amount of money she helped raise. I heard someone say they were considering naming a room in one of the shelters after her. It's pretty impressive stuff."

Ana sat back. Shit, maybe Rachel was actually a good person, which would really complicate the fact that Ana was already ridiculously attracted to her. What had she been thinking? If Rachel did reach out to her now, Ana would be faced with the impossible dilemma of responding and potentially getting involved with her walking-conflict-of-interest, or ignoring her and sending Rachel complete mixed messages. Maybe they could just be friends? Ana almost laughed at her own delusion. She knew she could never be just friends with someone she was so chemically drawn to. But how would she ever be able to say no to someone who was so morally and physically delicious? Lucky for her, Rachel had *not* texted and likely wouldn't. Ana convinced herself she was getting all worked up over a hypothetical that would never come to fruition. Right? Or what if Rachel had turned around and handed Ana's business card to her attorney the next day? What if this silence was the calm before the storm? Any day now she could get a letter from the ethics committee calling her in for a hearing.

"Oh, God," Ana said, letting her head drop into her hands. "Stella, I fucked up."

Stella sat down at one of the seats across from Ana's desk. "What happened?"

"Nothing I just...I kinda gave her my phone number at the event the other night."

Stella covered her mouth. "You didn't."

"I know, I know, it's just, I mean, you saw what she was wearing, right?"

Stella nodded. "Yeah, and did you see what *you* were wearing? I bet she texted you the second you walked away."

Ana shook her head. "Not a peep."

"Well, she's a doctor. Maybe she's just weighing all the options right now. We're not all as quick with our decision making as you. Some people actually like to think through the options before jumping off a cliff."

"Oh please, you are so not one of those people."

"Nope, I'm sure not. And that's why you're my best friend. But hey, next time you go cliff jumping, help a buddy out here. Her friend Charlotte is like, super hot. Don't leave me hanging."

"There isn't going to be a next time, don't worry."

Chapter Eighteen

"Good Shabbos!" Noa shouted as Rachel stepped into their parents' apartment.

"Good Shabbos," Rachel said as she carried the flowers into the kitchen and handed them to her mother before kissing her on the cheek.

"Auntie Rachel!" Estie squealed as she came running into the room with Benjamin toddling behind her.

Rachel bent down and scooped her up. "And good Shabbos to you, my little Esterina," she said. She kissed the little girl's cheeks so many times she started giggling and kicking until Rachel put her back down.

Rachel's mother walked over to her and grabbed her chin. "You're looking pale. Are you eating enough?"

"Oy vey, Ma, will you let her put her bag down first?" Noa chimed in.

Their mother threw her hands in the air. "Am I not allowed to make sure my eldest daughter eats enough? It's been ages since I've seen her."

Rachel rolled her eyes. "It's been barely a month, Mamala. If that."

Her mother shrugged. "At my age, a month may as well be a year."

Noa and Rachel exchanged glances. Their mother was in her midsixties and barely had gray hair, but the way she spoke you would think she was nearing a hundred.

"Where did my offspring go?" Jacob came stomping into the kitchen, his arms stretched out in front of him like Frankenstein's monster.

Benjamin and Estie jumped out from behind the small, round kitchen table, attempting to scare him. Jacob jumped back feigning surprise as he picked them up and carried them into the living room.

"Good Shabbos, Rachel!" he shouted from the other room.

"Yeah, yeah," she yelled back. She started arranging the flowers in a vase and asked her mother if she needed help finishing the meal.

"Check the oven for me, will you?" her mother said, pointing to the oven.

Rachel leaned down, pulled open the oven, and peered in to make sure the broccoli casserole wasn't burning. She smiled when she saw a loaf of challah on the rack beneath it. With so many kosher bakeries close by, her mother rarely made the challah herself these days, because of her "poor arthritic hands."

"Hello, hello!" Rachel heard the loud, booming voice of her father as he walked in the door.

Abraham Cohen was tall and thin and had a full head of thick gray hair that hung low over his deep blue eyes. He had a naturally cheery disposition and was the definition of a social butterfly. He and her mother, Hannah, could not be more opposite. Where Hannah was cold and standoffish, Abraham was warm and welcoming. Where Hannah was quick to judgment, Abraham was always one to hear both sides of the story. Where Hannah would rather stay home and play her piano, Abraham was always doing some sort of work down at their synagogue.

Rachel wished she could be more like her father. Warm and extroverted and kind. Unfortunately, she had inherited more of her mother's prickly tendencies, and most people said she was hard to read. Everyone except Noa, Charlotte, and her patients, that is.

Rachel had taken after her father in a physical sense, however. He was the reason for her slender, tall build, the light color of her eyes, and her knack for sports. Her fondest memories were playing basketball with him on weeknights after school at the local park. Even at the age of six, he wouldn't go easy on her. She could still remember him smacking the ball from her little hands, jumping up in the air to block every shot she took. If she cried, he would squat down on one knee and ask her why she was upset simply because she had been beaten.

"Failure is a part of life," he would say. "You cannot quit every time it happens. You must dust yourself off and you must try again. Always try again."

Rachel had repeated that mantra throughout her entire life. During her varsity basketball tryouts in high school, during her finals from undergrad, and then during her boards from Columbia. Every step of the way, her father's voice was always there to lift her up, to push her. He didn't expect things from her like her mother did. He didn't have a plan for her life that she had to follow. All he ever asked was that she give 100 percent of herself to whatever she did. To commit. To try. To fail. And to try again. And for that, she loved him.

"Tate," she said, as she leaned up and kissed his cheek.

"There's my favorite daughter," he said, and kissed the top of her head.

"Standing right here," Noa said from the sink without turning around.

Rachel's father looked down at Rachel and winked.

"How was work?" she asked.

"Oh, you know what they say, every time someone buys life insurance, an angel gets his wings." He let out a loud, boisterous laugh that filled the room.

Rachel's mother shushed their father and waved her arms in the air. "We're lighting the candles, come, come!"

Everyone left the kitchen and made their way into the dining room. The family gathered around the long, wooden table that had belonged to Rachel's grandparents and grew quiet as their mother lit the candles and recited the weekly prayer.

Rachel waved her hands in front of her face and closed her eyes. Shabbat dinner was one of her favorite traditions. She was sad she had missed it three weeks in a row. She loved that her family had a set time each week where they would gather together and just enjoy being around one another. Of course, it being on Friday night wasn't always ideal for her social life, but she rarely worked a typical Monday to Friday, anyway. It had bothered her more in high school, when her friends would go to movies and dinner and on dates and Rachel would be stuck sitting at the same table every week.

Her family was not so devout that they did not allow the lights to be turned on, but they had a strict "no technology in the house" rule for the entire evening, and something about that made Rachel happy. It was the gift of being present. The gift of being entirely in the moment with nothing existing beyond the four walls of her childhood home. She hoped she would host Shabbat dinners with her children one day and her grandchildren after that. But that would, of course, require her to actually date and produce children with someone, a prospect which seemed more than dauting lately.

"So, how was work for you?" her father asked once they were all seated in their unofficial assigned seats around the rectangular table.

"It's good. I had a very interesting case today. Triple bypass in a patient with arrhythmia." Rachel took a bite and smiled as the familiar taste of her mother's fresh challah filled her mouth.

"What about that awful lawsuit? Is that over now?" her mother chimed in.

Rachel's shoulders tensed at the reference, the bread growing sour in her mouth. "Actually, no, not yet. I still have to be deposed. The first time didn't exactly go according to plan and they had to reschedule."

She could feel Noa's eyes on her from across the table and intentionally wouldn't look at her. Noa had about as much of a poker face as their mother had patience.

"Such a disgrace." Her mother shook her head. "Suing innocent people like this, over a tragic accident. That lawyer should be ashamed of himself."

If only it was an accident.

She ignored the fact that her mother had assumed the attorney was a man. Not a sexy, curvy, five-foot-four Latina whose tongue did wonders between Rachel's legs.

She shoved a beet into her mouth to avoid having to discuss the topic any further. For once, her mother took the hint and changed the topic, but unfortunately for Rachel, the shift was not much of a reprieve.

"Did you meet any nice ladies at that fancy event last week?"

Leave it to her mother to distill a major award into just another "fancy event."

Rachel loved that her parents were so accepting of her sexuality. Acceptance was one of the many things she loved about her Jewish faith. What she didn't love was her mother's ambition to have more grandchildren than her friends down at the shul.

"We are so proud of you, Rachel," Noa added, lifting her glass of wine. Her parents followed suit. "It's incredible to win such an award."

"We truly are so proud." Her father patted her gently on the back.

"Well, did you?" Her mother pressed.

Again, her shoulders tensed. "There were a lot of beautiful people there, yes." She did her best at being vague. She still hadn't told Noa about running into Ana for yet a third time since their little interlude, and she certainly hadn't mentioned Ana slipping Rachel her number.

Not that Rachel still had her business card in her wallet or anything. And not that she had entered the phone number at least ten times that last week and typed out several different variations of texts.

"Hello, Counselor," she had typed on the first failed attempt.

Too flirty.

"Someone called for a doctor?"

God no, way too 1970s porno.

"Hello, Miss Mendez," another attempt read.

Too formal and possibly super creepy.

Finally, after talking herself in and out of it, she had decided to just let sleeping dogs lie and not text her at all. But she would still hold on to the card for good measure.

"Don't be coy, you know what I mean. You're almost forty. You should start taking this seriously. Your father and I have always supported whomever you choose to bring home, you know that. But bringing no one home? Not ever? That is simply unacceptable."

"Hannah, please," Rachel's father pleaded. "It's Shabbat."

"Actually, I did meet someone," Rachel said, her palms sweaty beneath the table.

A look of shock spread over Noa's face across the table, and Jacob stopped chewing mid-bite.

"She's great, and things are very new, so if you would just please leave it at that, I would appreciate it."

The room hung in silence for what felt like eternity, with only the sound of Benjamin slapping his hands down on the table and Estie scraping her plate with her fork.

What the hell am I doing?

"Well, okay then," her mother said. She seemed satisfied, if a little confused.

The topic quickly changed to Estie's school and when her next piano recital would be. Rachel was very thankful that her niece was a talker because by the time the meal was finished, there was no more space for follow-up questions on the topic of Rachel's love life.

"What the hell, sis?" Noa whispered, scraping the dishes into the sink after they had finished the meal. "You met someone? Since when do we keep secrets?"

Rachel glanced over her shoulder to ensure they were alone. "I'm not keeping secrets. It's no one you don't already know about."

She glared into her sister's eyes as if willing her to read her mind. Slowly, a look of understanding spread across her face.

"No way. The lawyer?" she shouted.

"Shh!" Rachel covered her sister's mouth with her hand. "You see why I don't tell you things?" She paused to see if their privacy would be interrupted, but the sound of Estie playing the piano in the living room ensured her parents would be entertained for at least another half hour. "I might have stretched the details a bit at dinner. I *did* see her at the event and she *did* give me her number, but I haven't even reached out to her."

Noa laid the plate down in the sink and set her hand on her hip in typical boss mom fashion. "And why not?"

"Oh, gee, I don't know, maybe because she's the *shameful* one our mother was just about to roast over a spit at dinner? Maybe because she does in fact still have to depose me? Maybe because she could single-handedly destroy my entire career? Maybe because I don't want her knowing what really happened in that OR—" Rachel stopped herself. She hadn't discussed that day with anyone. Not even Noa. She wasn't about to tell her what happened now. Especially not in their parents' kitchen.

"Or maybe because you might actually like her," Noa chimed in, a smirk plastered across her face.

Crimson spread to Rachel's cheeks.

"Auntie Rachel, come listen to me!" Estie shouted from the living room.

"Coming!" Rachel slapped her sister on the butt and left her giggling like a schoolgirl in the kitchen.

On the subway ride home later that night, Rachel pulled out her cell phone and sent the text she had been avoiding for an entire week.

Rachel: Hi.

It was the best she could come up with.

CHAPTER NINETEEN

Ana stretched her arms above her head. She had fallen asleep on her couch. Again. She looked around at the piles of papers spread across her coffee table and on the floor of her tiny living room. The mess made the already small space feel even smaller, but Ana was too tired to care right now.

It was super early on a Saturday morning, judging by the way the light hit the ceiling in her apartment. Most people would be passed out from the night before, but even with a west facing window, the sun burst through her room first thing in the morning, bouncing off the buildings across the East River.

She had spent last night working, as demonstrated by the mass of documents surrounding her like a moat. Not on the *Solomon* case. She had intentionally not looked at that case in weeks. Instead she had spent the night getting caught up on several of the "quick and easy" assignments Paul had given her in their last meeting.

"Should take you a few seconds," he would always say. "It'll be quick."

Really, she knew that was code for don't overbill the file and piss off the client, but also don't underbill the file and piss off the firm. It was a delicate balance, being a defense attorney, and Ana often wondered whether she should have gone into the circus, being so good at walking on a tightrope and all.

Ana sat up and found her phone on the floor. She had fallen asleep mid-text with her brother, and there were a dozen question marks on the thread now.

Such a drama queen.

She exited the thread and noticed another notification. A text from a number she didn't have saved.

Unknown: Hi.

Ana cocked her head sideways. It was a Manhattan area code, so it had to be someone local. Maybe a wrong number? Slowly, Ana's brain began to work through the possibilities. She considered just ignoring it until—

No way.

It had been a full week since Ana had given Rachel her phone number at the event. She assumed she had thrown her card away or forgotten it had even happened by now, but could it be that this was her? And what if it was her? Ana hadn't exactly thought this whole thing through. Last Friday she had been drunk on the mojitos, and the smell of Rachel's perfume, and the way her eyes matched her tuxedo perfectly, and the veins that rolled on the back of her hand when she grabbed her drink off the bar. Basically, everything had gone through her mind except what the hell to do if the woman did actually contact her.

Ana: New phone, who dis?

There was no way Dr. Rachel Cohen was actually texting her right now.

A series of little blue bubbles began to dance on her screen and stop and then dance again.

Unknown: It's Rachel.

Unknown: Dr. Cohen.

Unknown: I mean, it's Rachel Cohen.

Holy fucking shit, she was texting her right now.

Ana sat straight up and started fixing her hair.

She can't see you, you idiot, it's a text.

She started thinking about what to say. Maybe she shouldn't say anything right away Maybe she should play it cool. Make her wait a little while. Rachel had made Ana wait an entire week, for heaven's sake. But Ana didn't feel like playing power games right now. There would be time for those later, depending on how things progressed.

Ana: Well, well, Dr. Rachel Cohen, cardiac surgeon, hometown hero award winner. How are you?

Ana sat back into the couch, relaxing a bit now that the first text was off. She waited and watched as the bubbles jumped up and down on her screen again, a twinge of excitement filling her every time they popped up on her screen and a feeling of disappointment every time they disappeared again.

Rachel: I'm good.

The bubbles stopped. This was going to be harder than she anticipated. Ana bit her cheek and started typing.

Ana: I hear you're more than that. Word on the street is that they're thinking about naming a room at one of the shelters after you. The Dr. Rachel Cohen room. Nice ring to it.

Rachel: Oh God, who told you that? Nothing is official yet. And it would just be the Cohen room. That's more than I even want.

Ana: Is that humility I hear? I didn't think doctors had that gene.

Ana stood up to go make a cup of coffee, stepping over a stack of papers as she walked the two feet to her kitchen.

Rachel: Funny. And ironic, considering lawyers aren't exactly known for their humility either.

A smile spread slowly across Ana's face. They were flirting. Right? Weren't they?

Ana: If someone said I was humble, they lied.

Ana clicked on the number and added it as a new contact.

Ana: Speaking of lawyer stuff, we can't talk about the case. You know that right? You're represented by counsel and ethically I cannot speak to you about anything involving the litigation. Is that understood?

She hoped she hadn't scared her way but it needed to be said. She was already blurring the ethical lines by communicating with this woman at all. If anyone found out, she risked a formal complaint being filed against her with the bar, let alone what Paul would say. This was risky. Really, really risky.

Rachel: What case? I was texting you about your blood work results, obviously.

A wave of relief flooded Ana. Good. Now that was settled, they could proceed with being what? Friends? Friends who flirt? This was fine. Just like Stella said, she would have someone else do the deposition. The case would settle. The end. It was all going to be fine. Or so she tried to convince herself as she typed out the next text.

Ana: Blood work? Hmm sounds serious. Maybe I should be seen in person?

Rachel: Easy, killer. Maybe you should tell me your middle name first.

Ana hesitated. She wasn't sure she fully trusted the situation yet.

Ana: Trying to get all the information you need for a formal
bar complaint, Doctor?

Rachel: I would never mess with someone's career like that.

There was something pointed in the text, and she was obviously
implying that Ana was currently messing with her career. She set down
the phone. Maybe that was enough for one day. They had talked, but it
wasn't too late to turn back now. She could just tell her that this wasn't
a good idea and block her number. No rules broken.

Ana set her phone down on the counter and walked toward the
bathroom to take a shower, deciding to leave the text on read for a
while.

But before she even reached the door to her bedroom, she was
back typing out another text.

Ana: Sofia. My middle name is Sofia.

Her phone started buzzing in her hand. Her mother *would* be the
only one bold enough to call so early on a Saturday.

"Hi, mami," she said. She was also the only one Ana would pick
up the phone for so early on a Saturday.

"There's my favorite daughter. I was starting to think you had died
up there in that big city."

Ana shook her head. Aside from the fact that she was her only
daughter, she was annoyed at her mother's constant need for the
dramatics. "I texted Antonio last night, mami."

"And you think he tells me these things?" Ana could hear her
mother mumbling under her breath in Spanish. "The only thing he
wants to do is go work on that silly car with your father and take videos
on that ticky-tacky thing."

"TikTok, mami," Ana said, trying not to laugh.

"TikTok, tic-tac-toe, whatever you call it, it melts his brain."

"Well, you pay his phone bill, so who's to blame for that?" Ana
said.

Her brother's lack of motivation to move out of the house and start
an actual life of his own was a regular topic between the two of them,
but one that always had to be handled with care. Her mother might be
critical of Antonio in brief moments like this, but he was still her baby
boy at the end of the day.

"Dios mío, what am I going to do? A son who doesn't want to
leave home and a daughter who never wants to come home."

Ana rolled her eyes. This was why she didn't call home more
often. There was always some guilt trip associated with the interaction.

If she called once a week, she should be calling twice. If she called twice, she should be calling every night. And no matter how often she called, she should never have left Miami in the first place.

Ana's mom would have been happy if she had worked at one of those law firms you see on TV for when people get into car accidents, so long as it was just around the corner and she could come over for dinner every night.

Ana couldn't live that way. She felt suffocated in Miami, stifled by the fakeness of the area. The fake tans, the fake hair, the fake people with their fake money. She needed to experience something real, something uniquely her own. She needed New York, its grittiness, its rawness.

"I visit you as often as I can," Ana said, trying to keep the bitterness out of her voice. She loved her family so much, but moments like this were what kept her far away.

"I know, mija, I know." There was an awkward silence in their conversation and Ana checked her phone to see if Rachel had texted her again. She hadn't.

"Are you doing anything today?" Ana asked her mother to get the conversation flowing at a more casual pace again.

"The three of us are going to a car show in Pompano Beach. Your brother and father are making me go, claiming it's quality time. But I know they just want me there to take pictures of all the cars so they don't look uncool doing it."

Ana laughed. "That's probably true, actually."

The conversation carried on naturally from there, with her mother talking about the increasing prices at their local grocery store, their neighbor's granddaughter's baptism the next day at church, and endless stories about people Ana had only met once in her life. Ana just let her talk. She knew it must be lonely for her mother with her gone, being in the house with two men. She had friends in the area, but her mother wasn't exactly the social type, so she knew she probably spent most of her time watching her favorite soap opera on the TV in the kitchen or reading whatever romance novel she picked up at the thrift store that week. Ana didn't mind spending an hour of her Saturday morning listening, if it made her mother happy.

"Call me sometime? I miss you," her mother said, ending their conversation.

"I miss you too," Ana said sincerely.

When Ana hung up, she noticed four new text messages.

Rachel: That's a pretty name.

Rachel: Doing anything to enjoy the nice weather today?

Rachel: Not that you have to tell me your plans.

Rachel: All right, well, enjoy the day, take care!

Ana smiled reading Rachel's obvious nerves via text. She considered making her suffer a little while longer, but it had already been over half an hour since she last responded and she hated to be a tease. Well, not in this sense, anyway.

Ana laid the phone down on her kitchen counter and tapped her finger on the surface for a minute. She contemplated her next move, and before she knew it, she was hitting the call button at the top of the screen.

This is stupid. Just hang up. Say it was a butt dial. What are you thinking?

"Hello?" Rachel answered after the second ring.

"Hi," Ana said, trying her best to sound relaxed and not like she was about to have a heart attack.

"Hello, Counselor," Rachel replied, her voice sounding calm and natural. "Do I need to sign a contract or something for this phone call to happen?"

Ana smiled. "No, but we may need an NDA depending on how things progress."

There was silence on the other end.

"Sorry it took me so long, I was trying to get someone to stop talking to me."

Rachel cleared her throat. "Oh. I didn't realize you had company. I'll let you go."

Ana bit down on her thumbnail and grinned, sensing an opportunity to play a little. "Well, what can I say? Cuban women can be really demanding. And this one *really* likes me."

"Okay then, well, yeah, I am actually not sure what to say to that. So, yeah, um, you enjoy your day, Ana."

"Oh wow, I got the first name. I must be in trouble."

Rachel let out a sharp sigh. "This is what you do, isn't it? You just rile people up for fun. You called me to what? Throw it in my face that you had someone else in your apartment? To see if it would get some sort of rise out of me or something? Well, too bad, it didn't. I knew this was a bad idea. I should have never texted you in the first place."

"Whoa, whoa, back up. It was my mother. She called in the middle of our conversation, and I always try to answer when she calls."

There was a long pause on the other end of the line before Rachel spoke again. "Well, I didn't, I mean, I assumed—"

"You assumed I was an asshole. That's fair, and I technically am one, but I assure you, the only woman who has been here in the last month is you. Well, you and Stella, but she doesn't count."

Another long pause. "I'm sorry, I shouldn't have jumped to conclusions."

Ana walked over to her couch and plopped down, dangling her legs over the end. "Why don't we start over?"

"I'd like that," Rachel said.

"Hi, Rachel. I'm Ana. Tell me about your night last night."

CHAPTER TWENTY

The buzz of her phone was becoming a familiar feeling in her pocket as Rachel walked up the dark steps comprised of peeling concrete to the second floor of the hospital. She never took the elevator when she could help it. Just good practice for someone who saw inside clogged arteries a dozen times a week. Rachel waited until she got all the way to her office to pull the phone out of the pocket in her scrubs.

Ana: Is it too early for a drink?

Over the last week, Ana had become the first one to text her every morning and the last to text her at night. Inevitably one of them would call before bed. She was surprised how easily things had started to flow with her. They kept the topics mostly light. Ana would send a photo of a pathetic salad she'd picked up at Pret a Manger at four in the afternoon, saying she was finally eating lunch. Rachel would text her a picture of her eating a protein bar and calling it dinner. They talked about their commute, the weather, how people in New York represented both the best and worst of humanity. They told silly coworker stories and talked about how much better women's soccer was than men's. And of course, they talked about how much better women were than men overall. They had delved briefly into the topic of their families but only enough for her to learn that Ana was Cuban and from Miami. She had, in return, shared that she was Jewish and grew up on the Upper West Side.

They never crossed any lines, though there were certainly undertones to a few of Ana's messages, but Rachel made sure to keep things casual. And above all else, they did not mention anything about the case. Every time it crossed her mind, Rachel got a deep, sinking feeling in the pit of her stomach. She just kept repeating to herself that as long as they were keeping things friendly, and she wasn't revealing too much about herself, it was fine. It was a lie that was getting harder and harder to convince herself of. Because every night when it was time to hang up the phone and say goodbye to Ana, Rachel felt herself fighting back the urge to invite her over.

Rachel: Depends, I mean, I'm drinking already.

Rachel sent a photo of her coffee cup and a winky face emoji.

Ana: And I thought I was the silver-tongued lawyer here.

Am I rubbing off on you, Dr. Cohen?

A tiny jolt of electricity shot to Rachel's heart. She loved when Ana called her that now. Doctor. A word that once dripped with venom now felt wet with…something else? She wasn't sure why or how, but it had a markedly different impact on her than it once did. She closed her eyes and let herself imagine what it would sound like having Ana whisper the word into her ear, her low, sultry voice vibrating off the tip of her earlobe.

"Hey!" Charlotte entering her office made her jump from her daydream.

"Holy shit, you scared me."

Charlotte laughed. "I can see that. Zoning out at work already?" She checked her watch and smiled. "Was popping in to see if you needed coffee, but looks like you're all set."

Rachel glanced down at the cup on her desk. "I'd walk with you, but I have to be scrubbed in by eight for my first case today."

"No worries." Charlotte nodded.

Rachel felt a pang of guilt at the interaction. She hadn't told Charlotte about running into Ana at the event. They had left pretty much immediately after the exchange, and for some reason Rachel had wanted to keep the moment to herself. Charlotte had been her best friend since high school. They never held anything back from each other. She felt guilty lying to her friend this way. But she was allowed to have something that was just hers, right? Was it technically lying to omit a tiny part of something from someone?

"You good, Rach?" Charlotte asked. "You seem off lately. Distracted or something."

Rachel shrugged. "All good, just focusing on my cases, you know?"

Charlotte nodded. Rachel could tell by her body language that she wasn't buying it. If she kept talking to Ana this frequently, she would need to tell Charlotte. But for now, she would wait. Thirty minutes before surgery wasn't the best time, anyway.

"All right, well, let me know if you want to grab dinner this week."
Rachel nodded. "You got it."

Her phone buzzed again as Charlotte was leaving, and she could see her friend pause briefly at the door as if she was about to say something but decided against it. When she was gone Rachel let out a breath of relief and checked her phone.

Ana: Get distracted thinking of me rubbing off on you?

Rachel's cheeks immediately felt flushed. This was what she meant by some of the texts having questionable intentions.

Rachel: If you must know, Counselor, I was meeting with
    someone. Now go away. I need to focus and you're
    distracting me.

Ana: So bossy.

Rachel shook her head. What the hell was she going to do with this woman?

All three surgeries that day went off without a hitch. Rachel had done so many coronary artery bypass grafting, or CABG, procedures she could probably do them in her sleep. But she never took any case lightly. That was maybe the most important thing she had learned from that awful experience during her residency: Any procedure, no matter how routine or how simple, could go wrong if the surgeon wasn't properly prepared.

She loved surgery days. They seemed to make time fly by. Twelve hours would feel like two hours on those days. When she was in the operating room, it was like nothing outside those four walls existed. The sound of the anesthesia machine and the patient monitor was ASMR to her. Some surgeons listened to music when they operated, but not Rachel. She didn't need or want anything distracting her from what was right in front of her. In those hours when she was scrubbed in, nothing else existed. Nothing else mattered.

She waited to check her cell phone until she left the office. Charlotte had gone home hours earlier, as their shifts weren't exactly aligned this week, and her last surgery had run late due to a delay in getting an OR nurse over from another surgery.

It was almost nine o'clock by the time she nestled into her seat on the 6 train and headed north toward home.

She pulled out her phone to catch up from thirteen hours of missed social interaction.

She had about a dozen text messages, some from Noa, some from her mother, and some from another cardiac surgeon talking about a potential conference next spring. Rachel scrolled past all of them until she landed on the ones she had actually been looking for.

Ana: What a win. I'm actually eating lunch at a decent hour today.

There was a photo of Ana shoving a sandwich in her mouth.

Ana: What's your favorite kind of food? Don't say American. That literally does not exist.

Ana: I'm bored. Distract me from this endless career of torment. Tell me a joke or something.

Ana: Heading home. You should really get a job that gives you more free time. I mean, look at me? I've got loads of it.

Ana: Eating dinner. Have I mentioned I'm bored?

Rachel laughed at the slew of texts. She could picture Ana in her fancy office, with her tight little pencil skirt that hugged her ass in unfair ways, and her head dropped into her hand, complaining about being bored. Rachel had always envisioned lawyers to be a certain type of person, and at first glance Ana met all of those preconceived notions. Nice clothes, nice office, working long hours, always very put together, argumentative. But the more she got to know her, the more those notions began to fall by the wayside. She got bored just like everyone else. She got lonely. She got stressed. And she certainly got horny.

Rachel: Hi.

Ana: She's alive!

Ana added a GIF from an old Frankenstein movie.

Rachel: Barely. Thank God it's a short subway ride for me. Elijah is probably pissed.

Ana: Who is Elijah?

Rachel: Um we live together. I was pretty sure you knew I was married.

Ana: Oh really? You lick pussy pretty well for someone married to a dude.

Rachel nearly choked on her own spit.

Rachel: Thank you. I'll be sure to let Elijah know you think that. And she's a girl. Just fyi.

Ana: You're really not going to tell me who this person is are you?

Rachel: If you keep your panties on for a few minutes, I'll show you.

Ana: Hmm…Never had a woman ask me to keep my panties ON before. But I'll do my best.

A few moments later, Rachel pushed open the door to her apartment and dropped her bag. Elijah came running to the door to greet her, meowing loudly with each little bounce. Her primordial pouch swung back and forth like a punching bag as she ran, and Rachel made a note to cut down on the amount of food she was leaving out for her every day.

"Hello, my little lady bug," Rachel said, picking up the fluffy ball of fur. Elijah instantly began purring at the contact and Rachel buried her face in her neck and kissed her cheek. She lifted up her phone and took a selfie mid-kiss before setting the cat back down on the ground.

Elijah continued to circle her legs, leaving streaks of white, brown, and black fur on her pants with each passing brush.

Rachel: This is Elijah. Cute isn't she?

Rachel sent the selfie to Ana and set the phone on the counter so she could make herself dinner. She put a pot of water on the stove to boil and pulled out a box of whole grain pasta from the cabinet.

The sound of her phone buzzing repeatedly grabbed her attention. It was Ana calling.

"Yes?"

"Hold on. You have a female cat named Elijah?" Ana's enchanting voice echoed on the other end.

"If you must know, yes, I do."

She could hear Ana holding in a laugh. "One, how did I not know about this yet and two, tell me she came with that name."

Rachel's mouth dropped open. "I'll have you know this cat was named after a prophet."

"Mm-hmm, but the question still stands. Did *you* name the cat Elijah?"

Rachel paused. "Maybe."

Ana let out a loud laugh on the other end of the phone and Rachel couldn't help but smile at the warm, infectious sound of it.

"What? It's a cute story, okay?"

Ana stopped laughing eventually and continued. "Well then, I'm going to need to hear it."

"I'm making dinner, you know," Rachel said, trying to sound annoyed at the interruption.

"Oh please, we both know you're good at multitasking. Talk and stir."

Rachel shook her head, dropping pasta into the water. She proceeded to tell Ana the story of how Estie had opened the door for Elijah on Passover and how Rachel had essentially saved her sister from becoming a mom of two children and a cat all within one month. Ana didn't say anything until Rachel was finished.

"So, you have a sister?" Ana asked.

Rachel paused. She hadn't realized she had inadvertently revealed more about her family by telling the story.

"Mm-hmm," she said.

"What's her name?"

Rachel's defensive mode instantly engaged. "Why do you want to know?"

She regretted it, but she hadn't done it on purpose. She didn't like letting people in on her personal life. Even if Ana hadn't been the attorney suing her, she would still be reluctant to be so open with someone this way, especially this soon.

"I'm just trying to get to know you better, Rachel," Ana said, her voice soft and kind. Rachel ignored the feeling she got at the sound of her name slipping off Ana's lips.

"I'm sorry, I'm just protective about my family. And with you, I mean…"

"I get it," Ana said.

Rachel was taken aback by how patient and understanding Ana was being with all of this. Normally her quills popping up was the first thing that turned women off her, but it hadn't seemed to deter Ana at all.

"Well, I have a brother." Ana said. "Although maybe I've mentioned him before? His name is Antonio and he's about as useful as a Popsicle stand in Alaska. But I love him with all my heart, and if anyone tried to mess with him, I'd have them thrown in jail, or maybe get tossed in there myself."

Rachel laughed. "I actually completely understand what you mean by that. Sometimes I want to kill my sister, but if anyone looked at her wrong, I'd probably push them onto the subway tracks."

"That was oddly specific," Ana said before they both started laughing. "Let me guess, you were the kid who created a *Sims* character only to drown him in the pool by removing the ladder?"

Rachel burst out laughing and had to cover her mouth. "It was one time!"

By the time they had finished talking, Rachel had made and eaten her pasta, gotten into her pajamas, and crawled into bed. She didn't even remember hanging up the phone, but she must have at some point because when she woke up in the middle of the night to use the restroom, her phone was face down on the pillow beside her and the call had ended.

So much for keeping things casual.

CHAPTER TWENTY-ONE

A steady trickle of sweat dripped down Ana's spine as she walked up the stairs to the courthouse located at 60 Centre Street. The *Law & Order* courthouse, as it was known around the office, was a beautiful building, and normally she loved going to court there. However, the same architectural features that made the courthouse so distinctive also meant it lacked modern conveniences such as central air conditioning. During the summer, that meant coming ready to sit in a pool of your own sweat while waiting for your case to be called.

Saturday was just a few days away, and Ana was looking forward to having the day off. Normally her weekends passed unnoticed and she would work through the entire day. But this weekend she had decided to take her brother's advice and actually relax, maybe see a Broadway show or take herself to dinner. Stella had invited her to a cookout at her family's house in the Bronx, but Ana wasn't really in the mood to trek out that far. All of her other friends or colleagues were either working or had plans that she wasn't included in, so that meant Ana was on her own.

Ana waited for the small, crammed elevator to take her to the third floor and walked into the crowded courtroom to find both her adversary and her seat.

"*Reckson International Realty? Reckson?*" Ana shouted into the sea of lawyers.

When she saw no heads turn in response, she sighed and slid into one of the empty spaces on the wooden benches. The stiffness of the wood against her back reminded her of being in Mass as a little girl. She'd hated it, even back then. Her mother had always made her wear some sort of ridiculous dress anytime they went, and she could never follow along with when they were supposed to stand or kneel or go up to eat the cracker. It was no wonder Ana had stopped going the moment she moved to New York. She considered herself more spiritual than religious these days, a secret she would never tell her devoutly Catholic parents.

Ana pulled out her phone and typed out a quick text to Rachel.

"Ana Mendez," she heard someone say from behind her.

It was Sheryl Peterson, the attorney for the individual doctors in the *Solomon* case. Instinctively, Ana gripped her cell phone tight against her chest, the screen face down.

"Sheryl, so glad to see you're okay," Ana said politely.

Sheryl grabbed her neck. "Me too, asshole blew right through a stoplight, can you believe that? I'm in PT three times a week and chiro twice a week for this neck of mine. A buddy says I should sue for my injuries, can you imagine that?" She started to laugh, the wrinkles around the corners of her eyes spread wide across her tan, weathered face.

"It sounds like you're really hurt, Sheryl. Maybe you should talk to someone about it." Ana replied.

Sheryl waved her hand. "I'm too stubborn for that, though if I end up needing surgery, that'll be another story. Speaking of which, what's going on with you and Dr. Cohen?"

"What?" Ana nearly dropped her phone in her lap. She felt a low buzz as it vibrated against her chest. "What do you mean going on? Nothing is going on. What a strange question," Ana stuttered uncharacteristically.

Sheryl looked at her like she had lobsters crawling out of her ears. "I meant the deposition. Has it been rescheduled?"

A wave of relief flooded her entire body.

"Oh, the deposition! Yes, yes, well, you know, I need to talk to Paul about that, I mean, we do still want to depose her, it's just…"

Sheryl raised an eyebrow. "Well, if you don't think the testimony is worth it, you could always waive it and wrap up discovery. She wasn't individually named, so you wouldn't need to discontinue her from the case. Not that I would ever do David's job for him, mind you."

Ana nodded her head. David Blackstone, Rachel's attorney, had emailed her twice trying to reschedule the deposition, but she hadn't responded.

"Yes, I'll, um, I'll think about it."

Sheryl nodded. "Well, the note of issue isn't due until October, so you've got a few months to sort it out. Just don't wait too long. Doctors are busy people, you know."

"Good point, I'll reach out to both of you soon. It was great to see you, Sheryl."

Ana waited until Sheryl had left the courtroom before checking her cell phone.

Rachel: Morning. What time did I fall asleep last night?

Ana smiled remembering the sound of Rachel's voice getting sleepier and sleepier until her words had jumbled together and she was making absolutely no sense at all. Ana should have let her hang up at least thirty minutes before she did, but she enjoyed listening to someone who was usually so buttoned up become a little delirious with sleep.

Ana: Probably around midnight.

Rachel: Midnight? Good Lord, what could we have talked about for so long? It didn't feel that late.

Ana: What can I say, I'm great at small talk. You did confess something pretty embarrassing, though, if we're being honest.

Rachel: Oh God. What?

Rachel: Tell me!

Rachel: Ana Sofia Mendez.

Ana held in a laugh as she watched the doctor unravel in a series of anxious bubbles bouncing across her screen.

Ana: First of all, calm your tits. I'm in court. Second of all, you told me that Dorothy was your favorite Golden Girl. Everyone knows Blanche is the best.

Rachel: First of all, stop thinking about my tits in court. Second of all, Dorothy is smart, sarcastic, and a great daughter. Some might say there are some similarities between you two.

Ana blushed. She could definitely get used to this. Flirty texts during the day, long conversations at night, a beautiful woman complimenting her. She had been waiting for the other shoe to drop ever since the exchange between them had begun. But so far, Rachel was kind and smart and caring. The more Ana learned about her, the more she liked her.

"*Jameson v. Reckson International Realty*? *Jameson*?" a young male attorney shouted from the door to the courtroom. Ana put her phone back in her bag. Now she really had to stop thinking about Rachel's tits in court.

When her conference was over, Ana jumped on the 6 train to make her way back up to the office. Even the subway was hot, and the tiny windows were thrown open at the top of the car to allow air to circulate through the hot box that now soared up the East Side. The smell of sewer and body odor flooded the crowded compartment, and Ana did her best to breathe through her mouth.

Whoever said New York was beautiful in the summer had clearly never been to New York in the summer. The streets smelled like the bags of garbage that lined the sidewalk, and the tall buildings meant any breeze from the Hudson and East River was cut off if you weren't literally walking right beside one of the rivers or in one of the city's wind tunnels.

Ana liked going down to Battery Park when it was hot like this. It was cool and open. She liked looking out across the water to see Ellis Island and the Statue of Liberty gleaming in the sun. She wished she was heading that way now, instead of back uptown to her office.

Ana wiped a bead of sweat from her forehead and pulled out her phone.

Ana: What are you doing this Saturday?

She sent the text before even fully thinking it through. *She's probably working. Or volunteering. Or saving abandoned puppies from beneath the Manhattan Bridge.*

Rachel: Sorry was with a patient. I actually have no plans.
     You?

Ana: Let's hang out.

Ana: You in?

She smiled as the bubbles did their usual appearing and disappearing act across her screen.

Rachel: Yes. It's a date.

Chapter Twenty-two

Rachel ripped off her tank top and tossed it on a pile in the corner of her bedroom. Elijah watched, her thick tail swaying back and forth as her green eyes seemed to judge every top that ended up across the room.

"It didn't match the shorts, okay?" Rachel said to the curious feline.

Elijah stood up from her curled position and slowly walked over to the pile of clothes. The sound of purring coming from the stack a few seconds later told Rachel that she was making biscuits among her discarded shirts.

She had tried on at least a dozen mixtures of tops and shorts, sundresses, and maxi dresses and none of them were meeting her expectations.

They were just having a picnic in Central Park. Rachel knew there was no need to get so stressed out over it. But it was hot. Like really, really hot. Which limited the options severely. Eventually Rachel gave up and slipped on a long, blue maxi dress with a floral pattern. It was cool and comfortable but still cute. Not that this was a date or anything. Even though she had said it was in her last text to Ana. Technically she had no idea what this was. All she knew was that when Ana expressed an interest in spending a Saturday afternoon with her, Rachel had immediately said yes. She slipped on a pair of white Keds and fluffed up her hair in the mirror.

They were meeting near the park at twelve thirty, the hottest time of day, of course. Rachel applied a third layer of deodorant and shoved the sunblock into her backpack. She'd asked Ana if she should bring anything, but Ana had said she would take care of it. The assertiveness in the way she had said it was very much a turn-on. Rachel was used to having to be in charge of everything in her life. Her commute, her schedule, her patients, even her cat's meals. It was nice to have a day she hadn't planned and organized for once.

She walked the few blocks from her apartment to where they were meeting—the steps at the Met. It was much easier than meeting inside the park, considering how massive the thing was, and as a *Gossip Girl* fan, Rachel was more than okay with the meeting place.

Walking the ten blocks west to the park, Rachel could already feel a trickle of sweat start to form down her back. She slowed her pace and extended her arms to allow some ventilation and hopefully prevent further perspiration.

After a few moments, she was at her destination. She looked around, squinting beneath her sunglasses to search for Ana. It didn't take long. Ana stood out like a beacon of light among the crowd of tourists lining up to enter the museum. Not that she blamed them. With the temperature almost in the nineties, she envied the blast of AC they would be met with when they entered those revolving doors.

Ana looked over at her and smiled. Rachel told her feet to keep moving toward the striking woman who was now standing up from the steps, a large tote bag tucked under one arm. She was wearing overall shorts with a red spaghetti tank top underneath. Rachel enjoyed the way the tank cut low across the top and underneath Ana's arms, which allowed her breasts plenty of room to sway and bounce as she walked toward her. Her long, black hair was pulled up into a messy bun on the top of her head, and Rachel could see honey brown streaks shining in the sun's reflection for the first time. She wore black Wayfarer-style sunglasses that covered a large portion of her face, much to Rachel's chagrin.

"Hi," Ana said as she leaned in to hug Rachel.

Rachel inhaled the sweet smell of Ana's perfume and tried to ignore the loud beating of her own heart as she felt Ana's warm body pressed against her. She wished she wasn't already starting to sweat and she hoped she had applied enough perfume and deodorant to offset the smell of the city that probably already clung to her.

"Hi," Rachel replied, after Ana had stepped back again.

Ana lifted her sunglasses and shoved them on top of her head, allowing her brown eyes to shine as she slowly looked Rachel up and down.

"You look great," Ana said.

Rachel looked down. "Thanks. You look—"

"Like a bum, I know. I wanted to wear my hair down, but it's just too damn hot for that, I'm sorry. The high school cheerleader hair will have to do."

Rachel laughed as they turned and started to walk toward the park. "Bum is a bit of a stretch for how you look, but duly noted that you were a cheerleader."

"Okay, technically I was, but I only did it so I could get out of class early and hang with this girl I had a massive crush on who was the flyer. If you saw the view I got at the base of that stunt, you'd have been a cheerleader too."

Rachel laughed and shook her head. As they walked behind the Met, Ana pointed in the direction of a shady area about halfway across the park. Rachel hoped they would be able to find a spot under a tree or something, but it was crowded, so she wasn't holding on to too much hope.

"So, you've always been this impulsive, then? Doing a sport just to see a girl's ass. Taking strangers home from bars. Slipping your number to people you're supposed to be deposing."

Rachel looked to Ana to see if she had overstepped the mark with her last comment. When she saw Ana blush slightly, she counted it a victory.

"Well, generally yes, although you have been an exception to many rules, that's for sure."

Rachel tucked a hair behind her ear. "Ditto."

They walked in silence for a few seconds.

"Anyway," Ana said, picking up the conversation again, "that's why Stella and I get along so well. She's my"—Ana snapped her fingers—"get up and go friend."

"You two never...?"

"Me and Stella?" Ana let out a laugh but didn't immediately protest. "We gave it a go when we first met. Went on a few dates, hooked up briefly. I mean, we were basically the only two openly queer women at my firm for a while. Well, until Darcy came out of the closet, anyway."

Ana started to walk faster in the middle of her sentence and tossed her tote under a vacant tree.

"Ha, all ours," she said, with an edge of competitiveness in her voice.

Rachel took off her backpack and dropped it next to the tote bag while Ana bent down and pulled out a large blanket, spreading it out in the shady grass.

"Who's Darcy?" Rachel asked, taking a seat on the blanket and sliding her backpack in front of her.

"She was one of the managing partners at my firm. A bit of a trailblazer, you might say. She was the first female managing partner and she was a total lez. Everything was fine and dandy until she started hooking up with one of the junior associates." Anna wiggled her eyebrows playfully.

Rachel's mouth dropped open. "Okay, that sounds like a Lifetime movie or something."

"More like a porno," Ana said, laughing. "Anyway, they're both gone now. Last I heard they were still together, at least that's what all the junior associates and paralegals say. I'm not big on social media, so I'm out of the loop. And as for me and Stella? Well, that was over before it even began." Ana's eyes lingered on Rachel's for a second. "Plus, she's not really my type."

Rachel looked away, trying to avoid the burst of warmth that spread to her heart when Ana looked at her that way. "Sunblock?" she said as she pulled out the lotion.

"I'm good, I don't really burn," Ana said. She extended her arm, displaying her naturally tan skin.

"Melanoma doesn't care if you're Cuban, Miss Mendez," Rachel said, with a reproachful look. "Trust me, I'm a doctor."

"Sure, a heart doctor." Ana laughed in the way that made Rachel's insides turn to mush. The way she had laughed at the awards ceremony. "Besides, I'm more than happy to help you apply that to your lily-white skin."

Rachel could feel her cheeks turning red.

"Is that sunburn already?" Ana said, reaching up and gently touching her cheek. Rachel could smell Ana's perfume on her wrist and closed her eyes just for a second, soaking in the scent before snapping back to reality.

"Must be. I better start applying this." Rachel turned her back to Ana, hoping avoiding eye contact for a few seconds would give her some respite. But within seconds, she could feel Ana scooting closer behind her.

"Here." Ana reached around her side, barely grazing against her arm. She held out her hand and wiggled her fingers. "Let me get your back. You're gonna fry in this little spaghetti strap dress of yours. Even in the shade."

Rachel cleared her throat but handed the sunblock over to Ana without protest. She focused all of her energy on not reacting when Ana's warm hands began to slide across the top of her back and shoulders and up around the bottom of her hairline. She ignored the urge to moan when Ana's hand lifted up the straps of her dress one at a time and moved her hands slowly beneath them. She tried to keep her mind from drifting back to the night they had spent together, but the feel of Ana's hands rubbing against her now was almost too much.

Jesus Christ, Rachel, it's just sunblock, your mother has done this to you hundreds of times.

But there was nothing motherly about the thoughts that were coursing through Rachel's mind. She closed her eyes and leaned her head to one side, giving herself just a few seconds to enjoy the feeling of Ana's hands against her until, almost as soon as it began, it was over.

"All set," Ana said, rubbing her hands together and scooting back across the blanket.

"Thanks." Rachel picked up the sunblock and turned back to face Ana.

Now it was Ana's turn to look down as she wiped her hands on the shorts of her overalls and began digging in the tote bag. Was she nervous? Rachel was still learning Ana's personality traits, but she hadn't anticipated nervousness to be one of them. If anything, the woman had an excess of poise and confidence, but now she was fidgeting and moving things around in the tote bag like she would rather do anything but look at Rachel. Maybe Rachel wasn't the only one struggling to not think of their first night together.

Ana pulled out a two liter bottle of pink lemonade and two red Solo cups. Next there was a Tupperware filled with carrots, peppers, and hummus, then a loaf of French bread followed by a second Tupperware filled with four different kinds of cheese, all sliced. Last but not least, she whipped out a bag of grapes and set it in the middle of the blanket.

"Lunch is served," Ana said, proudly displaying the picnic like she was a host on a game show.

Rachel gave her best golf clap and smiled. "This is actually impressive. You managed to bring stuff I like to eat."

Ana pulled open the containers one by one. "Well, I assumed you didn't eat pork, which actually kills my Cuban soul by the way, so I figured I should nix the charcuterie meats and head straight for the cheese and veggie vibe."

"Learning my Jewish culture, very nice. Although I actually don't keep kosher. You're right, though, I don't eat pork or shellfish, but I can't say no to a cheeseburger. If you wanted to go out somewhere next time, don't feel like you have to pick a kosher place."

Rachel caught herself and stopped speaking, but it was too late.

Ana smirked as she popped a carrot into her mouth. "Already planning our next date, Doc?"

Rachel narrowed her eyes. "Are you implying this is a first one?"

Ana shrugged, unabashed. "It's whatever you want it to be."

Chapter Twenty-three

Lemonade?" Ana untwisted the cap and poured some into a red Solo cup.

Rachel extended her hand and took it, the tips of her fingers grazing Ana's for a moment. Ana told herself to keep her cool. To not let this woman rattle her. She was just a woman she had hooked up with in a bar. Just a woman she had talked to almost every night. Just a woman she was struggling to not pin down to the ground and fuck right there in the park. They were just hanging out. The lawsuit didn't exist. Only this day existed. There was no pressure here.

Ana watched as Rachel took a deep sip of the drink and choked.

"Oh, did I not mention there was tequila in it?" Ana feigned a look of innocence.

Rachel wiped her mouth and raised an eyebrow. "No, actually, you seem to have omitted that part."

"Do you not like tequila?"

Rachel shook her head. "I love tequila. But tequila, well, I think we both know how the song goes."

They sang the chorus in unison and began to laugh.

"My brother and I used to make this when we were in high school." Ana steadied her hand as she poured herself a drink, ignoring the nerves that caused it to shake. "We thought we were so slick, mixing it with lemonade, like our parents wouldn't know." Rachel rested her chin in her hand, seeming interested in the story, so Ana continued. "Then one day, maybe a week before my high school graduation, my dad confessed that he had known all along what we were doing. He just never told our mom. He had even lied and said he drank some of the tequila once when she asked where it was all going."

Ana laughed as she took a sip, feeling the warm liquor land in her stomach. "My brother was so shocked that he hadn't ratted us out, but

I knew better. Papi was always the cool one between the two of them. Plus, he'd never do anything to upset my mom. He even bought me a bottle of tequila when I graduated law school as part of our inside joke."

Ana realized she was rambling and cleared her throat. "Anyway, that's the drink's origin story for you."

"It's a good story. Somehow it doesn't surprise me that you were a wild child."

Ana took another sip. "Oh yeah? And let me guess, you were Little Miss Straight A's and home by eight every night?"

Rachel shrugged. "Definitely a yes to the straight A's. And on Fridays and holy days, most definitely home by eight, sometimes even earlier if it was winter. We have to be home by sundown those days, so the time changes, but yeah, safe to say my nights out in high school consisted of playing basketball or studying."

"Somehow, that doesn't surprise me either," Ana replied. Her eyes lingered on Rachel's for a moment, and she felt her heart beating louder the longer Rachel looked at her. For the first time, she was very aware that their knees touched, and wished she could reach out and lace her fingers in Rachel's.

"It's wild we both went to Columbia, you know," Ana said, attempting to change the subject.

Rachel leaned forward. "Been googling, have we?"

Ana smirked. "Maybe." She waited to see some sort of reaction from Rachel and watched as Rachel's eyes darted down to her lips and then back up again briefly.

Ana sat back and looked around. She had picked the perfect spot for this. They were close enough to the Great Lawn that they could see the city surrounding them, but they were also near the Turtle Pond and the Delacorte Theater, which gave them shade and the fresh smell of water. A cool breeze wafted through the trees, and Ana watched as Rachel leaned her head back and inhaled the fresh air.

Suddenly, Rachel's eyes shot open. "Did you know it's basically impossible to get lost in this park?"

Ana reeled back at the sudden burst of excitement. "Pretty sure a lot of *CSI* episodes would beg to differ."

Rachel waved her hand. "Ignore that part. But really, come look." Rachel stood up and waved Ana over to a lamppost not far from where they were sitting. Ana wiped her hands and complied, standing up from the blanket and following Rachel.

She pointed to a series of numbers printed on the lamppost.

"You see these here?" Rachel said, her voice elevated. "These are the key to knowing where you are at all times. The first two or three numbers will tell you the closest street, and the last number indicates if you're on the east or west side of the park. Odd numbers are for the west side and even are for the east side. Pretty neat, huh?" Rachel's blue eyes danced with excitement.

Ana smiled, understanding for the first time that this sexy, brilliant woman was actually just a total dork. *I wonder if she knows how adorable she looks right now, all giddy over numbers on a lamppost.*

"I'm not gonna lie, I was today years old when I learned this," Ana remarked.

Ana was impressed with the revelation. It was always a turn-on when someone could teach her things she didn't already know. Something told Ana that there was a lot that Rachel could teach her. First, she was a surgeon, so basically the entire medical field was her playground. Then there was the fact that she was Jewish, a culture she knew very little about, aside from the recently discovered fact that they didn't eat pork or shellfish. And now, Ana knew that Rachel, as a local New Yorker, could teach her a lot about the place she'd called home for the last eight years. All of this only compounded the realization rushing through Ana at that very moment: Rachel Cohen was a catch.

She walked back over toward the blanket and sat back down, patting the ground beside her. She hoped Rachel would take the hint and come closer to her this time. Lucky for her, she did, and when Rachel sat beside her and crossed her legs, their knees knocked together. Ana smiled at the proximity and the feeling of the light, soft caress of Rachel's knee rubbing against her skin.

"Do you come here often?" Ana asked.

"Yeah actually, I run here almost every morning. Just around the pond mostly."

Ana nodded slowly. "Well, that explains it, then," she said.

Rachel tilted her head to the side. "Explains what?"

"Gee, maybe the washboard abs, or ripped quads, or like total lack of fat on you? Your body is"—Ana paused for a moment, looking Rachel slowly up and down—"incredible."

Rachel looked down and tucked a strand of hair behind her ear. She had done that at least ten times since they had first sat down, so Ana deduced it was a nervous tic. *Does that mean I make her nervous?* Ana hoped so, because right now she was sure her heart was beating so loud, Rachel wouldn't need her stethoscope to hear it. *Oh, God, I forgot she has a stethoscope. That is so hot.*

"Thank you," Rachel said her cheeks a bright pink. "I could say the same about you."

Okay, she was definitely blushing, not sunburned. Ana took the little ray of hope she could and continued.

"So, say it." She leaned closer, looking directly into Rachel's eyes as if daring her to reciprocate.

In all of their interactions up until this point it was always Ana taking charge. Ana making the flirty jokes, Ana blurring the line between friendship and more, Ana asking her on the picnic today, Ana giving her number to Rachel. She wanted to see what Rachel would do when the ball was in her court.

Rachel picked at the cuticle of her thumbnail. "Your body is incredible," she said quietly without looking up.

Not fully satisfied with the lack of assertion, Ana decided to push her luck.

"I'm sorry?" Ana lifted her hand to her ear and leaned in closer to Rachel. "I couldn't hear you, Dr. Cohen, what was that?"

Rachel shook her head and laughed but still looked down. "Your body is incredible," she said, just a tiny bit louder.

"Gosh, this hearing aid of mine just will not work." Ana tapped playfully at her ear and leaned so close she was inches away from Rachel's face.

Finally, Rachel looked up. "I said—" She paused and her voice seemed to catch in the back of her throat when they made eye contact.

Ana felt her breath hitch in her chest as she stared into the bluest eyes she had ever seen. There was no shyness in them now. No reservation or fear. Ana knew that look anywhere. That was the same look Rachel had given her in the bar the first night they met. She knew it because she felt it herself in that moment. The look of desire was spread all over Rachel's face, and Ana bit her lip to keep from leaning over and pressing her lips into Rachel's.

"Go on," Ana managed to say, her voice cracking.

"Your body is incredible," Rachel replied in no more than a whisper.

Ana gulped slowly, searching Rachel's face for something telling her to stop. To lean back. To *not* make a move right now. But there was nothing. Slowly, Ana began to inch closer, her gaze now traveling from

Rachel's eyes down to her mouth. She was so close she could smell the tequila on Rachel's breath, and she began to close her eyes, readying herself for the inevitable touch of Rachel's lips on hers.

"Heads up!" Ana looked to her right just in time to see a soccer ball come flying at them, bouncing across the ground at lightning speed and plowing through their entire picnic, sending both women sprawling back on their hands.

A teenage boy came running toward them and jumped over the banket, following the ball. He grabbed it before it reached the pond and ran back in the direction of the Great Lawn, never once stopping to apologize for the mess he'd just made.

"Little shit!" Ana yelled after the kid, wiping hummus from her leg.

She began muttering in Spanish under her breath, sounding just like her mother, and searching around for more blotches of hummus. It was no use. The picnic was ruined. The cheese had been squished by the ball and the Tupperware had been knocked over, spilling the carrots, hummus, and peppers all over the place. The only survivors were the grapes.

"At least we saved the alcohol?" Rachel said, lifting the bottle of tequila-infused lemonade in the air. Ana stopped mumbling to herself and looked over at Rachel, who sat smiling with a glob of hummus stuck on her right cheek. Immediately, they both burst into laughter.

Ana reached over and wiped the hummus from her face with her thumb. "Is now a good time to mention that I forgot to bring napkins?"

CHAPTER TWENTY-FOUR

Rachel couldn't stop smiling as she walked down the hall at work the next day. She'd had a great run around the park that morning and was feeling energetic. Her schedule that week was Sunday to Thursday, which meant she would have Friday night off to spend with her family, which made her happy. It also meant she would be off again on Saturday. A major win considering she had some weeks that were fourteen days in a row. She nodded in friendly acknowledgment at the nurses who passed as she made her way down the fluorescently lit path toward the staff lounge.

After their picnic had ended abruptly, Ana and Rachel had packed up the sad remains of the food and walked around the park a bit. Well, first they snagged some napkins at a roasted peanuts stand, and then they walked around the park a bit.

She was shocked at how easy being around Ana was. Normally on a first date, Rachel struggled to fill in the awkward gaps in conversation. She hated the typical "what's your favorite color" questions and always felt pressured to carry on the conversation, even if it was forced. Probably yet another reason why she had given up on dating long ago. But with Ana everything felt smooth, natural, fluid even. She didn't have to make conversation with Ana because the conversation just sort of happened. They had spent almost the entire day together just walking and talking without Rachel even realizing how much time had flown by. It was only the gurgle of her stomach reminding her that she hadn't eaten anything since the few carrots back at the picnic that told her she should probably go home.

Rachel thought back to the moment before the soccer ball had come crashing through their little lunch. Was Ana really going to kiss her? It had sure felt like it and, God, Rachel had wanted her to so bad. But there was a small part of her that felt a wave of relief when the universe had intervened and prevented the connection. Things with Ana were murkier than ever, and adding a physical element to the mix might be more than her overly compartmental brain could handle right now. The lawsuit itself had been enough to give Rachel anxiety, she couldn't imagine adding a sexual element in the middle of all that stress. But for some reason, being near Ana seemed to have the opposite effect on her nerves. In fact, whenever they spoke, Rachel felt a sense of calm like she had never felt before. Her overactive brain went silent and all of her worries seemed to disappear. It was disarming, distracting, and alluring all at once.

Would she have really been able to say no to Ana if she had tried to kiss her? She knew the answer was no. She knew she would have suggested they go back to her place, which was a whopping ten minutes away. She knew they would have spent the rest of the day in bed together. She could imagine Ana wrapped in her arms, naked, their bodies dripping in sweat with nothing but the warm summer air flowing in from her open windows to cool them off. The mental image was enough to drive Rachel wild as she poured herself a large cup of coffee.

"Long time no see."

Rachel jumped, a little dribble of coffee escaping her mouth as she did. Charlotte entered the break room.

"Hey, Char," Rachel replied.

"How was your weekend?" Charlotte said, pouring her own cup of coffee.

Rachel took a loud slurp. "Good," she answered vaguely. "Went to the park for a bit."

Charlotte nodded. "Cool." She took a sip and looked at Rachel as if waiting for her to say more.

"Okay, I can't take it any more. Come with me." Rachel grabbed Charlotte by the arm and dragged her down the hall into her office.

"Can you keep a secret? Like pain of death secret?"

Charlotte rolled her eyes. "Please, don't you remember when we were in tenth grade and we told our parents we were sleeping over at each other's house but we snuck out to the park to smoke weed?"

Rachel crossed her arms. "You smoked weed. I kept looking out for cops the entire time."

Charlotte looked like she was contemplating the memory for a moment. "Okay, yeah, that tracks, but whatever. The point is I can keep a secret. So spill."

Rachel scooted closer to Charlotte. "Okay, so, I've kind of been talking to someone."

Charlotte's face lit up in excitement. "Oh my God, who? Tell me everything. Is she tall? What does she do? How old is she? Is she Jewish?"

Rachel laughed. "Easy, easy. Okay, so first of all, just try to keep an open mind here."

Charlotte furrowed her brows skeptically. "Pretty sure between the two of us, you're the one with the stick up her ass. My mind is an open book."

"Valid," Rachel replied. "Okay, it's sort of Ana."

Charlotte paused for a moment, seeming to ponder the name before a look of realization spread across her face. "Holy shit, the sexy lawyer?"

"Yes, okay, yes. The sexy lawyer who is still very much supposed to depose me at some point in the very near future." Rachel ran her hand through her hair. "I mean, it's a terrible idea, right? I know it is, I just, I don't know, we talk all the time and this weekend we went to the park together and she was going to kiss me until a soccer ball kinda interrupted us and wow I really wanted her to kiss me and I know it can't possibly go anywhere but I—"

Charlotte's face grew into a wide Cheshire Cat grin.

Rachel dropped her hands to her side. "What?"

"Rachel Cohen, you're totally falling for sexy lawyer lady!" Charlotte threw her arms around Rachel and pulled her in to a suffocating hug.

"Did you not hear anything I just said?" Rachel said into Charlotte's neck, struggling to breathe.

"Oh, I heard," Charlotte said, releasing her. "I heard you going on and on about someone like you've never done before. And I heard you, as usual, trying to overanalyze what could actually be a good thing."

"Good? How on earth could this possibly be good?"

"Shh, shh, shh." Charlotte bopped Rachel gently on the tip of her nose. "Turn that Ivy League brain off for a minute and just enjoy the now. You like someone. She likes you. Just let it be and let everything else run its natural course."

Rachel sighed. "Easy for you to say, you aren't hiding some big secret from her and at the same time risking your career."

"What big secret?"

Rachel straightened her shoulders. She was surprised she'd let herself slip like that. "Nothing." Rachel cleared her throat. "It's just a bad idea is all."

Charlotte shrugged. "Maybe, or maybe not. Guess you'll have to try it and find out."

Rachel's alarm buzzed, reminding her that she had a patient to get to, so she said her goodbyes to Charlotte.

Her patient was a seventy-four-year-old man undergoing a septal myectomy. He had presented with hypertrophic cardiomyopathy months ago, and the non-surgical treatment options hadn't worked. The procedure would take around four hours open to close, and Rachel spent the next half hour reviewing his chart before heading to the operating room to scrub in.

It was an open procedure, which meant a large incision would be made along the patient's sternum. The sternum itself would then be cut in half and spread open, allowing Rachel and the vascular surgeon to access his heart. He would then be hooked up to a heart-lung machine that would breathe for him and keep his blood circulating during the surgery. After that, Rachel would carefully remove the thickened portion of the septum, close the sternum, sew him up, disconnect the machine, and all would be well. It was an intense but not overly complicated procedure, and Rachel had performed it dozens of times.

Once she was fully scrubbed in, Rachel started the official time-out.

"This is Angel Martinez. He is seventy-four years old and he is having a septal myectomy." The nurses, the assisting surgeon, and the anesthesiologist all nodded in assent. "Let's begin."

Four hours and twenty four minutes later, Rachel was back in her office decompressing from the operation. She rubbed the back of her neck and reached around to massage her shoulder as best she could. Her intense focus in surgery made her good at her job but a ball of tension and knots every other time of day. She wished she had time to get a massage, but in her line of work, it was a waste of money. She would need to get one every week.

The buzz of her phone made Rachel smile.

Ana: Hi.

Rachel: Hey you. Just finished my first case. How are you?

Ana: Working on a few cases of my own just different kinds. Lol.

Rachel: True, I actually never thought about us both having cases before.

Rachel wasn't shocked Ana was working on a Sunday. The woman seemed to work almost as much as Rachel did, but somehow, she still found time to text her randomly throughout the day. The effort wasn't lost on Rachel.

Ana: I had a great time yesterday.

Warmth spread through Rachel's heart and she could feel her cheeks burning. She knew it meant she was blushing even though she couldn't see herself.

Rachel: It was all right, I guess.

Rachel sat back in her chair and watched anxiously as Ana typed back.

> **Ana:** Oh yeah? Maybe I should track that high schooler down and kick his ass.

> **Rachel:** No medical care. Please.

> **Ana:** Fine. But only because it would keep you busy and I'd have to go to sleep without hearing you blab on about whatever episode of The Nanny you've watched for the hundredth time.

> **Rachel:** What? That show is a modern classic.

> **Ana:** I'll take your word for it.

> **Rachel:** Hold on…you've never seen The Nanny?? I think I can hear my mom yelling from here.

> **Ana:** We were more of a telenovela casa, if you know what I mean. But I'm willing to give it a go, if you're offering.

Rachel tapped her finger on her phone.

Is she implying what I think she is?

It was tempting, the idea of Ana coming over to her apartment, cuddling up on the couch, eating popcorn, and watching TV. But she knew that if Ana ever stepped foot in her apartment, the last thing that would be happening would be an innocent 90s TV show binge fest. Plus, they had just spent almost the entire day together yesterday. Did Rachel really want to be the epitome of the U-Haul lesbian cliché? And with Ana of all people?

Rachel: Hmm…what did you have in mind?

Rachel smiled at her decision to play coy. She wasn't usually one to lead someone on, but she felt like Ana could handle much worse and might even enjoy a little game of cat and mouse.

> **Ana:** You're going to make me spell it out, aren't you?

> **Rachel:** I couldn't possibly know what you mean, Counselor.

Okay, now she was just being mean.

Ana: Fine. How about I come over tonight and you can show
    me what's so great about this flashy girl from Flushing,
    Queens?

Rachel: Hey! You have seen it. Mean.

Ana: Relax. I googled the theme song. So…are you going to
    make me ask twice?

She really wanted to say yes. What did she even have going on tonight, anyway? It was a Sunday night and she was off work in a few hours and then what? She'd go home and make a salad to eat with Elijah? How pathetic was that? She wanted Ana to come over. She really, really did. But there was a part of her that just wasn't ready for that yet. She liked what they had. She liked getting to learn about Ana from a safe distance. There was no chance in either of them risking their careers this way. If they took things to the next step, it would get complicated, and Rachel really didn't like complicated.

Rachel: How about we reach a settlement here?

Ana: Oh God, now I know we've been talking too much.
    You're really starting to sound like a lawyer. What are
    your terms?

Rachel: 8:00 FaceTime? We push play on Netflix at the
    same time?

It was the best she could do, and she hoped Ana would understand her need to keep some physical distance between them. But when five minutes passed before a response, her anxiety started to kick in. What if that meant she was losing interest? Maybe it was too romantic a suggestion? Maybe it freaked her out or pushed her away. Before she was able to unravel too far, her phone buzzed.

Ana: Sorry, had to finish focusing on an email. 8:00 it is. I'll
    be sure to put my finest pajamas on.

CHAPTER TWENTY-FIVE

Ana closed her laptop around seven. She had billed about six hours, which was pretty good for a Sunday, but she knew she could have billed ten if she hadn't been distracted by a certain redhead all day. Usually, a distraction in the middle of trying to get work done would cause Ana an unbelievable amount of stress. She was the one who silenced her phone all day so she could keep her head down and not worry about mindless conversations with friends or her brother sending her a silly photo of him covered in grease. But lately, when she heard the soft buzz of her phone on her desk, a warm sensation had started to spread to her heart. Now she got excited when her phone lit up in the middle of drafting a motion or reviewing a contract. When it was a text from Rachel, that excitement doubled, and when it wasn't, a feeling of disappointment replaced it.

When she first gave Rachel her number, she hadn't expected all of this. She figured maybe they would flirt a little—heck, maybe eventually even meet up for another round of mind-blowing sex—before never seeing each other again or mentioning a word to anyone about it. But she hadn't expected to actually develop feelings for her. And yet, over the last few weeks of getting to know Rachel, she couldn't deny that they were there. Yesterday at the park, she was so close to kissing her she could practically taste her ChapStick. If that stupid little twerp hadn't ruined everything, who knows how the day would have turned out? Maybe they would have done more than kiss.

And then what? They would stop talking until after the lawsuit? Or worse, they'd keep talking during the lawsuit? Ana shoved down the thoughts that made her question whether all of this was really worth risking her career over. She had never met a woman like Rachel. She could flirt with danger a little longer, right?

She was afraid she had blown her shot by not making a move

later in the day, but Rachel's little Netflix and chill compromise had given her renewed hope. Besides, Ana wasn't one to back down from a challenge, especially one as potentially rewarding as Rachel Cohen.

She walked into her bedroom, slid open the door to her closet, and leaned down to dig around in her bottom drawer. The room was too small for a dresser, so Ana had saved space by putting her dresser inside the closet. She had less space for hanging her dresses and suits, but at least she didn't have to get dressed in the living room every morning.

"Gotcha," Ana said, as she successfully found what she had been looking for. It had been a long time since she had worn this for anyone, and she had never worn it for someone who was only going to be on a tiny little phone screen. But Ana was willing to make the effort tonight.

Rachel had wanted the kiss just as much as she had. She just knew it. This would be the ultimate test. If the outfit caused a reaction, then Ana would know Rachel was struggling with this whole "not crossing any lines" charade they were both playing. No one had ever been able to resist Ana in this thing. She couldn't wait to see Rachel try.

As she slid on the getup and applied lotion to her legs, Ana thought back to yesterday. Not just to their *almost* kiss, but to the afternoon when they had walked and talked. That was maybe the craziest thing about Rachel. Ana was content to just walk around a park and talk to her for hours. And Rachel seemed just as happy to do the same with her.

Normally, Ana was always having to plan some event for her dates. Something to do together or place to go. A Broadway show, or the ballet, or a Knicks game. Something to really wow the girl she was seeing. But there was no pressure to show off for Rachel. No need to impress or woo her. She just enjoyed getting to know more about her.

So far she had learned that Rachel would rather sit on a beach and read a good book than hike in the woods. She learned that not only did she not eat shellfish but was actually allergic. She learned about her high school basketball team making it all the way to the state championship her junior year and how they had lost by just two points. And she learned just how much being a surgeon—a good surgeon— really meant to Rachel. She cared about her patients, not just during the operation but long after.

The revelation gave Ana a sinking feeling in the pit of her stomach when she thought of the lawsuit that was still pending between them. She owed David Blackstone an email this week, she knew, but the more she learned about Rachel, the harder it was to believe that she had anything to do with Mark Solomon's death. There was just no way someone so good and pure of heart could have any idea of what went wrong in that operating room. She considered not pursuing the deposition at all but knew she could never explain that change of heart to Paul, and the effort wasn't worth the risk.

Soon Ana's alarm went off, telling her it was now seven forty-five. Time for her to put on her finishing makeup touches and get ready for this FaceTime.

She leaned over her bathroom mirror, applying her standard shade of red lipstick, and ran her hands through her hair so that it fell down in front of her chest in waves. It was so long it almost looked like she didn't have anything on underneath. At least until you saw the black leather corset.

Ana walked over to her couch, turned on her TV, and opened the Netflix app. She tried to ignore how loud her heart beat in her chest as she waited.

Relax, you've worn this thing plenty of times. Everyone loves it. She's going to love it.

Her phone rang at exactly eight p.m., because of course it did. The fact that Rachel was punctual was no surprise to Ana. The woman seemed to have every aspect of her life buttoned up into neat little compartments. She had never seen her apartment, but she imaged she was the type to label the sections of her cupboard and have a crisp white duvet over a plain down comforter. Meanwhile, Ana struggled to put the dishes in the dishwasher most nights and constantly had stacks of laundry lying around waiting to go into the drawers. She wasn't messy per se, she was just way too busy to care about silly things like being neat.

Ana positioned herself so that her phone was angled just the right way for her boobs to look their best. She slid the screen to accept the call.

"Hello?" Ana said, trying to make her voice sound sultry.

But there was no one there. Just an empty living room. Apparently, Rachel had called her and then set her down on her kitchen counter and walked away. Perturbed at the lack of immediate gratification she was seeking; Ana cleared her throat.

"Playing ding dong ditch, are we?"

"Sorry!" She heard Rachel's voice echo from somewhere in the apartment. "Just feeding this little gremlin so she'll be quiet during the show." Ana heard the sound of a cat meowing and the *plop, plop, plop* of wet cat food hitting a dish.

She waited in silence, listening to Rachel talk to Elijah in a completely different voice than she had ever heard before. She covered her mouth and tried not to laugh as the cardiac surgeon with a medical degree from an Ivy League school called her cat a "little fluffy muffin lumpers" in a baby voice.

"Wow, can't wait to hear what pet name you give me," Ana said, unable to keep in her laughter.

"*You* don't get a pet name because only good—" Rachel appeared on the screen and froze mid-sentence.

There's the reaction I wanted.

"You were saying?" Ana said. She watched as Rachel's eyes darkened on the screen, a look of desire and lust taking over her usually gentle face.

"I..." Rachel stammered, lowering her glance down to Ana's chest. Ana tilted the camera for just a second and then raised it back up to her eyeline again.

"Finish what you were saying, Doctor."

Rachel gulped and blinked, looking as if she was trying to remember what she had said in the first place.

"Why don't I get a pet name?" Ana raised a single eyebrow, continuing to watch Rachel writhe on the screen.

"Because only good girls get pet names," Rachel said, her voice low and raspy.

Ana sank down on the couch a little so she was reclining and angled the camera down so Rachel could see more of her cleavage and the corset she was wearing.

"Are you saying I'm not a good girl?" She smirked a little at the power she had taken so easily from Rachel.

"I'm saying I could think of a lot of things to call you right now, and good wouldn't be one of them."

Checkmate.

CHAPTER TWENTY-SIX

Rachel was pretty sure this was what a heart attack felt like. All the clinical signs were there. Her chest was tightening. It was difficult to breathe. Her fingers were going numb. As the logical side of her brain took control, she reminded herself that she was an extremely healthy woman in her mid-thirties, which meant cardiac arrest was highly unlikely. What was more likely was that Ana was causing Rachel so much fucking gay panic right now she felt like was going to explode, and this was her body's way of handling said panic.

Luckily, she had carried her phone over to sit down on her couch when her knees started to go weak upon first seeing Ana on the screen wearing nothing but a black corset that pushed her breasts up so high, she looked like she belonged in a nineteenth century saloon. Not that she was complaining, but holy shit, this was not what she had anticipated when she had suggested they FaceTime and watch a silly TV show together.

"So, this is your idea of comfy pajamas?" Rachel asked, narrowing her eyes.

Ana shrugged, feigning ignorance. "I said finest pajamas. Trust me, this thing is anything but comfy."

Rachel shook her head. "I knew better than to become involved with a lawyer. Remembering every word like it's written in blood."

Ana stuck out her bottom lip. "Are you saying you don't like my pajamas?"

"Definitely not saying that," Rachel said a little too hastily. "Just wasn't expecting them, that's for sure."

Ana sat up on the couch, placing her phone on her coffee table so that Rachel could see her full body for the first time. The heart palpitations returned and Rachel focused her energy on not rubbing her legs together to satiate the growing need manifesting between her legs.

"I guess I could take it off, if you really don't like it."

More heart palpations.

"You're cruel, you know that?" Rachel said, scooting down on her couch, unable to keep her hand from tracing the inside of her thighs.

Ana just barely spread her legs, and Rachel squinted, trying to mentally zoom in on the image. Ana tossed her head back and let out a low laugh, the kind of laugh that always drove Rachel to madness. Surely she must know that by now?

"I take it by how hard you just squinted that you want to see more?"

Rachel was unable to speak. She gulped and nodded in silence, watching as Ana picked up the phone again and brought it close to her face. She tilted the screen down and began to play with the top of the corset, where her nipple was just barely covered. Slowly, she moved her hand beneath the thin piece of leather and started rolling her fingers over her nipple, letting out a weak moan as she did.

Rachel moved her hand beneath her shorts and bit down on her lip. She had never really done anything like this before, and she wasn't sure what the protocol was for when she was "allowed" to start touching herself, but if it didn't happen soon, she might combust on her couch.

"Teasing isn't showing," Rachel said, challenging Ana in the way she knew Ana liked.

"Patience," Ana said, removing her hand from the corset. She lay down on the couch on her stomach and angled the phone along her back, allowing Rachel to see for the first time the back of the thong she was wearing. Her round, tan ass was on full display, and Rachel inhaled sharply at the sight.

"How's that?" Ana asked, swinging her legs back and forth, a pair of black high heels popping in and out of the tiny screen.

Rachel was getting light-headed. Ana's ass was possibly her favorite physical feature on her, aside from her long fingers. God, what she would give to get a hand—or two—on that ass right now. Rachel squirmed.

"It's good," she said, trying her best to remain still but having a difficult time controlling her facial expressions and her body at the same time.

"Are you touching yourself?" Ana licked her lips subtly.

"Do you want me to?" Rachel replied, trying to hide the desperation in her voice. *God, please say yes.*

"Hmm," Ana said, swaying her feet again. "If I say no, will you obey me?"

Rachel shook her head. "At this point, probably not, no."

Ana laughed again. "Maybe I'm not the only bad girl here, then." With that, she lifted two fingers to her mouth, slowly sliding them inside and sucking on them briefly before moving them between her legs where she lay, still face down on the couch.

Rachel strained again, trying to see exactly where her hand had ended up, but the movement of Ana's ass made answered her question. Rachel slid her hand beneath her underwear, now knowing she had full permission to pleasure herself. She was soaked. Normally she needed some sort of lube when she got herself off, but not this time. This time she had to force herself to go slow when she started rolling her fingers across her clit. She had to remind herself to breathe and pace herself or she would finish in ten seconds just watching the way Ana rolled her hips.

Rachel threw her head back, listening to the sounds of Ana. Whimpers, gasps, and a few moans mixed in with the sound of Rachel's fingers sliding in and out of her wet folds. She closed her eyes and soaked in the image of Ana in her corset, the sounds coming from the phone in her hand. She imagined they were together, and it was Ana's fingers slipping in and out of her right now.

Soon, too soon, she was close and she looked over at Ana on the screen. Her face was down and she was still grinding against herself, faster now. She had apparently grabbed a pillow at some point and was now biting into it, muffling the moans and profanities coming from her pretty little mouth. The sight was enough to make Rachel come undone, and no amount of focus or breathing could abate the inevitable.

"Ana, I'm—"

"Me too, come with me," Ana groaned.

That was all it took. Within seconds Rachel was tumbling over the edge and into bliss, her legs trembling and twitching. The sound of Ana screaming her name on the other side of the screen took her to another level of pleasure, and she closed her eyes for a moment, letting herself soak in what had just happened.

There was no going back now. There was no doubt that they were way more than just friends. Rachel would let herself focus on the implications of all that later. For now, she rolled her head to the side and looked at Ana, who had flipped onto her back and was smiling.

"You know what?" Ana said, a smug look of satisfaction on her face. "Maybe I do like this show after all."

CHAPTER TWENTY-SEVEN

Ana sauntered into her office with an extra pep in her step. She tossed her bag on the floor against her desk, plopped down into her chair, and clicked on her computer to wake up the screen. She hadn't worked any more last night. How could she? She hadn't been able to think about anything but Rachel all night. Ana thought about Rachel as she showered. She thought about Rachel as she tried to fall asleep. She thought about Rachel on the 7 train into work that morning. She thought about Rachel as she waited for her computer to load.

And unfortunately, she thought of Rachel as soon as she opened her emails.

From: David Blackstone
To: Ana Mendez
CC: Sheryl Peterson
Re: Dr. Cohen Depo

Good morning, Ana and Sheryl,
I am once again following up on the deposition of Dr. Cohen. She would like to put this matter behind her as soon as possible. It has been over a month since we last spoke. Please advise as to your earliest availability within the next two months.
Kind regards,
David Blackstone

"Fuck," Ana said as she finished reading the email, a wave of dread now washing over her, threatening to erase her peppy mood. She knew this day was coming. She had been ignoring it for over a month now, all the while growing closer to Rachel.

To: David Blackstone
CC: Sheryl Peterson
Re: Dr. Cohen Depo

Good morning, David,
*   I understand. Let me check my schedule and get back*
to you.
*   Best,*
*   Ana Mendez*

Her finger hovered over the send button for a few seconds before she finally pressed down and watched the email disappear from her screen. That would buy her a few days at least, but she really needed to get a handle on what the hell she planned to do about all of this.

When Stella had initially presented her solution to just have a junior associate cover the deposition, she hadn't exactly accounted for the hoops she would have to jump through to make that happen. First, the partner, Paul, would have to approve it. Then the client, Martha Solomon, would have to approve it. She'd have to explain to both of them why she, the attorney handling the case, could not cover the final deposition. Then whatever poor, unsuspecting junior associate she cornered to take on the task had to agree to it. She rubbed her neck and sighed, figuring she would get the first hurdle out of the way that afternoon during her meeting with Paul.

Rachel: Good morning.

A wave of relief flooded over Ana with that simple, two-word text. She instantly forgot the massive amount of anxiety she had as it pertained to this woman and instead focused on the little butterflies that now fluttered their way across her chest and down into her stomach.

Last night had gone much better than she could have ever anticipated. She had planned on just teasing Rachel a little bit. Getting her riled up, hopefully a little turned on, and then turning off the camera, changing into some shorts and an oversized T-shirt and actually watching *The Nanny*. But one look at Rachel's face, flushed with desire; one little bite of her perfect, plump lower lip; one gasp at the sight of Ana in her corset, and Ana was past the point of no return.

On the bright side, there was no question that Rachel had feelings for her. On the downside, there was no avoiding the massive iceberg called the *Mark Solomon* case their ship was heading full steam toward.

Ana: Morning sleepyhead.

Ana snapped a selfie of her making a kissy face at the camera, making sure her chest was pushed out in her low-cut red blouse and black blazer.

She watched and waited for the next text, hoping for a selfie in return. Maybe Rachel was still in bed, the sheets wrapped up around her half-naked body. What did her bed even look like? Ana laughed, imagining anything but neat, crisp hospital corners on Rachel's bed. The thought just seemed out of place. Ana had only seen glimpses of her apartment last night, and frankly she hadn't been paying much attention to anything but Rachel's crystal blue eyes and freckled cheeks, but somehow, she just knew the woman had an all-white bed that was made in perfect military style every morning.

She imagined Rachel was the type of person who washed her sheets and towels no less than once a week. She probably even had special hand towels with little cursive initials on them for when company came over. Ana let herself drift off, envisioning the type of environment someone as meticulous and dedicated as Rachel Cohen probably lived in.

Her phone buzzed and Ana perked up with excitement before unlocking the screen.

Rachel: Who's sleepy? Not this girl. Went for a nice run this morning.

There was a selfie, but Rachel was far from bed. She was seated in her office sipping a full cup of coffee, her scrub cap already on her head and a wide grin spread across her porcelain face. Then a second photo came in that must have been taken on the run Rachel mentioned. The sun was rising over a tree in Central Park, the sky painted an eerie shade of pink and orange hues. It took Ana only a second to recognize the location. It was where they had their first hangout. She sent a heart back in reply to both photos.

Ana smiled wide at the photo. It made her feel good to know that this—whatever it was—meant something to Rachel too. That Ana wasn't the only one getting sentimental over things like a tree in Central Park. Then her thoughts drifted back to the previous night. After they had both recovered from what was probably the kinkiest FaceTime of Ana's life, they'd talked and flirted until around midnight, when Rachel fell asleep on her couch mid-sentence. Ana should have woken her up and told her to go to bed, but she hadn't wanted to hang up. She'd wanted to stay that way, watching her breathe slowly, in and out, a strand of red hair flowing in and out of her mouth. But she reminded herself that one, that was super creepy, and two, she needed to shower and get ready for work the next day.

Judging by the wide-eyed expression featured in the selfie, Rachel wasn't exactly lacking energy, so Ana's decision to let her sleep where she was wouldn't be held against her.

Ana sat back feeling a sense of satisfaction. She too had felt a renewed level of energy this morning. Something about the day felt crisp, fresh, and alive. They had drawn a new line in the sand last night and left all other lines in the rearview mirror. They hadn't exactly discussed what that might mean for them officially, but for now it just felt really damn good to know that a sexy, smart woman fifty blocks north of her office was moaning her name as she came last night.

Remembering that Rachel had an early surgery that morning, Ana copied and pasted the Hebrew phrase for *good luck* from the internet to make sure she had spelled it right and pressed send.

Rachel: Wow, wishing me luck in Hebrew? I'm impressed. I guess this means I should learn some Spanish then?

Ana: I might know someone willing to give you some one-on-one lessons. If you can afford her, that is.

Rachel: Oh, I don't know…how experienced is she? I mean, I wouldn't want someone who doesn't know what they're doing. Especially if it's going to cost me.

Ana: Trust me, you'll be more than satisfied with the services she provides.

Ana smirked, leaning back in her chair. She loved this little dance they did. The flirting, the double entendres, the tight squeeze that seeing the bubbles dance on the screen caused in her chest.

Rachel: Hmm…I'll think it over. If last night was any indication, I'm definitely interested.

Ana felt warmth spreading to her chest. She leaned forward preparing to type a response but the loud *ding!* of an incoming email refocused her attention on work.

The remainder of the morning passed without much interruption. Rachel hadn't texted her any more, probably indicating she was in surgery. Ana responded to a few discovery demands, sent out several good faith letters, reviewed a lease agreement for a new case she had just been assigned, and most importantly, planned what she was going to say to Paul when she stepped into their meeting in exactly two minutes.

She held her shoulders back and inhaled slowly before opening the heavy glass door to his office. He was on the phone but waved her in with a frown and gestured toward the empty seat across from his desk.

"Listen, Patrick, we both know what happens to this case when it gets in front of a Westchester jury. Think it over and get back to me. If I don't hear back in a week, the offer is rescinded and we will see you at jury selection."

Paul hung up the phone and shook his head. "Man, some people just do not know when to hold them and when to fold them."

"Trial?"

Paul nodded. "Yeah, an old case of Darcy Hammond's that probably should have settled ages ago that I got stuck with when she left. Anyway, what's on the agenda for us today?"

"Just a few cases, *Neprati, Jones*—"

"What's going on with the *Solomon* case?" Paul interjected. She wasn't surprised. He rarely let her drive in their meetings. He'd ask if she had any cases she wanted to go over with him and before she could even finish saying the case name, he'd move on to the topics he really wanted to discuss. Her list of questions was of no concern to him, so long as his list of worries and fears was pacified.

"I actually wanted to talk to you about that one today," Ana said, readying her nerves for the sales pitch about to spring from her lips. "Discovery is basically wrapped up. We just have that one deposition of a surgical resident."

"Dr. Colleen?" Paul asked.

"Dr. Cohen," Ana corrected. Saying Rachel's name to Paul made her shudder slightly. It was impossible to now distinguish the surgical resident Dr. Cohen from the Rachel Cohen who had made her scream into a pillow on her couch last night.

"Cohen, Cohen, yeah go on." Paul started to fidget with his pen as she continued.

"Anyway, she's pretty insignificant in all of this. I'm not even sure we really need her deposition, honestly." She paused for a moment, seeing if Paul would take the bait. When he stared blankly at her, she proceeded to plan B. "But I know we want to be thorough. I think it would be a good deposition for a junior associate to cut their teeth on. You know, get some experience deposing a doctor. It's not a risk to the case since she's such a peripheral party in all of this."

"She?" Paul asked.

"Yes. Dr. Cohen is a woman."

Paul nodded. "Oh, yeah right, right," he mumbled.

Ana waited again, picking at her cuticle. She could tell by the wrinkled expression on his face that he was contemplating what Ana had said.

Please say yes, please say yes.

"I'd get them fully up to speed, so there would be no double billing," she added, trying to sweeten the pot.

Paul sat back in his chair and crossed his arms.

"All right," he said skeptically. "Get the Willis boy to do it. He's got a bright future here, what with his father being a judge and all. Get him up to speed, make sure he doesn't overbill on the prep time, and he can handle the deposition."

Ana felt like a millstone had just been taken off her neck and sighed an audible breath of relief. She hated Micah Willis with a passion, but anything was better than having to depose Rachel herself at this point.

"Great, no problem, I'll make sure he's ready to go."

Paul nodded. "And what about the *Mereen-Morris* case? Any movement on settlement there?"

Ana nodded, inwardly accepting that she had just tackled the first major hurdle of avoiding this huge conflict of interest staring her in the face.

One down, two to go.

CHAPTER TWENTY-EIGHT

Rachel sank down into her office chair, twisting her head from side to side, massaging the back of her neck. Long procedures like today's made her shoulders and neck feel like there were little rocks lodged under her skin, not just from the stress of knowing that if her finger moved a centimeter to the left, a critical artery would be nicked, but also just from the physical posture of surgery itself. Thank God for good sneakers and massagers. She opened her drawer and pulled out a curved stick with a ball on the end and tucked it around her back. It hurt as she dug into one of her more prominent knots, but in all the right ways. She'd found this little contraption at REI a few months back and it had changed her life. No more relying on Charlotte to dig into the places on her back she couldn't reach. This sucker let her do it all herself. The perfect tool for someone as stubbornly independent as Rachel.

After a few minutes of kneading, her vision started to go blurry and she stopped, drinking a full bottle of water to flush out the toxins she had just released. She picked up her phone from her desk and checked back in with the world. She landed on a text from Noa and opened it first.

> **Noa:** Estie would like me to tell you that she would like you to come have dinner and play unicorns this Wednesday night.

Rachel laughed, imagining the exact conversation that had prompted the text. She read on.

> **Noa:** Benjamin says he too would like to play unicorns with you and Estie.

> **Noa:** Jake says he feels left out and would also like to join in the unicorn fun. This Wednesday. You free?

Rachel shook her head and started typing immediately.

Rachel: If my diva commands. This Wednesday it is.

Rachel: P.S. I hope Jake knows I meant him.

Rachel exited the thread and scrolled some more, landing on several unopened texts from Ana.

Ana: I know you're probably busy playing Victor Frankenstein over there, but just wanted to say hi and see if you were free Wednesday night? They're doing Othello for Shakespeare in the Park and it happens to be my favorite.

Rachel did a literal face palm and typed back.

Rachel: I just committed to someone else that night. Rain check?

Bubbles started to appear on the screen instantly.

Ana: That's cool, no worries, I'll ttyl.

Rachel pulled her head back. She was being short with her. Why? Rachel scrolled up again to soothe her anxiety that was quickly taking the driver seat at the control panel of her mind.

She read Ana's text and then her reply. She had been polite, she'd said...she'd said she had committed to someone else. Oy vey. Rachel shook her head and smiled, realizing the faux pas that was likely the cause of Ana's consternation.

Rachel picked up the phone and called Ana. She hated miscommunications over texts. She knew it was untoward to call her in the middle of a work day, but she took the risk anyway. It only rang once before Ana answered.

"Is that jealousy I detect, Miss Mendez?"

"I thought we said no calls at work."

"Well, maybe I decided to break the rules this time. Now, answer my question. Unless you're busy."

"No, I'm just in my office. The door's closed." Ana let out a loud sigh. "I mean, am I even allowed to be jealous? We never said we were exclusive. So it's cool."

Rachel chuckled to herself. *So that's how she's playing it. Miss Cool and Aloof and oh, nothing bothers me.*

"You sure about that, Counselor? You seem pretty miffed over there. Pencil skirt in a twist?"

Ana lowered her voice. "Is this your way of trying to ask what I'm wearing?"

"If I wanted to know that, I would just ask for a picture, which you're welcome to send after this phone call, by the way. But quit deflecting. Why don't you want to ask about what I'm doing Wednesday night?"

There was a pause. "If you wanted me to know, I'm sure you would have told me."

She liked hearing Ana get all flustered and jealous. She was always the calm and collected one, and Rachel was the one usually fumbling to find the right words in her mind. When Ana walked into a room, people noticed. Heads turned and eyes shifted and conversations stopped at her mere presence. Meanwhile, Rachel once had a classmate sign her senior yearbook "HAGS, Raquel." They had been in the same school together since kindergarten. She didn't mind having this little ounce of control over Ana right now.

"Well, if you must know, she's very beautiful. She has long, brown curly hair and brown eyes, and she's Jewish. Plus, she's super creative and funny and way smarter than me."

"Damn, way to kick me while I'm down. Aren't doctors sworn to do no harm?"

"Yeah, only problem is…she's five years old."

There was silence on the other end of the phone.

"It's my niece, dummy. She wants me to come play unicorns with her and Benjamin. Kinky stuff, I know."

Ana let out a loud huff. Rachel could almost see her gritting her teeth and rolling her eyes through the phone. It was cute to imagine.

"I really don't like you sometimes, you know that?"

"That's not what you said last night."

"You sure you want to go there?" Ana's voice was cool and steely again. Just like that, she was back in control.

Rachel felt a twinge of fear. She wasn't sure she was ready to challenge Ana to this battle just yet. She would likely lose, and her office wasn't exactly the best place for her to get all hot and bothered.

"Fine, we will leave it at that. But you should probably know that I'm not seeing anyone else." Rachel paused, waiting for some response from Ana. When she didn't get one, she kept talking. "Just thought you should know."

Rachel bit down on her thumbnail and waited for a response. They hadn't even gotten close to defining anything yet, and she hoped she hadn't said too much too soon. Ignoring her inner saboteur that was yelling at her, she waited through the endless seconds of silence.

"That's good to know," Ana replied, her voice still calm and collected, but with a slight elevation at the end of the sentence. "I'm not either. Just so you know."

Rachel smiled and felt her cheeks begin to burn from happiness. "Okay then, I guess we should both get back to work, huh?"

Ana chuckled. "Yeah, those scumbag doctors aren't going to sue themselves."

CHAPTER TWENTY-NINE

"Hey, scoot over," Stella said in between bites of chicharrones.

"God, how can you eat those things?" Ana asked, turning up her nose as Stella squeezed into the bleacher seat beside her.

Shakespeare in the Park was perhaps the most "New York" thing she had done since moving there for law school eight years ago. In fact, it was the only thing she could afford to do during those three years of law school, since the tickets were free. Even after starting at Byron & Browning, it had remained one of her favorite ways to pass a warm summer night in the city.

She wasn't kidding about *Othello* being her favorite Shakespeare play, and there was no way she was missing it, even if Rachel was busy tonight. Luckily, Stella was in between random hookups, for the time being at least, and was free to be her plus one. She knew absolutely nothing about the play, or Shakespeare in general, but had agreed to come because it was a nice night and, as Stella so delicately put it, "Theater chicks are hot."

"What?" Stella said, popping another fried pork rind into her mouth and chewing loudly on purpose, a sly smirk crawling up from the corner of her mouth. "Your family doesn't eat chicharrones back home?"

Ana wrinkled her nose again. "My brother does. He used to chew them until they turned into paste and then open his mouth to show me and pretend it was vomit."

She shivered at the memory.

"Ah," Stella said, swallowing deeply. "Well, I'll do my best not to trigger you with my snack, Mendez."

Ana bumped her shoulder into Stella playfully and ignored the wafting smell of the salty food as it drifted up from the plastic bag and into her nose.

"So," Stella said mid-chew, "you gonna give me an update about your little mermaid or what?"

Ana blushed and looked down. She had intentionally been keeping Stella out of the loop on this topic lately. Mostly she didn't want anything getting back to Stella if the shit hit the proverbial fan at work, and also, she was slightly terrified to admit what was going on between them. What *was* going on between them? They had hung out once. It was *not* a date. At least, she was pretty sure it wasn't a date. But then there was the whole FaceTiming and mutual orgasms thing that had kinda made things complicated, totally her fault, by the way—who could resist a woman in a corset? And then they had both agreed they were talking with only each other. But were they dating? More than dating? Ana really wasn't sure.

"What do you want to know?" Ana answered coyly.

"Oh, come on. Don't be shy, now. You're never one to hold back on hookups."

Ana remained quiet and inhaled slowly, unsure of where to even begin when it came to this topic.

"Listen," Stella continued. "Do you remember that time you took that hot little junior associate dancing? And then you made out with her on a park bench after?"

Ana cringed. "Her name was Lizzy, and yes, I remember. The next day she told me she had been too drunk to remember what happened. Thanks for bringing up that scarring memory."

"Exactly," Stella said. "And then a few months later you found out she had been screwing your boss all along?"

Ana nodded. "Yes, yes, thank you for reminding me of all of these exciting details of my failed love life."

"Right," Stella said. "My point is, whatever it is you and Dr. Quinn Medicine Woman have going on, it can't be as bad as that, right?"

Ana let out a loud laugh, and a few people sitting around them turned to shoot her a dirty look. The show hadn't started, but New Yorkers could be real assholes sometimes.

"When you put it like that, I guess you're right." Ana let out a slow breath before continuing. "Okay, fine. We hung out here at the park a couple of weeks ago. Just over there, actually." Ana motioned to a grove of trees behind where they were sitting on the elevated bleachers.

Stella nodded. "And?"

"And it was nice." Ana took a sip of the bottled water she had brought and averted her eyes.

"And…" Stella said, pressing the issue.

"And…we kinda," Ana lowered her voice, "had FaceTime sex the next night?"

Stella dropped the bag of chicharrones and covered her mouth. "No fucking way."

There were more dirty looks from their snooty seat neighbors.

"Shh!" Ana held a finger up in front of her mouth. "God, you have no volume other than loud."

Stella picked up the bag off the floor and rolled it closed. "Valid, but damn, what did you expect? I mean, talk about hitting the gas pedal. You went from hanging in the park to fucking on the phone."

"Shh! Please stop saying *fucking* so loud," Ana said, turning red.

"Fuck, my bad," Stella said, dipping her head and finally lowering her voice. "So, what's next, then?"

The sound of the orchestra warming up indicated to Ana that the conversation was over for now.

"Well, right now we watch *Othello* and we beware of the green-eyed monster." Ana wiggled her eyebrows, waiting for a reaction from Stella.

Stella had a vapid look on her face and Ana rolled her eyes. "You really know nothing about this play, do you?"

"Nope." Stella shrugged. "But I hope the chick playing Juliet is hot."

Ana shook her head. "I think you mean Desdemona."

"Whatever, nerd," Stella replied as she leaned back and crossed her arms.

The play began and Ana let all thoughts of Rachel, work, her family, or even her friends leave her. For the next hour and a half, she wasn't clawing her way to a promotion for a job that she really wasn't at all passionate about. She wasn't jeopardizing said job by continuing to become more and more involved with a woman she was supposed to be deposing in an important lawsuit. She wasn't a constant disappointment to her mother. She wasn't being nagged and asked when she would be home again. She was in Cyprus. She was Desdemona in all her naivete and hope. She was Othello in his ambition and envy. She was Iago in his malice and plotting. She was everyone and anyone except herself. That was why she loved the theater.

One of the things that had excited her most about living in New York was her easy access to Broadway. Nowhere else in the world could a person be so lucky. Sometimes on Saturdays when Ana had convinced herself to take a day off work, she would go down to the theater district and buy last minute matinee tickets for shows that were starting in half an hour or less. She knew the look on the scalpers' faces as they started to get desperate with showtime approaching, and she used her negotiation skills to broker some pretty great deals on orchestra seats.

It didn't matter which show. It was all an escape to Ana. She had seen *Wicked* at least six times, *Les Misérables* three, and her personal favorite, *Phantom of the Opera*, over a dozen times before it tragically left Broadway forever. She never paid more than forty bucks a seat. Sometimes she went with other people. She had convinced Stella to see *Aladdin* with her a few years ago, and Stella went because she liked the movie as a kid. She had seen *Six* with a girl she dated briefly last year. And yes, months ago she used the firm's connections to see *Moulin Rouge* with a junior associate named Lizzy who had quickly thrown her over for Darcy Hammond. But that was ancient history now.

She hadn't done much theater in school aside from the required plays in elementary school; she'd dabbled in a few classes in middle school, but nothing serious. She wished she had, though. She wished she had allowed herself a little bit of room to just be creative when she was younger. To enjoy being a kid. But growing up in a poor family didn't allow much room for passion projects like theater. She was too busy learning economics and the stock market. Or running her own lemonade stands on the weekends to make money off tourists. She was born a hustler. Always working, always trying to turn one dollar into ten. That was why she wanted to become a lawyer in the first place, so she could give her own family the financial stability she never had growing up.

By the end of the play, Ana was fully enraptured by the story and had completely forgotten about the outside world. When the bright lights over the Delacorte Theater came on, she blinked rapidly to remind herself where she was.

"What did you think?" Ana asked, still soaking in the afterglow of another amazing performance.

"Depressing as hell," Stella said. She grabbed her empty plastic bag and crumpled it up. "I mean, why did the hot girl have to die?"

"Desdemona," Ana replied.

"Yeah, desperate Mona over there being all, no he didn't kill me, I killed myself. And then the main dude kills himself anyway. Basically, moral of the story, everyone dies. The end."

Ana chuckled. "That is certainly one interpretation of it."

When they got through the crowd of people leaving, Ana pulled off to the side to check her phone for the first time since they'd sat down.

> **Rachel:** Just got to Noa's. Hope you enjoy the play. Just remember…I am not what I am.

Ana smiled at the quote from *Othello*, adoring the fact that she not only knew the play but knew it well enough to quote Iago. She kept scrolling.

> **Rachel:** Putting the wildlings to bed.

There was a selfie of her and two little kids with stickers on their faces, in matching pajama sets. One was a little girl, who Ana assumed was Estie, and the other a little boy a few years younger. They both had dark, curly hair that fell in perfect ringlets around their large brown eyes. They didn't have Rachel's more prominent features—her red hair, her blue eyes—but they both had her nose, and Estie had freckles like Rachel's.

She found herself being a lesbian cliché and imaging what Rachel would be like as a mom. She could see it easily, a pair of bouncing little kids running around her as she got dressed for work. Would she want to raise her kids Jewish? Ana assumed so. Heck, Ana didn't even know if she wanted to raise her own kids Catholic, she hadn't been practicing for so long. Would she still work or would she want to take time to raise her kids? Would she want her wife to stop working so she could keep working? Would she hire a nanny to watch them full-time? Ana thought all of this and more as she zoomed into the little crease on Rachel's face where a faint crow's foot formed in the corner of her eye.

She stopped looking at the photo long enough to lift her head to see Stella staring at her, an all-knowing eyebrow raised over her dark lids.

"Sorry, just, um, catching up on emails and stuff."

"Uh-huh," Stella said, crossing her arms. "Well, I better get going and let you handle those…emails." She winked and reached out her arms for a hug.

"See you tomorrow," Ana said as Stella released her grip.

"You betcha," she replied, as she started to saunter away. "Oh, and Ana? Next time there's one of these dorky Shakespeare things, do me a favor and *don't* invite me."

Ana laughed and shook her head. "Deal."

Chapter Thirty

G od, you make the best cheesecake," Rachel said, spooning another helping into her mouth.

Her sister smiled as she took her own smaller bite. "That must be true if you're eating a whole piece, Little Miss Health Nut."

Rachel made a face at Noa like they did when they were children, and Noa aped the expression back to her. As much as her erratic work schedule could often hinder a social life, Rachel was grateful for it on nights like tonight, when a Wednesday night was actually her Friday night, since she was off on Thursday. She'd normally be fast asleep in bed by now, but with a free day tomorrow, she poured herself another glass of wine.

"And they're finally out," Jacob said, reentering the room. "Two hours to make them fall asleep, that has to be a new record for their stubbornness."

Noa shook her head. "Estie is teaching Benjamin her tricky ways."

Jacob turned to Rachel. "Well, it doesn't help when someone gets them all worked up with a violent bedtime story."

"Who, me?" Rachel tossed her hands in the air feigning innocence. She had read both kids a story from one of their *My First Bible* books. Benjamin had requested she read Jonah and the big whale, but Estie wanted to hear about her namesake, Queen Esther, and how she saved the Jews of Persia. Rachel had eventually compromised with Daniel in the lion's den. Maybe not the wisest choice for a five-year-old and a two-and-a-half-year-old.

They shared a room, which worked for now, since they were finally on the same sleeping schedule, but Rachel knew the family would soon outgrow this two-bedroom brownstone they rented in Brooklyn. They talked about moving to New Jersey a lot lately. Jacob's company had an office in Secaucus, and Montclair was a nice school district, or so she'd heard them say repeatedly the last several months at Shabbat dinner with her parents.

It made Rachel sad, the idea of her sister and the little ones not being a subway ride away, but she knew they would never be able to afford a house in Brooklyn on Jacob's salary, and in New Jersey the kids would have a nice big back yard to run around in. They could even get a dog, which was all Benjamin had been asking for since he could speak.

"My riveting storytelling wasn't enough to knock them out?" Rachel asked, as she finished off the cheesecake.

"Don't feel too bad," Jacob said, rolling up the sleeve of his collared shirt. "I'm kind of a big deal around these parts." He did his best at a cowboy accent, and Rachel shook her head.

"So." Noa rested her head in her hands on the kitchen counter and faced Rachel. "What's the tea with Law and Order? Have you seen her again? Are you two, like...going steady?"

Rachel burst out in laughter. "Going steady? My God, who are you, Uncle Moishe? Who the hell talks like that this side of the twenty-first century?"

"Go easy on her," Jacob added. "She's the youngest member of our temple's mah-jongg club and I think it's getting to her. Last week she ironed my boxers."

"Hey!" Noa swatted at Jacob as he walked by. "You wear tight pants to work, excuse me for assuming you wouldn't want anyone to think your ass is wrinkly at the age of twenty-nine."

"Now there's a mental image I could have lived without." Rachel blinked her eyes and started wiping them roughly.

"Please, you wish your ass was this smooth." Jacob leaned over the sink, sticking his butt out and rubbing his hand over it pretending he was a model.

"All right, you two. Jake, stop distracting her with your butt. Rachel, focus." Noa wrinkled her forehead and stared at her sister.

"Ugh, fine. Yes, I've seen her."

Noa slammed her hand down on the counter. "I knew it! Tell me everything. I need to live vicariously through you. The most exciting thing happening in my life right now is a five-year-old's piano recital and Jake's stupid summer work party at Yankee Stadium."

"Hey!" Jake chimed in from across the room.

"No offense," Noa added flippantly.

Rachel tucked a strand of hair behind her ear. "I mean, what's to tell? Well, you know a little already, that she's a lawyer. She's thirty-one. She's from Miami—well, a little town just outside of Miami. She has a brother who's younger than her. She was raised Catholic but isn't practicing anymore. She speaks English and Spanish. She's smart and gorgeous and actually shockingly considerate for someone with such an awful career. And she does this little thing when she gets excited about something where her voice goes up super high."

She looked over at her sister and Jacob, who both now stood frozen with their mouths open staring at her.

"What?"

"Oh, you've got it bad, little sis," Noa said.

"Kay, first of all, I'm older than you. Second of all, what are you even talking about?"

Jacob walked across the room and put his hand on her forehead. "You feeling okay? Do you need something? Because I think you may be...lovesick!" He bent over laughing and gave Noa a high five. The two stood beside each other beaming with pride at his ridiculous dad joke. Rachel crossed her arms.

"You two are as mature as the kids sleeping in the other room, you know that?"

"And *Ana* you glad we are?" Jacob added, which prompted a *heyoooo* from Noa as the two continued to laugh at their own humor.

Rachel shook her head. "You asked about her and I answered. It's not my fault you guys are reading way too much into my words."

"It's not that, silly, it's your face. I mean, did you know you light up like a menorah talking about this woman? I haven't seen you this head over heels about someone since that girl in medical school. What was her name again?"

"Leah."

"Leah! God, how could I forget? Rachel and Leah, the worst Jewish couple names ever. Imagine the jokes at temple?"

"I hate you. You know I hate you, right?" Rachel said, staring at her sister.

Noa shrugged. "Yeah, but you love me too. And you *love* Ana."

Rachel checked her smartwatch and faked a yawn. "Oh wow, would you look at the time, I better get going." She pulled out her phone and opened a rideshare app, ordering a car to take her home. It was past ten and she didn't feel like taking the subway this late at night.

Noa and Jake started singing about her and Ana kissing in a tree in while Rachel distracted herself by checking her phone.

She noticed she had a notification on her work email, which was odd considering she had just cleared her inbox on the subway ride over. Fighting off the little voice inside her head that told her she wasn't required to check her emails this late at night, she clicked on her inbox.

From: Mount Sinai ER
To: Dr. Rachel Cohen

Hey, Dr. Cohen, this just came in. I thought you would want to know.

Rachel scrolled down to see a medical chart that had been attached.

Patient: Henry Wentz
Age: 77 years old
CC: Chest pain
Narrative: Pt came to ER via ambulance with complaints of CP. Has history of AAA with Dr. R. Cohen. Pt had been experiencing CP for past several days. Family urged him to be seen sooner but pt refused. Pt collapsed at dinner tonight and was rushed over. Pt initially responsive upon arrival, but shortly after fell into cardiac arrest. Chest compressions performed for three mins. AED performed for two mins. Pt expired at 21:34 PM. Family in waiting room. Will notify PCP and Cardio.

Rachel froze. Mr. Wentz. Her patient asking for pudding and ice cream. She had just seen him a few weeks ago for a post-op. He was fine. He was great, actually. He was working out regularly on his stationary bike, he was mowing the lawn, he was spending time with his grandkids. He was seventy-seven years old, not eighty-nine. Rachel knew patients died, but when they were eighty-nine it was a lot easier to accept than when they were only seventy-seven. Rachel remembered him showing her photos of his wife and grandchildren. She thought of them now. Of the pain they must be experiencing at his loss.

"Rach?" Noa asked coming to her side. "You okay? You look as pale as a ghost."

Rachel nodded, staring at her screen. "One of my patients, he… he died tonight."

Jacob walked over to her now too. "Oh Rach, I'm so sorry." They both wrapped their arms around her and squeezed for a moment before letting go.

"Do you need anything? Was he older?"

Rachel shook her head. "He was only seventy-seven." She bit down on her nail, contemplating what she had just read. Soon, she started to pace frantically. "What if I made a mistake? What if I missed something? What if this is like the Solomon surgery all over again, except what if I'm Dr. Schumacher this time?"

"Rach?" Noa said softly. "Honey, what happened that night? You never talk about it."

"Don't," Rachel snapped. "Don't ask me about that night. Never ask me about that night. Especially not now. Not with Mr. Wentz and Ana and—"

Rachel dropped her head in her hands and pinched the bridge of her nose, focusing on her breathing. It was all crashing down around her. This delicate little world she had built. She couldn't let it happen. She wouldn't let the doubt creep into her mind. Not now. She wasn't Dr. Schumacher. Sometimes people just died. She was a good surgeon. She told herself every day that she was a good surgeon.

Noa rubbed circles on her back slowly. "Okay, we won't talk about it. But why don't you stay here tonight? We'll pull out the couch for you. We've got an extra set of sheets ready."

Rachel took a second to collect her thoughts before putting her phone in her bag. "No, I'm good. My car is pulling up now, I'm gonna go." She hoisted her bag up onto her shoulder and started walking toward the front door, silent.

"Rach, don't leave like this. Stay, please," Noa pleaded, uneasiness ringing in her voice.

Rachel turned to face her sister and gave her a reassuring hug. "Noa, I'm fine, really. This stuff happens. I'm a cardiac surgeon. Patients die. It's part of the job." She shrugged, doing her best to remain stone faced so her sister wouldn't worry.

But Rachel was not okay. She was never okay when a patient died, especially after a procedure had gone so right. She remembered that surgery. Everything had gone perfectly, from open to close. She remembered every post-op visit too. Had there been something she had missed? Should she have followed him more closely after the surgery?

Rachel let out a loud sigh and turned to leave.

"Please text me when you get home safe?"

She nodded and let the door close quietly behind her. She slid into the back seat of the silver Toyota Camry, confirmed her name was showing on the driver's screen, and shut the door. The car proceeded toward the Manhattan Bridge, the quiet lull of music coming from the radio. Rachel tuned it out. All she could think about was Mr. Wentz. What had gone wrong? She would have to check his chart thoroughly. She had to have missed something. She must have done something wrong. She could have done something to prevent this. She should have… Oh, God, what if she really did do something wrong? What if this ended up haunting her just like the Mark Solomon surgery?

No. This wasn't like the Mark Solomon surgery. That was a mistake. A major mistake. And she had just been a resident then. She wasn't the operating surgeon. She wasn't the one who had messed up. She wasn't responsible for that. She wasn't—

Her mind came to a jolting halt and she drifted back to the present. The words to the song started to echo in her ears. She couldn't understand them. They were singing in Spanish, but the music was soft and low, with the sound of bongos drumming softly. The music made Rachel's hips want to sway. It was Cuban music.

Rachel picked up her phone and without thinking hit the call button.

"Hey," she said, "I know this probably sounds random, but what are you doing right now?"

"Um…is this a booty call?"

"No," Rachel replied, her voice earnest. "I just…I need to see you. Is it okay if I come over?"

There was a pause on the other end of the phone. "Of course, please, I mean, yes. Come over." Ana sounded flustered, and Rachel hoped she wasn't imposing.

"If you're busy, it's really fine, we can talk later, it's just—"

"Rachel. It's 10:24 on a Wednesday night. I'm surrounded by stacks of papers, not dancing women. I'll text you the address. See you soon."

Rachel felt relief at the levity in Ana's voice, and she smiled briefly before hanging up. Within a matter of seconds, the address came in.

"Driver?" she said leaning forward. "Change of plans, can you take me to Long Island City instead? This address here?" Rachel leaned forward and showed him the screen.

"I still have to charge you the same amount," he said.

"That's not a problem."

The man nodded and typed in the address into his phone. Rachel focused on breathing as the realization of what was happening slowly began to hit her. She was going to Ana's apartment. And she was going to tell her the truth about what happened to Mark Solomon.

CHAPTER THIRTY-ONE

Ana couldn't remember when she had moved so fast. She had no idea what time Rachel would get there. She had been so shocked by the fact that she was asking to come over, she'd said yes without asking any further details like when would she get there? Was she hungry? Was she okay?

She scurried around her tiny apartment, turning the many large stacks of papers into one massive stack on the floor at the end of the couch. She ran into the bathroom and started spraying cleaning solution all over the counter and toilet and wiping it down with the quickest available thing, toilet paper. Then she scurried into her bedroom to quickly make her bed, something she had neglected to do that morning. Tossing a stack of dirty clothes into the hamper in her closet, she slid the door shut and looked around. A rogue bag of chips on her nightstand caught her attention and she snatched it up just in time to hear the doorbell buzz loudly.

Rachel was downstairs.

Shoving the half-full bag into the cupboard, Ana walked over to the beige call box on the wall and pressed the dingy round button.

"Hello?" she said, trying to hide the fact that she was struggling to catch her breath.

"Hey, it's me…Rachel. It's Rachel."

"Hi, come on up." She pressed the second button on the box and a loud buzz echoed through the apartment. She counted to five to give Rachel enough time to get through the first door, the entryway, and the second door before releasing the button and jetting back into her room. She sprayed a quick dash of perfume and looked at herself in the mirror.

Shit. She had already washed all of her makeup off from the day and wasn't even wearing a bra. Her baggy Fleetwood Mac T-shirt had been her dad's back in the 80s, and it sagged off one shoulder. She had shorts on, but barely, considering they were leftovers from law school. A faded baby blue "C" on the left leg was the only way to tell what school she had even gone to.

Ana pulled open her drawers attempting to select a better outfit, but there was no time. As she reached for a new shirt, there was a soft knock at her door. Rather than keep Rachel waiting, she shoved the drawer closed and walked over to let her in.

"Hi," Rachel said.

Ana inhaled deeply, unable to avoid the instant reaction her body had to seeing Rachel standing in her doorway. She wore a pair of khaki chino shorts that hit her mid-thigh and a navy blue polo top. A pair of dark brown Sperrys confirmed that yes, she was definitely the put-together little preppy girl Ana had always imaged she was outside of work, and she couldn't help but think how adorable she looked in the simple getup.

"Come in." Ana stepped to one side.

Rachel smiled, but it didn't reach her eyes. Something was wrong.

"Can I get you a drink? Water? Or um…" She leaned down into her fridge. "Beer?"

"A beer would be great, honestly," Rachel said, dropping her bag on the couch. She looked exhausted in a way Ana had never seen her look before. She was used to Rachel being tired—after all, the woman was practically Supergirl for all she did in her daily life. But this was something different. She looked drawn out, and there was a puffiness around her eyes that looked like she had been crying.

Ana walked over to the living room and sat down beside her on the couch, extending the cold beer to Rachel and cheersing with one of her own.

Rachel took a deep sip and then started fidgeting with the label.

"Everything okay?" turned to face Rachel more.

Rachel shook her head. "One of my patients died today."

A sudden stream of tears burst through her blue eyes and she dropped her head into her hand. Ana scooted closer and wrapped her arms around Rachel, pulling her close so she could rest her head on her shoulder.

"I'm so sorry, Rach," Ana whispered, stroking her hair and kissing her on the top of the head. It was forward, she knew, but she couldn't help but want to pull Rachel close right now. Seeing her like this, so vulnerable and crushed, was more than Ana could stand.

"Did something happen in the operating room?" Ana asked.

"No, I hadn't seen him in weeks, he was—" Rachel jolted upright. "Wait." Her voice went steely and cold. "Why would you assume it was in the OR?"

Ana was taken aback by the reaction and struggled to find her words. "I didn't, I just didn't know if that's why you were upset or..."

"I was with my sister tonight. Do you think I would be playing with the kids if I had lost a patient on the table earlier today? Jesus, what kind of a monster do you think I am?"

Ana reeled. "I don't. I don't know, I was just..."

"This is because of the lawsuit, isn't it? That *thing* we don't talk about. I knew it would come up sooner or later, I knew it. You think because Mark Solomon died on the OR table, all of the patients I treat will end up dead."

Rachel stood up from the couch and started walking toward the door.

"Whoa, whoa, whoa," Ana said, walking after her. "Rach, just wait a second."

Rachel whipped around, tears streaming down her face. "What?" she snapped. Ana held out her arms and touched Rachel's elbows. It was as close as she dared to get.

"Please don't go," Ana said, unable to hide the desperation in her voice. "Please. I want you to stay."

Rachel dropped her head and exhaled, covering her face with one hand. "God, I'm sorry," she said, her voice sounding back to normal. "I'm such an idiot."

She took a few steps closer, and Ana wrapped her arms around her and pulled her close.

"You're not stupid, Rachel. Very far from it," she whispered, rubbing her hand up and down on Rachel's back. "I'm so sorry this happened."

Ana was trying very hard to be a good friend for Rachel right now. That's what she needed. Not someone who wanted to carry her to the bedroom and make love to her all night, even though that was definitely what Ana wanted to do. She tried to ignore the smell of Rachel's shampoo as it wafted into her nose while Rachel sobbed gently against her neck. She tried to ignore how warm Rachel's skin felt beneath the thin polo shirt as she moved her hand along Rachel's spine. Ana tried to ignore the little vibration that tickled her neck each time Rachel exhaled into it. And she tried really, really hard to ignore how indescribably turned on she was getting, standing so close to this woman.

Focus, she told herself as she steadied her breathing. *Think of things that don't turn you on. Think of abuelita, or Antonio, or Paul. Think of Shakespeare or Broadway shows or—*

Her thoughts were interrupted by the feeling of Rachel's hand gripping her waist. Ana's breath hitched in her chest as Rachel ever so slowly moved her hand from Ana's hip bone to the middle of her back. She had stopped crying, but she still had her face buried in Ana's neck.

Was Rachel feeling the same way? She had been so upset a few seconds ago, but was it possible that she was just as turned on as Ana was right now?

Ana tilted her head up slightly. Their height difference was more apparent than ever now that Ana wasn't in heels, but when she looked up, she was only inches away from Rachel's face. She gulped loudly as Rachel's gaze darted from her eyes down to her lips and then back up again.

Ana bit her bottom lip, attempting to hold back the thing she really wanted to do. Rachel licked her lips slowly and gripped Ana's waist hard with her other hand, so that now she was fully holding on to her.

"I, um—" Ana started to say, but Rachel's hand came up and she placed a finger over her lips.

"Don't talk," Rachel whispered.

Ana inhaled slowly and watched as Rachel slowly moved closer until finally their lips were almost touching. When she was only centimeters away, she said softly, "Kiss me."

Slowly Ana pressed her lips against Rachel's. A surge of electricity shot down her spine at the contact, and she reminded herself that she needed to go slow. Rachel was vulnerable right now. She was fragile. They would take their time. They could just kiss and not do anything else. That was fine with Ana. That was all she needed.

But within seconds it became clear that Rachel was anything but fragile. She reached up and pulled Ana's face into hers, forcing Ana's lips open with her tongue. Ana responded by pushing her body against Rachel harder than she intended, sending them both spilling back.

Rachel let out a loud grunt as she slammed into the front door, Ana's body pressing against her, her hands fully exploring Rachel's body.

Ana didn't want to stop to process everything that was happening right now. How Rachel had gone from crying to defensive to vulnerable to horny all in a matter of seconds. Or how she had been sitting on her living room floor half an hour ago reading medical records for a plaintiff she was deposing next week and now she was kissing the woman she had been thinking of kissing for almost two months. She didn't care about any of that right now. Right now, all she cared about was getting her hands down Rachel's pants and finding out if she really tasted as good as she remembered. She continued to let her hands enjoy the sculpture of a woman she had pressed against her door, and she reached around, grabbing a handful of Rachel's ass, letting out a satisfied moan as she did.

"Getting déjà vu?" Rachel said, biting down gently on Ana's ear.

Ana smiled between kisses, remembering their first time in this exact position. Only that time, Ana had been the one pressed against the door.

"Depends," Ana said, her voice husky and low as she nipped at Rachel's neck. "You going to sneak out in the middle of the night on me again?"

Rachel leaned her head back and grabbed Ana by the chin. "Not a chance."

Chapter Thirty-two

She had gone there to tell Ana about the Mark Solomon surgery. She really had. But now Mark Solomon, or any man for that matter, was the farthest thing from Rachel's mind. The only thing she could think about was Ana. Ana's hands working their way beneath her shirt. Ana's mouth tracing kisses up her neck and around her clavicle. Ana's voice whispering softly into her ear.

Rachel rested her head back against the door and let herself immerse fully in the sensation that was Ana Mendez. They had both been yearning for this moment for so long, perhaps even since that first day when Rachel walked into Ana's law firm. Maybe even before then. Maybe since Rachel had snuck out of that very apartment in the middle of the night and regretted it the next morning.

Ana started to lift the bottom of Rachel's shirt and paused for a moment, asking silent permission. Rachel nodded and Ana continued to slide the shirt slowly up over her torso and head until it was eventually discarded onto the floor.

"Take me to bed," Rachel said, her voice pleading.

"So bossy," Ana said playfully and held out her hand before leading her into the bedroom.

From there things moved slower, and when Rachel reached over to turn off the light on the nightstand, Ana stopped her.

"Oh no, you don't. I didn't get to enjoy looking at you last time. I'm going to take my time now."

Rachel blushed and looked down, confirming that she was at least wearing a semi-cute black bra. Her khaki shorts indicated she wouldn't be so lucky on the bottom half, and she hoped her plain white underwear wasn't a complete turn-off.

Ana sat down on the bed and rose to her knees. "Come here," she said firmly, motioning for Rachel to obey with a single finger.

Rachel acquiesced and moved to the bed where Ana was waiting. Kneeling on the soft comforter, she reached out and felt Ana's arms wrap around her. Soon her bra tumbled to the floor beside the bed, her pale breasts exposed to the soft glow of the light.

She let her own hands do some exploring—after all, she was half naked while Ana was still fully clothed. But when she felt beneath Ana's oversized T-shirt, she realized that her assumption had not been entirely true. A full breast and hard nipple met Rachel's hand, and she pulled back slightly to look at Ana.

"No bra?" Her voice was low and excited.

Ana raised an eyebrow. "Are you complaining?"

"Definitely not," she answered firmly.

She lifted off Ana's shirt, exposing her full breasts. She tried not to stare, but it was difficult. Ana had the most beautiful body she had ever seen on a woman. Her full figure was such a contrast to Rachel's more lean build, and it was everything Rachel could want. Where Rachel's body was hard and toned, Ana's was soft and supple. Where Rachel had small breasts, Ana was well endowed. They fit together like two magnets, able to resist any force of nature trying to force them apart.

Closing the remaining space between them, Rachel gently pushed Ana back onto the bed and slowly crawled on top of her. Ana spread her legs instantly, allowing Rachel's leg to slide between them with ease. Rachel lowered herself and it only took a few seconds before she could feel Ana's breasts moving against her bare skin. The feeling sent shivers down her spine, and warmth started to gather between her legs. She kissed Ana's neck, taking her time to press her lips fully against each inch of skin she touched until finally she reached Ana's left nipple.

A ripple of pleasure tore through Rachel as she felt Ana's body tighten and then release as she sucked on the peaked mound. Ana used her hands to guide Rachel's head as she continued to roll her nipple in her mouth.

"Fuck," Ana hissed.

Rachel paused just long enough to move to her other breast. Simultaneously she moved her hand down Ana's thigh and beneath the thin pair of shorts she was wearing, where she was met with confirmation that Ana was just as turned on right now as she was.

"You're wet," Rachel said, removing her mouth from Ana's breast.

"Can you blame me?" Ana growled.

Seemingly having enough of Rachel's teasing, Ana rolled both of them over, pinning Rachel beneath her with both hands. She moved off her briefly and slid off her shorts without leaving the bed. Soon she was back on top of Rachel, her full breasts pressed against her. Rachel spread her legs, allowing Ana to slide one leg between them as she had just done to Ana a few seconds ago. What was once a slow, dull warmth between her legs was now a pulsing, throbbing ache, and she shifted upward to create some friction against her growing need. Seeming to feel her desire, Ana began to grind against her.

She moved her hand back to Ana's center and made slow, intentional circles on her clit as Ana moved on top of her. This only elicited more expletives from Ana, who moved harder against Rachel's hand.

"I can't take much more of this," Ana whimpered above her.

"Me neither," Rachel said, her voice shaking.

Rachel took the hint and pressed two fingers to her entrance. She had to fight the urge to go inside her but paused to wait for Ana's consent.

"Please," Ana said, fumbling at Rachel's underwear as she desperately tried to match Rachel's pace.

Rachel slid a single finger into Ana, feeling her wrap tightly around her with each inch. Soon, Ana's fingers found their target and began to circle Rachel's clit as they moved together. Rachel slid a second finger inside and Ana moaned on top of her. Rachel curled her fingers deep inside with each movement Ana made on top of her, letting Ana do the work to create her own pleasure. But Rachel's own excitement was starting to build now. As if sensing her pending orgasm, Ana slid two fingers deep and hard inside her, slowing her search for gratification.

Now it was Rachel's turn to be vocal. "You feel so good," she groaned, trying to focus only on her fingers as they moved inside Ana. But it was impossible to focus on her own pleasures and pleasing Ana all at once, and eventually she had to concede and fully surrender to the pleasure Ana was giving her.

A soft laugh of satisfaction rolled from Ana's throat as she continued to both work her clit and move deep inside her.

"I knew I'd win," she said as Rachel started to build again.

"Kinda feels like I'm the one winning right now," Rachel managed to say.

Within seconds Ana pushed her past the point of no return, and she couldn't fight off the sensation that was crashing all around her.

She pulled Ana down so she was breathing heavily in her ear. She wanted Ana to hear what she sounded like as she made her come. She wanted Ana to hear her scream her name, which, based on her physical response right now, would be in a matter of seconds.

"Ana," she whispered.

She gripped Ana's back and bit down on her shoulder. She was building too fast, there was no going back at this point. Rachel held off for a few more seconds. She moved her hands down to Ana's bare ass and gripped her firmly while Ana thrust deep inside her, and finally, after months of anticipation, she unraveled into Ana's hand.

Ana stayed quiet for a few seconds, her slick body pressed against Rachel, fingers still deep inside her, before slowly withdrawing them inch by inch. She nestled down beside Rachel, kissed her neck, and gently moved a strand of hair from Rachel's face to tuck it behind her ear.

"How do you feel?" Ana asked, concern ringing in her voice.

Rachel turned and faced her. "Like I'm floating."

"You sure you're okay?" Ana asked, stroking Rachel's cheek. "You were so upset earlier, I wasn't expecting…well, this."

Rachel rolled onto her side and rested her head on her hand.

"I'm okay, I promise," she said as she leaned over and kissed Ana.

She did want to tell her what had happened in that operating room. She really did. That was the reason she had gone over there in the first place. But for now, she just wanted to see what Ana tasted like. She would talk to her another time.

Rachel awoke the next morning to the smell of coffee. She rolled over and looked for Ana but was disappointed to find the bed empty. Stretching her hands above her head, she took a moment to observe her surroundings.

The bedroom was small, as she already knew, but this was her first time actually seeing it in the light of day. There wasn't room for much else aside from the bed, a closet, and a small nightstand that housed a lamp, a phone charger, and a single photograph of Ana draped in familiar baby blue robes and a rounded cap. She had a black stole and a purple hood draped around her shoulders and she wore a proud smile across her beautiful face. She looked younger but still very much the same, her dark eyes shining bright with the potential of her future. On both sides of her were two people who Rachel assumed were Ana's parents and a guy probably a few years younger than Ana. He had shaggy hair and a patchy beard. Rachel guessed this was Ana's brother, Antonio.

"Morning," Ana said, walking into the bedroom, a cup of hot

coffee in her hand. She sat on the edge of the bed and handed the mug to Rachel.

Rachel took a sip and scooted up so her back was resting against the headboard, taking care to pull the sheet up around her chest. She was still naked and felt a little vulnerable now that Ana was back in her baggy T-shirt.

"I always forget you went to Columbia too," she said, motioning to the photo.

"Indeed I did. I bleed baby blue too, Dr. Cohen. You didn't think you were the only Ivy Leaguer in this relationship, did you?"

Rachel blushed and looked down at her coffee. The word "relationship" would normally make her clam up after such a short time, but with Ana it had the opposite effect. Her fight or flight hadn't kicked in yet, and she was wondering if it ever would with this woman.

"Surprised you didn't notice these babies last night," Ana said, lifting her shirt to reveal a pair of faded blue shorts with a worn-out "C" with a little crown on the leg.

Rachel set the coffee down on the nightstand and leaned over to touch Ana's exposed leg.

"Well, I was more focused on getting them off than what was on them," she said, leaning up to kiss Ana.

Ana kept kissing her until they both fell back flat onto the bed. Ana's long, black hair tumbled around her shoulders and onto Rachel's chest. She was glowing, lying on top of Rachel. She had a look of total bliss that Rachel had never seen before. She wasn't aware she was capable of making anyone that happy, let alone feeling so happy herself.

"What time do you have to get to work?" Rachel asked, playing with a strand of Ana's hair that had fallen into her face. She didn't know what time it was, but she knew Ana was probably late by now.

"You know, it's the strangest thing," Ana said, leaning down to kiss Rachel's cheek. "I woke up feeling super under the weather today." She sat up and let out a weak cough before lowering herself again and kissing Rachel's neck.

"That is strange," Rachel said, tilting her head back to allow more of her to be exposed for Ana's taking. "Maybe you should see a doctor?" she added playfully.

Ana took a little nip at Rachel's throat and moved to her ear. "I was thinking the same thing," she whispered.

Rachel pulled Ana so that she was straddling her. "I happen to know someone who does house calls. I mean, she is off work today, but she may be able to make an exception for the right woman."

Ana looked down at her, moving her hands to Rachel's breasts, which had now made their way out from beneath the sheets.

"And how much does this doctor charge?" Ana said, allowing both hands to gently trace the outline of Rachel's nipples.

Rachel tried to focus on keeping a straight face, but she could already feel the familiar pulse of desire thrumming between her legs.

"Oh, I'm sure you could work something out. Maybe a tit-for-tat type payment system?" Rachel reached her hand to the hem of Ana's shirt. "For example, she probably wouldn't like that you're dressed," she said, slowly tugging the shirt above Ana's head. Rachel was pleased to see she hadn't decided to put a bra on, allowing her full breasts to drop just inches from Rachel's face as she removed the garment.

"Hmm." Ana leaned away from Rachel. "Then I guess she really wouldn't like me having these shorts on still, right?" She stood up slowly and walked over to the doorway. Her hair fell down just enough to cover her exposed chest, and Rachel could barely see her nipples peeking through the tangled forest of black.

"She would hate that," Rachel said, propping herself up on her elbows. Her voice was uneven with lust as she watched Ana slowly bend over and remove her shorts.

She wasn't wearing any underwear either. Rachel inhaled slowly at the sight of Ana standing before her, fully naked, looking like something out of the Garden of Eden.

"Well," Ana said, sticking the tip of her finger into her mouth and biting down playfully. "Then I guess you better come punish me."

"Be careful what you wish for." Rachel tossed back the sheets and chased after her.

Chapter Thirty-three

Ana stroked Rachel's hair as she lay on the couch with her head in her lap.

"I just don't get how anyone could like Rose more than Blanche," Ana said. She popped a piece of kettle corn into her mouth.

"What? She's no Dorothy, but she's way better than Blanche."

After several long hours of sex, sleep, and more sex, they had finally decided to order Chinese and watch the TV shows they were supposed to have watched during their little FaceTime fuckery a couple of weeks earlier. They had started with *The Nanny* before moving on to *Designing Women* and were now in a heated debate over *The Golden Girls*.

Ana laughed as Dorothy walked out onto the screen wearing a turkey costume.

"Betty White is an icon," Rachel said, stealing a piece of kettle corn.

"Fine, but that's not the discussion. The discussion is Blanche v. Rose. I mean, look right here." Ana pointed to the screen. "Look at her in that Goosey Loosey costume. Tell me she isn't rocking those feathers."

Rachel shook her head. "Fine, but look at Rose in that Henny Penny getup. I mean, you can tell she was a dancer back in the day. Look at her legs."

Ana cast Rachel a sideways glance. "Betty White, huh? That's what does it for you, babe?"

Rachel smacked Ana on her arm and laughed. "Don't be jealous of Betty. She's timeless."

"Hey, I get it, I mean Fran was doing things to me with those little skirts a few hours ago."

"It's the big hair, isn't it?"

"Or maybe I just like Jewish girls from Queens." She winked at Rachel and leaned over to kiss her forehead.

"I'm from the Upper West Side." Rachel narrowed her eyes.

Ana shrugged. "Potato, potahto."

Rachel lay down and rested her head in Ana's lap. "I think you mean laytkes, latkes." She smiled as Ana continued to play with her hair.

"Tell me more about when you grew up," Ana said softly.

Rachel looked up at Ana. "What do you want to know?"

"I don't know. I mean, you grew up in Manhattan. That had to be pretty cool, right?"

Rachel grabbed Ana's hand and started playing with her finger-nails, smoothing her hands over them one at a time.

"In some ways, sure. I was very privileged growing up. I went to a private school my entire life. Even my university was private and right here in the city. I've never known anything else. So I guess you could say I've never had to experience the real world like most people in this city."

"Is that why you spend so much time volunteering? You feel guilty for not needing anything as a kid?"

Rachel appeared to think about it a second. "Maybe? I don't know. I guess I always carry a certain level of guilt around with me on a daily basis. I see others having so little, and I know that the only reason I am where I am today is because I was blessed with so much early on in life. If I can help others get a little leg up, to me that's worth the effort."

"You also worked really hard, Rach. I mean, medical school at Columbia couldn't have been easy. I doubt they care if you went to private school. The classes aren't easier because of it."

Rachel nodded. "True, but I wouldn't have even been considered for Columbia if I hadn't come from those private schools in the first place. It's just how the system works. The very flawed, very prejudiced system."

Ana contemplated what Rachel said for a second. She had never thought about it that way before. She had always taken pride in earning everything she got in life. She was, after all, a product of the American dream. Her parents had always raised her to think that if you worked hard and applied yourself, anything was possible. She had never considered the game being rigged before she sat down at the table to play.

"What about being Jewish? Did you ever experience any type of discrimination because of that?"

Rachel laughed. "What? You mean people *don't* like Jews? That is so shocking to me." Her voice was monotone as she looked up at Ana. "Of course I experienced discrimination. Not at my schools, obviously, but in the little places we forget about, it was there. On the subway when I'd hear someone whisper 'Jew' as I got off at the stop where my temple was, wearing my yarmulke. And in the swastikas that I still see graffitied on the subway walls in Brooklyn when I go to visit Noa and Jacob. Antisemitism is everywhere. It's never gone away."

Ana waited in silence for her to continue.

"I used to see the girls in my school and be so jealous. The shiksas, my mom would call them in her more judgmental moments. She always wanted to send me to a Jewish school, but my dad said it was good for me to get a secular education. They'd all go on dates on Friday nights and they didn't have to go to things like Hebrew School on Sundays. I always wanted to be more like them. To me they were normal and I was the oddball."

"And now?" Ana asked, taking Rachel's hand and lacing her fingers with hers.

Rachel sighed. "And now I love being Jewish. It's part of me, it's part of my family. And it will be part of my children one day. I love singing our prayers, cooking our food, speaking our language. I love it because it *is* me. It's not even a choice at this point. I love it in the same way a fish loves the sea or a bird loves the sky. Does that even make sense?"

Ana nodded. "It makes a lot of sense. Growing up in Miami, nobody cared that I was Cuban. Heck, you got more attention in my neighborhood if you were white than if you were Latin or Black. But when I moved to New York, I felt this need to blend in. To kind of whitewash myself. I stopped speaking Spanish and worked really hard to make sure I didn't have an accent. I didn't want people to look at me and instantly know I was Cuban. My parents always raised me to be so proud of my heritage, but when I moved here, it felt like I was ashamed of where I came from. Then when I started working at Byron and Browning, which is possibly the whitest, straightest firm known to man, those feelings only got worse. It felt like if I didn't look like them or sound like them, I'd never really fit in."

"And now?" Rachel asked, looking up at Ana.

"And now—" Ana exclaimed something in Spanish, laughing at herself as she finished the sentence.

Rachel smiled and stared up at her.

"It means 'I am proud of who I am.'"

"Good," Rachel said before adding a phrase in Yiddish. Ana raised an eyebrow. "It means 'I'm proud of you.'" Rachel kissed Ana gently.

Ana felt her chest swell as Rachel's soft lips traveled across hers. She opened her mouth for her, slowly letting Rachel's tongue enter to explore inside, feeling her trace the roof of her mouth.

She stopped for a second, just long enough to look into Rachel's eyes. They were the clearest eyes she had ever seen, and there was something in them today that made Ana weak. They were soft, docile and vulnerable. She knew there was nothing between her and Rachel now except the few layers of clothing they had on.

"Hey," Ana said, "I know we don't talk about this, and that's good, but I wanted to tell you something about the litigation."

Ana felt Rachel tense in her lap. "It's nothing bad," she said and saw Rachel relax, but only slightly. "I just wanted to let you know that I worked it out. I won't be deposing you anymore."

Rachel sat upright fully and faced Ana. "What do you mean? Did you drop it? Are you…are you off the case?"

"No." Ana shook her head. "I can't really say much else, other than I talked to my boss and he's okay with someone else doing the questioning."

Rachel nodded seeming to soak in Ana's words. A worried look spread across her face.

"Hey," Ana said, scooting closer and cupping Rachel's face in her hand. "This is a good thing. It means we can spend less time worrying about that and more time focusing on what matters."

Rachel nodded silently. "Yeah, totally."

Ana could tell that Rachel was still processing everything. Maybe it had been a mistake to bring up the litigation after such an intimate night together. But she had hoped bringing it up would be a relief to Rachel, not a new burden. Maybe she just needed time to take everything in. To process and absorb. Not everyone handled new information like Ana did, and not everyone had been trained through working in litigation to roll with the punches and move on.

"You okay?" Ana asked, reaching out and taking Rachel's hand.

Rachel nodded again. "Yeah, everything's fine."

Ana wrinkled her brow. She wasn't buying Rachel's response, but she didn't want to push the issue. Whatever was the matter, she trusted Rachel to be honest with her about it whenever she was ready. Deciding to *not* cross-examine Rachel, she shifted her attention back to the TV show.

"I still say Blanche is better," she said, resuming their normal playful banter.

"And you're still wrong," Rachel added.

CHAPTER THIRTY-FOUR

Rachel dropped her purse on the floor as she walked into her apartment. Elijah came up to her meowing, clearly angry that she hadn't been home to feed her supper last night, even though there was a full bowl of dry food out for her at all times. The picky little thing only liked wet food and would loudly protest whenever it was a second late.

"Oh no." Rachel bent down to scoop her up. "Did you starve to death, my poor little fluffy lumpers? Have you been abused and neglected all night?" She placed a series of rapid kisses on her furry cheek before setting her back down on the floor. Elijah began to clean her face where the kisses had been placed, a look of irritation on her tricolored face.

Rachel walked into her living room and turned on the floor lamp before dropping onto her couch, letting out a long exhale as she did.

Ana had asked her to stay for dinner and even promised to cook real food instead of heating up their leftover Chinese food, but Rachel had said no. She loved spending the night with Ana last night and she really loved lounging around her apartment half naked all day, taking breaks to talk about their childhood memories and trying several new positions Rachel had never done before. But she missed her bed, her apartment, and yes, even her needy cat. Plus, she had a full day of work tomorrow, and staying out late wouldn't be wise.

She pulled out her phone to check her schedule for tomorrow. When she opened her emails, the message notifying her of Mr. Wentz's death was still open. A cord wrapped itself around her chest and began to tighten. She swiped out of the email and closed her phone.

Why had she not been honest with Ana about the Mark Solomon surgery? Was she really just trying to protect her career? Or was she afraid of something far worse? She knew telling Ana the full story would put Ana in a compromised position, but was that really all there was to her silence? Rachel knew it wasn't. She knew deep down the real reason she had chickened out of telling Ana the truth last night was because she was afraid that if she was honest with her, she would lose her. And Rachel cared way too much about Ana at this point to risk losing her.

In fact, Rachel cared about Ana more than she had ever cared about anyone before. Noa had compared her to Leah, a girl she dated in college for a short time. Their love had been intense, yes, but it had been fleeting, like loading a firepit with paper and striking a match. It had burned hot and bright but soon faded into nothing but ash. This thing with Ana felt different. It was a wildfire spreading its way through her heart, seeking out any crevices or crannies where Rachel had kept her deepest secrets. She hated keeping something this big from Ana, but it was the only way.

Her phone buzzed in her hand. It was Noa. She hadn't exactly told her about her little sleepover at Ana's last night, and understandably her sister was worried about her.

Noa: You okay over there?

Rachel: Yeah, just got home. Made a pit stop last night.

Noa: Oh reallyyyyy???

Rachel: Lol yes. I'll tell you everything later.

Rachel: Okay, well not EVERYTHING.

Noa: Oh, come on. I'll tell you all about the time Jake had to stop mid foreplay to run to the bathroom.

Rachel: Annnnd on that note, I'm going to take a shower.

Rachel tossed her phone on the coffee table and walked to the bathroom. Once inside the shower, she let the water run so hot it turned her skin red. She slammed her eyes shut tight against the liquid as it poured over her face. She didn't want to think about Mark Solomon or even Henry Wentz anymore. She wanted to turn off her brain and think back to last night, the touch of Ana's hands as they made their way beneath her shirt and up her back. The smell of her shampoo as Rachel moved on top of her, her face buried in Ana's neck as she moaned and ground against her. The way Ana scrunched up her face just before she finished, looking like she was trying to hold back the pleasure as long as possible until finally collapsing under the weight of it.

She could still smell Ana's laundry detergent on her now, even as she began to scrub her skin with her own body wash. She liked the smell. It was warm and sweet. She didn't want it to go away. She wanted to race back to Ana's apartment and wrap herself up in her sheets and pretend the sun would never rise tomorrow.

But it would rise. It would rise, and she would go to work. She would call Henry Wentz's children and give her condolences. She would perform another operation tomorrow afternoon. She would be focused and calm. She would forget all about how she was feeling right now. She would do her job to the best of her ability. She would do everything in her power to make sure she didn't lose another patient.

She finally stepped out of the shower once the hot water began running lukewarm and wrapped herself in her towel before walking into the kitchen. Elijah was standing by her empty food bowl, yelling up at her.

"Okay, okay, now I'll give you wet food." Rachel tucked her towel into itself and opened a can. "You do know you have dry food right over there, right?" She pointed to a bowl across the room.

Elijah stared blankly at her, twitching her tail.

After feeding the cat, Rachel picked up her phone from the coffee table to see a missed text from Ana.

Ana: Thinking of you.

There was a photo of her in bed, sheets draped across her otherwise naked chest, barely covering her dark nipples. The photo made Rachel feel like she needed to jump back in the shower again, and she could feel herself moisten at a single glance of Ana's raven hair draped around her bare neck and shoulders.

Rachel: You are stunning. And ditto.

Rachel untied her towel and used her bare hand to cover her breast, spreading her fingers just enough for her pink nipple to peek through the cracks. She snapped the photo and sent it back to Ana, smirking at the idea of her reaction.

Would she get as turned on as she just had? Approximately two seconds later, and Rachel had her answer.

Ana: You're killing me. Come back here and get into bed
　　　with me.

Ana: Now.

Rachel smiled and walked into her bedroom to slip on a T-shirt and boxers for the night. It wasn't late, but suffice it to say she hadn't gotten much sleep last night and she needed to get her rest before work tomorrow.

Rachel: So bossy.

Rachel pulled back the sheets and slipped between the covers, feeling the cool cotton press against her warm skin.

Ana: You like that I'm bossy.

Rachel: I do. Why should I come to you though? I just left. Isn't it your turn to travel?

Ana: Touché. Next time, your place.

Ana: After I take you on a real date, that is.

A shiver of excitement crept up Rachel's spine. A real date?

Rachel: Hmm…what did you have in mind?

Ana: Nice try, but you'll just have to wait and see.

Rachel: Rude.

Rachel shook her head and sent a photo of her blowing a kiss at the camera before telling Ana she was going to sleep. Ana made one final joke about wearing her out, but Rachel didn't see it until the next morning. She was already dreaming when the text came in.

CHAPTER THIRTY-FIVE

Ana strutted into the lobby of Byron & Browning, a sway in her hips as her heels clacked on the tile.

"Good morning, Marjorie," she sang to the receptionist as she pranced past her.

"Morning, Miss Mendez," Marjorie replied with a wide smile.

As Ana made her way down the long hall past the rows of external offices, she held her shoulders back and sang one of her favorite songs quietly under her breath.

"Good morning, Jackson." She nodded to a strawberry-blond junior associate. He shoved his glasses up on his nose and waved awkwardly at her.

She swung around the doorway to Stella's office, popping just her head inside.

"Buenos días, Miss Torres," Ana crooned.

Stella's eyebrows shot up. "Buenos días, indeed." She crossed her arms and leaned back in her chair. "Someone's feeling chipper this morning. Wouldn't have anything to do with your little sick day yesterday, would it?"

Ana shrugged coyly. "Maybe."

Stella's mouth dropped open and she began waving her arms for Ana to come in. "Shut the door, shut the door!"

Ana complied after adjusting the bag on her shoulder.

"Sit. You have tea to spill."

Ana shook her head. "Can't, gotta go track Micah Willis down first thing to see if he'll cover this depo for me."

Stella nodded. "Operation Little Mermaid still a go, then?"

Ana gave her a thumbs up. "A major go. Paul gave me permission to have the little prick cover the depo. And Rachel and I are officially... well, we're not officially anything yet, but you know."

"But you got laid."

Ana rolled her eyes. "God, you are such a frat boy sometimes."

"What?" Stella lifted her hands in innocence. "What do you want me to say? You made sweet love down by the sea? I'm a lawyer, not a poet."

"Clearly." Ana shifted the bag on her shoulder again and peered out the glass door.

"Well, you can't just pop into my office and give me literally no details. How was it?"

"I'm definitely not divulging *every* detail, but I will say it was absolutely amazing." Ana smiled so hard her face would hurt if she did it too long, but she couldn't help it. Thinking about Rachel had had that effect ever since she left her apartment yesterday evening. "I mean, her body is incredible, duh, but I've learned so many things about her. Her background, her struggles, her mind. She's such a beautiful person, inside and out. And her eyes, I feel like I could get lost swimming in them when she's looking at me."

Stella swayed back and forth in her chair. "Look at you, swooning over there. My little baby is all grown up and in love."

Ana shushed her. "Nobody said anything about love. Besides, you could settle down and find someone steady yourself, you know."

"Find someone steady? Yikes. That just made my legs clamp up faster than a trip to my gynecologist."

"I'm just saying, you don't have to try to sleep with every woman in the city."

"Do or don't do, Ana. There is no try."

Ana shook her head. "Yeah, yeah. Well, listen, I'm gonna go suck up to this douche canoe and then get some actual work done today."

Stella gave her a sharp nod. "You got it, boss. Drinks later this week?"

Ana tilted her head. "Maybe. Might have a date, though."

"And so it begins!" Stella hollered as Ana left.

Ana walked down to her office, dropped her bag on the floor and opened her emails. She didn't bother reading any of them; she knew it would just result in her getting sidetracked and responding to them, and before she knew it the day would be gone and she'd forget all about Micah.

It didn't take long to find him. Junior associates shared offices and Micah shared one with Jackson, whom she had passed earlier, and another associate named Efe, who was quiet as a church mouse.

When Ana stuck her head into their small internal office, she was glad to see only Micah was there.

"Micah," Ana said, stepping into the room. "Mind if I speak to you a moment?"

Micah tossed his head back and smoothed out his long, blond hair. He usually wore it in a ponytail, but today he had brushed the locks out, giving him the look of a Greek god—at least, that's how he carried himself. His navy blue tailored suit jacket was hanging on the chair behind him, and his light blue collared shirt and navy tie made his annoyingly blue eyes jump out.

He was quite possibly the cockiest person Ana had ever met, even more than Stella, and if she had her choice she would have asked literally any other attorney at the firm but him to do this for her. But Paul had specified him, due to his daddy being a judge, and who was she to go against hundreds of years of patriarchal bullshit all in a single morning.

"Come in," he said smoothly, motioning to a chair squeezed between the three desks in the room.

Ana took a seat and crossed her legs. "I was wanting to talk to you about something. Actually, I've been meaning to bring it up for a little while now."

"I think I know where this is going," Micah said, folding his hands and sitting back in his chair.

"You do?" Had he already spoken to Paul or something?

"Of course," Micah said. A smug smile spread above his perfectly chiseled jaw.

"Alright, well, in that case I'll just—" She was going to say she'd drop the file off at his office later and draft a memo on things he needed to know about the case, but before she had a chance, he cut her off.

"Shh," he said. Ana's spine stiffened. "I've been trying to avoid this too. I mean, ever since the whole Lizzy Taylor debacle over winter, I know you've been hurting. And I know in times of hurt, a woman—a beautiful woman like yourself—needs a man to lean on."

Ana stood frozen by shock and confusion.

"I'm sorry. What?"

Micah nodded. "You're asking me out, right? I mean, it totally makes sense. We're easily the hottest two people in the office. Oh, but you should know, I'm really not looking for anything serious."

"Oh, wow," Ana replied, unable to keep her jaw from dropping. "That is...wow."

"The answer is yes, by the way." Micah added, putting the nail in his proverbial coffin. "I would love to *hang out* sometime." He added air quotes.

She stood up and straightened out her skirt. "I'm not asking you to fuck me," she said. She stared down at the young man who now bore a confused look across his face. "I'm asking you to cover a deposition for me." Ana paused. "Telling is actually the more correct term, considering I'm a rank above you, but I initially wanted to assuage your ego and pretend you'd be doing me a favor. I now see your ego needs nothing more than a swift kick in the ass."

Micah sat back reeling in shock. "Wait, hold on—"

Ana walked toward the door. "I'll have someone drop the file off later today and I'll email you everything you need to know. Should be a straightforward deposition. The deponent was a resident who had nothing to do with the surgery." She tried not to understate Rachel's involvement too much, but it was getting harder to do.

She paused at the door. "Oh, and Micah?"

Micah stared at her.

"Darcy Hammond may have been comfortable sleeping with a subordinate, but if you ever confuse me with her again, I'll have you fired. I don't care who your father plays golf with."

With that she swiveled on her suede pump and left. Walking back to her office she chuckled to herself, imagining the look on Micah's face. She was probably the first woman in his entire life to reject him. She also had to laugh at herself a little bit, casting aspersions on Darcy and Micah when she herself was crossing all sorts of professional boundaries these days. She had been so judgmental when the truth had come out about Darcy sleeping with a junior associate, but now, well, now she felt guilty for being so harsh back then. The heart wants what it wants, ethics be damned.

Everything was going to work out perfectly, Ana told herself as she took a seat at her desk. She ran her hands through her hair and picked up her phone to text Rachel. It had been less than twenty-four hours since she last saw her, but already she missed her.

And who could blame her? The sex had been really, really good. Like even better than their first hook-up, which was already leaps and bounds above many others. And what was that thing she did with her tongue? Ana felt her pulse begin to race just thinking about it. She wondered if Rachel had a strap-on, and if so, how long it would be before they used it. What was the appropriate number of dates before strapping it on these days, anyway? She figured Stella would know, although Stella probably never went on enough dates with the same person to find out.

Ana let her mind wander to a fantasy of Rachel coming home in her scrubs, her hair slicked back from a long day. Ana imagined waiting in her tiny kitchen wearing a full June Clever style dress and apron, bending over into the oven to pull out some dish she probably had never heard of before.

"How was your day, dear?" Ana would say. She would wear her bright red lipstick and set her hair in big rollers the night before.

"It was shit," Rachel would say, slamming the door shut.

Then in an instant, Rachel would strut across the room and take Ana up in her arms and lift her effortlessly onto the kitchen counter. Only then would Ana see the hard, stuffed bulge jutting from Rachel's scrub pants.

"Oh no, Doctor," Ana would say. "What can I do to relieve some of your stress?" She'd slide her hand down her pants, just enough to feel how ready Rachel was for her. Then Rachel would shove her legs open and—

"Ana?"

Ana jumped in her seat at the sound of someone's voice at her door.

"Ay, dios mío, " Ana said, clutching at her invisible pearls in fright. She adjusted herself, hoping her face wasn't as red as she assumed it was right now.

"You all right?" the woman standing at her door asked. "You're all flushed."

Well, that answers that.

"Fine," Ana said shortly, looking up at the young woman she had only seen a few times in passing. "What did you need?"

"Oh, Micah sent me to grab your file on the *Solomon* case. He said he wanted to start reviewing it today."

Ana turned around to the bookshelf behind her desk and grabbed a large Redweld file stuffed with medical records and deposition transcripts.

"Here you go," she said, handing the heavy folder over to the young woman. "Too scared to come get them himself, huh?" Ana asked, and raised her eyebrow.

"What do you mean?" the woman asked.

"Never mind."

As the woman left her office, Ana took several steady breaths to remind herself that she was in fact in her office. Not being fucked senseless by Rachel on her kitchen counter, much to her dismay.

But no mind, there was plenty of time to live out that fantasy and more. The deposition was taken care of. Next, she had to plan a great first date.

CHAPTER THIRTY-SIX

Rachel dropped her keys into her desk drawer and pulled her phone out of her pocket. She knew it was Ana without even looking. She had convinced herself that the way her phone buzzed against her thigh felt different when it was a text from Ana. A completely illogical conclusion, she knew, but one she had a hard time denying either way.

Ana: Hi.

Rachel: Hey you. Just got back from a coffee run. How's work?

Ana: You free Saturday night? I know Friday is a no go unless you want me to meet your family for our first date.

Rachel: Jumping right past pleasantries now, I see? And no, not Friday, I wouldn't put you through that. Saturday is great.

Ana: Sorry. How is the coffee?

Rachel: Iced and delicious.

Ana: I would, you know. Meet your family. I mean, if you wanted me to.

Rachel: You are just really not in the mood for small talk this morning, are you?

Rachel felt a strange feeling spread into her chest. Meeting her family was a huge deal, and normally anyone suggesting it at this stage of a new relationship would terrify her, but with Ana it didn't. Even though she wasn't Jewish, the image of Ana sitting at the dinner table in her parents' house celebrating Shabbat just made sense in her mind. She could see her sitting next to her, waving her hands in front of her face during the prayers, and laughing as they told stories from Rachel's childhood. She could picture her roughhousing on the living room floor and playing unicorns and Barbies with Benjamin and Estie. She could see Ana talking with her father talking about their days at the office and gossiping with her mom about the neighbors. She could see Noa sharing her famous cheesecake recipe with Ana. She could see it all playing out perfectly in her mind, even now. Maybe that was the part that actually terrified her.

Ana: I miss my face pressed between your legs. How's that for small talk?

Rachel nearly choked on her coffee and had to set the cup down and wipe her mouth before responding.

Rachel: That's small talk I can get behind. Or in front of. Or anywhere you'd like me to be.

Ana: Mmm now we're talking. How about bent over? Could I have you that way, Doctor?

Rachel: I think I proved last night that you most certainly can, Counselor.

"All right."

Rachel nearly dropped her phone at the sight of Charlotte walking into her office.

"I'm single, I'm horny, and I have a thirty-minute break. I need an update. How is operation sexy lawyer going?"

Rachel set her coffee down and placed her phone beside it on her desk. "Good morning to you too."

Charlotte stared blankly at her.

"I might have stayed at her place this weekend."

Charlotte's face lit up and she shifted in her seat. "And how was it?"

Rachel tried to hide a smile, but to no avail. "It was phenomenal," she said. "I mean, we talked, we had sex too many times to count, we ate Chinese food, we watched stupid 90s shows. It was amazing."

Charlotte clapped her hands like a giddy schoolgirl. "When do you see her again?" She reached over and took a sip of Rachel's coffee.

"She wants to take me out Saturday night. She won't tell me where we're going."

Charlotte nodded approvingly. "A woman of mystery. I like that for you. Hey, you think her friend is still single? The hot one with the fade?"

Rachel laughed. "Stella? Oh, I think she's perpetually single."

Charlotte bobbed her head casually. "Great, maybe we can double sometime."

Rachel winced. "Let's just take this one step at a time. Maybe she and I have our first real date and then we talk about expanding the clan?"

"Fine, fine. Well, do yourself a favor and wear a dress to whatever this date is. You've got great legs. Show those babies off."

"I'll see what I can do."

Chapter Thirty-seven

Ana checked her watch and bit at her cheek. It was seven on the dot. Rachel wasn't late, Ana was just always early, which meant when people were on time, to her it felt like they were late. Plus, maybe she was a little bit anxious about this date. Why? She had no idea. She had already seen Rachel in more positions that she'd seen most of her exes in, and vice versa. You'd think this would be the easiest, most relaxed date of her life. But instead, it felt like the exact opposite. Ana, who was usually cool, calm, and collected. Ana, who once made a grown man cry at a deposition. Ana, whose looks could melt steel. That Ana now stood at the corner of Thirty-Seventh Street and Sixth Avenue with sweaty palms and antsy legs over a redheaded woman who was, as of thirty seconds ago, one minute late to their first real date.

Tapping her foot in her trusty all black, high top P.F. Flyers, Ana took a second to adjust herself and make sure she looked perfect. She had on high rise ripped jean shorts and a tight-fitting black top tucked in. It had a mock turtle neck and was sleeveless, which had the double benefit of making her boobs look big and her waist look small. She was going for tomboy chic tonight, but as the late summer heat pressed against her neck and her long, black hair began to stick to her skin, she was quickly becoming more "sweaty boy" than "cute tomboy."

"So sorry I'm late." Ana heard Rachel's voice from behind her.

Ana turned to see her date and had to take a second to catch her breath. Rachel was wearing a sundress, shorter than the one she had worn at the park, and this one was emerald green and had the sides cut out with a white floral print. When Ana leaned in to hug her, she could feel that it also had the entire back cut out. A quick glance below Rachel's collarbone confirmed she was not wearing a bra. It was a perfectly benign first date outfit, except for the fact that Rachel was wearing it, which instantly made Ana want to rip it off of her.

"You look gorgeous," Ana said, instead of resorting to physical aggression against the innocent dress. The stupid dress that got to be pressed against Rachel's naked breasts all night. The dress that could feel her bare legs wisping past it as she walked. The dress that made her pale skin look like flawless porcelain. Her hair was down and wavy, with a natural, messy, beach kissed look, even though Ana knew she had spent all day in an operating room and not lying in the sand. She had on smoky black eye shadow, which gave her a sense of elegance that made Ana feel underdressed.

"I should have dressed up more," Ana said. She felt uncharacteristically insecure.

"No," Rachel said, reaching out and grabbing Ana's arm. "I like you just like this," she said, as she stepped closer and wrapped both arms around Ana.

Ana leaned up and placed a gentle kiss on Rachel's neck, absorbing the familiar smell of coconut that she now knew came from Rachel's shampoo.

Ana settled back down onto her feet and held Rachel's hand.

"Shall we?" she said gesturing to a set of revolving doors a few feet away.

"You got us a hotel room for our first date? That's bold, even for you," Rachel said, walking through the doors to the Embassy Suites.

Ana smirked. "I figured why waste time, you know?"

They walked across the lobby to a set of elevators with a gold button labelled "Skylawn."

Ana pushed the button and waited while the elevator came down to them and the doors opened. They both stepped inside and Ana pressed the button for the third floor in silence.

She watched Rachel out of the corner of her eye. She could tell she still had no idea what they were doing.

Good. She had wanted to surprise her. It was tough planning a date for someone who had spent her entire life in the city. She was glad she had at least managed to find something Rachel had never done before.

As the doors to the elevator opened, Ana watched as Rachel's face lit up.

They stepped out onto the small rooftop to rows of lawn chairs, strings of overhead lights, music playing, twenty or so small tables, and a giant inflatable movie screen.

"Are we seeing a movie on a rooftop?"

Ana nodded. "We sure are."

Rachel looked around in awe and excitement, apparently rendered speechless.

Ana pulled out their tickets on her phone and showed them to a man wearing a black vest who escorted them to their seats near the middle of a large group of chairs, and they both sat down.

"Care for a drink?" Ana asked, handing Rachel a menu that had cocktails with kitschy names like the Casablanca Margarita and Tito's Ferris Bueller.

"What are you getting?" Rachel asked, a high pitch of giddiness in her voice.

"Guess." Ana narrowed her eyes at Rachel and bit her lip.

Rachel raised an eyebrow and examined the menu. "Well, the Goodfellas Sour has bourbon in it, and it's a little warm for bourbon. The Castaway Sunrise has rum, which I think you'd like, except it might be too sweet. Oh, I know! The 500 Days of Summer Mojito?"

Ana clapped softly. "Muy bien. Wow, am I that predicable already?"

Rachel shrugged. "You were drinking a mojito the first time I met you. And you also ordered one for both of us at the Center awards dinner. Remember?"

Ana leaned in closer to Rachel and whispered, "I was a little too distracted by how hot you looked both nights to remember what drink was in my hand."

Rachel closed the rest of the gap and placed a soft kiss on her lips. "You're telling me. I couldn't wait to get that pretty blue dress off you that first night."

Ana leaned in for another kiss, but Rachel sat back and raised an eyebrow. "Excuse me, I believe you owe me a drink. It's your turn to guess."

Ana sat back in her chair and wrinkled her forehead in discontentment before grabbing the menu from Rachel. She looked at it for less than five seconds before handing it back to her.

"Easy. The Great Gatsby Martini. You like martinis, you had a long day at work, and you love that stupid book. Give me a challenge next time."

Rachel's mouth dropped open. "I'll have you know *The Great Gatsby* is—"

Ana held up her hand. "Let me guess. A classic? Timeless? A work of literary genius? An age-old story of how far a man is willing to go for the woman he loves?"

Rachel crossed her arms. "No," Rachel pouted. "That is not at all what I was going to say."

"Sure, sweetheart," Ana said playfully. She leaned over and kissed her cheek before patting her on the leg and getting up to walk to the bar.

She looked over her shoulder when she was halfway across the lawn and winked at her, watching as crimson spread up Rachel's chest and into her cheeks.

After waiting in line and ordering their drinks, it was almost time for the movie to start. She carried both drinks back across the rooftop and sat down next to Rachel, who was apparently still bitter about Ana's distaste for one of Rachel's favorite books.

"How's your timeless, age-old, classic martini?" Ana baited, watching as Rachel took a sip of the drink.

"Orgastic," Rachel replied smugly.

Ana rolled her eyes at the *Great Gatsby* reference. "Nerd." She smiled and sipped her own perfectly minty mojito.

"So, what movie are we seeing anyway?" Rachel asked, setting her drink on the small table beside her.

"Oh, you could say it too is a classic, just a classic of another era."

A look of concern spread over Rachel's face. "Oh, God, don't tell me it's a Monty Python movie?"

Ana started to laugh. "No, but I'm glad someone else hates those movies as much as I do. No, this type of classic I think is right up your alley."

Just then, as if Ana had timed it herself, the string lights hanging overhead turned off and the opening credits began to play. Within seconds, Rachel had identified the movie.

"*Notting Hill*? Holy shit, I love this movie. It *is* a classic!" Rachel happily scooted down into her chair and picked up her drink to take another sip.

Ana reached out and held her hand while she listened to the opening song play as clips of Julia Roberts flashed across the screen.

Chapter Thirty-eight

"Are you crying?" Ana asked, as a smile spread across her face.

"What? No!" Rachel wiped her eyes. "It's just allergies."

"Sure it is," Ana said, while stroking the back of Rachel's hand.

Rachel fought back more tears as images of Hugh Grant and Julia Roberts sitting on a park bench reading to each other played across the screen. Soon the screen went dark and people were applauding. The string lights came back on and the music switched to the Michael Bublé version of "Can't Help Falling in Love."

"Okay, now I'm going to cry," Rachel said as she stood up from her seat. "This is maybe my favorite love song ever."

All around them people began to pack up their bags and leave.

"Come here," Ana said, holding out her hand.

Rachel took it and Ana pulled Rachel close as they started to sway gently to the music. She was dancing with her. Right there, in front of people who were just trying to leave and go home. Ana didn't care and no one else seemed to care either. They just smiled and walked around them. Off in a corner, an older couple followed their lead and started to dance too. Rachel leaned down and rested her head against Ana's, soaking in the sound of the music mixing in with the sirens and horns that were ever present in the city. The sounds of her home.

As the song came to a close, Ana kissed Rachel. It was slow and deep and intentional. Rachel bent down and wrapped her arms around Ana, pulling her close against her.

Ana broke the kiss sooner than Rachel wanted and rested her forehead against Rachel's.

"I was planning on taking you to dinner after this," Ana said, a familiar sound of longing in her voice.

"I'm not hungry," Rachel replied firmly. "Not for food anyway."

Taking the hint, Ana nodded, and soon they were downstairs

hailing a cab and flying up Third Avenue to Rachel's apartment. She hadn't thought to clean it before she left, but she didn't care. She needed Ana now, and her apartment was closer.

They hadn't stopped touching since they left the movie. Ana's hand fit perfectly into Rachel's the entire cab ride north. When they finally reached Rachel's apartment building, she couldn't pull her keys from her purse fast enough. By the time they reached the elevator, Ana's hands were on her again. Rachel let out a loud huff as she fell back against the wall of the small elevator. They only had a few floors to ride up, but it was long enough for Ana to get Rachel completely soaked through her underwear.

Finally they tumbled their way into Rachel's apartment. Rachel pushed Ana against the door as soon as she closed it and began untucking her shirt. She bit down on Ana's neck gently and could feel goose bumps on Ana's arms in response.

She was just about to take Ana's top off when they were interrupted by a loud meow coming from the living room.

Ana stopped and looked over Rachel's shoulder.

"Oh hello!" Ana slid out of Rachel's grasp and walked across the room. Rachel stood frozen, turned on and alone, facing her apartment door. Ana was already gone to greet the cat, who stood rubbing her face against the corner of the TV stand/bookshelf.

"Wow, leaving me for my cat?" Rachel said.

"Excuse me. She has a name. Introduce us, please. Don't be rude."

Ana knelt down and held out her hand, waiting for Elijah to come and greet her on her own terms. A few steps and sniffs later and Ana was gently petting her head.

Rachel sighed and walked closer to them. "Elijah, this is Ana. Ana, this is Elijah."

"So nice to meet you, little lady," Ana said, scratching beneath the cat's chin. "I've heard a lot about you." Elijah purred approvingly and began rubbing her face against Ana's legs and knees where she squatted.

"She's just using you because she thinks you're going to feed her, you know."

Ana tsked under her breath. "Do you hear these lies she's telling about you, Elijah? Defamation is a tortious action, you know. You call me if she does it again, okay?"

Ana stood and wiped her hands off on her shorts. Rachel remained in the kitchen with her arms crossed.

"What?" Ana replied innocently.

"Oh nothing, just never been rejected for a cat before."

Ana walked across the room and wrapped her arms around Rachel's waist. "Such a crybaby," she said, bringing Rachel's face down to hers. "Why don't you stop being jealous of your cat and show me your bedroom?" Ana asked, a little sparkle behind her deep brown eyes.

"Gladly."

Rachel walked Ana down the short hall past the bathroom and into her bedroom. She shut the door behind them to ensure there would be no interruption from Elijah and lit the candle on her dresser. Ana looked around briefly and started laughing when her gaze landed on the bed.

"What?"

Had she left out a pair of underwear or something embarrassing? Rachel did a quick survey of the room. Her bed was made, as usual. There was nothing on her nightstand aside from the book she was reading and a lamp and her phone charger. She had nothing but the candle and a photograph on her dresser. No dirty clothes on the floor. All in all, the place was pretty clean considering she hadn't expected company tonight.

"Nothing," Ana said taking a few steps closer. "I just...I fucking knew you had a white down comforter."

Ana wrapped her arms around Rachel's waist and looked up at her.

"What's wrong with a white down comforter?" Rachel asked, reaching around and grabbing Ana's ass with both hands. She loved that she was taller than Ana. It gave her a great angle to grab the best parts of her.

"Nothing. This place is just so you. So neat and tidy and organized. I love it." Ana kissed her.

"I'm glad." Rachel replied between kisses. "Because I plan on keeping you here for a while."

Ana leaned back, still in Rachel's arms. "Oh really? Some prisoner fantasy I should know about?"

Rachel laughed. "More like, it's a Saturday night and I'm hoping you don't have plans tomorrow?"

Ana paused, seeming to run through a mental calendar in her mind before answering. "Nope, I'm all yours."

"Good," Rachel said. "Now take your clothes off."

"Bossy as always," Ana said, taking a few steps back so she was next to the bed. "How about this. For every article of clothing you want me to take off, you say it in Hebrew, or Yiddish, your choice. If I guess what it is correctly, I take it off. If I guess incorrectly, you have to take it off instead, thereby teaching me what the word means."

Rachel raised an eyebrow. "And what do I get for my Spanish lessons?"

Ana licked her lips in a way that made Rachel want to shove her down on the bed and never let her sit up again.

"Maybe we can do body parts for that instead?"

Rachel inhaled sharply, and her eyes trailed the line of Ana's legs.

"Fine," Rachel said, "But I'm wearing a dress, so the math isn't mathing. You have more clothes on than me."

Ana looked her slowly up and down. "Then it'll be a quick game if I guess wrong."

Rachel narrowed her eyes. Only Ana could turn sex into a competition, and only Rachel would be indescribably turned on by it.

"Shirt," Rachel said firmly in Hebrew.

Ana paused, seeming to consider the word, then slowly began to lift her shirt.

Rachel nodded in approval as Ana continued to take off her top.

"Bra," Rachel said next in Yiddish.

Ana hesitated and then unbuttoned her shorts and let them drop to her feet.

Rachel waited a moment, taking in the sight of Ana in her black bra and black bikini underwear. She shook her head slowly.

"That means bra," Rachel said. "But I'm not wearing one."

"Oh darn," Ana said, stone faced. She motioned to Rachel's dress.

Slowly, Rachel slid the long dress off her shoulders, watching as Ana's eyes greedily explored her exposed shoulders, breasts, and stomach before the dress dropped to the floor.

Ana crossed the room and wrapped her arms around Rachel's neck, bringing an end to their little lessons for the day. Their kisses were hard and sloppy at first, with Ana grabbing at any inch of Rachel's skin that she could get her hands on. She pushed Rachel back onto the bed and climbed on top of her straddling Rachel's hips.

Rachel reached around to unhook Ana's bra with one hand, then fell back down on the bed and let Ana's full breasts fall on top of her. Her soft, cool skin pressing against Rachel sent shivers down her spine. She could feel her nipples harden against Ana's and reached up to push back a handful of Ana's long hair that now tumbled down in front of her face.

Ana smiled before kissing her neck and chest and slowly made her way to Rachel's breasts. Rachel felt Ana's hand start to make its way between her legs, but before she got too far, stopped her.

"Everything okay?" Concern rang in Ana's voice.

Rachel nodded and pushed Ana's hair behind her ear. "I want you to wear something for me."

A look of excitement spread across Ana's face at the apparent realization of what Rachel was referring to. Ana rolled off to the side, and Rachel opened the bottom drawer of her nightstand, pulling out a realistic-looking strap-on and handing it to Ana. Ana inspected it for a second and then stood up. She slid the harness over her bare thighs and adjusted it until it fit her.

Then Ana was back on top of her, and this time Ana's desire was more than palpable between her legs. Rachel spread her legs wide and Ana resumed kissing Rachel's nipples as she had been before the brief intermission. She kissed all the way down her stomach and moved between her legs, placing gentle kisses everywhere but the one place Rachel needed her.

She was teasing her, Rachel knew, and it took all she had not to grab her face and shove it down onto her pulsing pussy. But she resisted and let Ana take the reins. Finally, Ana ended her torment. She moved her tongue slowly at first, making light caresses over her clit, which only made Rachel's hips buck more with desire. Picking up on Rachel's not so subtle hints, Ana slid her tongue completely inside her. Rachel's back arched with pleasure as Ana entered her again and again, pausing each time to suck on her clit. Rachel tangled her hand in Ana's hair and looked down at her. Their eyes met as Ana moved in and out, up and down. Rachel clenched her hands tighter into Ana's hair and watched as Ana lifted her face briefly, displaying a tongue full of Rachel's pending climax.

She slammed her eyes shut, sending all of her energy into not exploding onto Ana's face. It would be such a waste of a perfectly good strap-on if she came too soon. Sensing Rachel was getting closer, Ana stopped, enjoying one final taste of Rachel's wetness with a slow, long lap of her tongue.

Then Ana moved back on top of Rachel, and pressed her mouth against Rachel's ear. Rachel looked down and saw her slide a finger slowly into her own pussy. She moaned slightly in her ear and, when she was done, rubbed the residual wetness onto the tip of the strap-on. The image made Rachel light-headed with pleasure and she spread her legs wider, ready to accept all of Ana.

"You ready?" Ana asked gently.

Rachel nodded. "Yes."

Ana kissed Rachel's neck and slowly slid the tip into her. Rachel moved her body in response, tensing at first and then relaxing as Ana slowly worked her way inside, inch by inch. Ana stayed that way for a few seconds, allowing Rachel time to really open up, before she started moving in and out.

It was painful at first; it always was with the strap-on, and Rachel hadn't let anyone use it on her in over a year. She was tight, but Ana seemed to know that and took her time letting Rachel shift from pain into pleasure.

Soon all traces of tension left Rachel and she grabbed Ana's ass, pulling her harder into her. Ana responded by moving faster, a slow trickle of sweat beginning to form down her spine as she did. Rachel moaned in her ear as the thrusts grew deeper and harder.

"You like that, baby?" Ana whispered in her ear, her voice low and commanding.

That was the first time Ana had ever called her that. The softness of the new pet name combined with the dominance in her voice pushed Rachel to the brink of oblivion as Ana moved in and out of her, pressing her down into the bed.

"Yes, fuck yes," Rachel whimpered in reply.

"You like my cock in you?" Ana demanded.

Again, Rachel felt her body's climax grow close in response to Ana's words. The sound of Ana's voice growling in her ear felt almost as good as what she was doing between her legs right now.

"God, you feel so good inside me. Please don't stop." Rachel grabbed Ana's ass again and started breathing harder. Ana moved her hand down to her clit and started rubbing against her gently, a sharp contrast to the other movements she was making. The sensation of her clit being barely touched combined with the deep penetration from the strap-on was too much for Rachel to stand. She was getting close now and wasn't sure how much longer she could last, especially with Ana talking like she was in her ear. She slid a hand up Ana's back. Slick and warm, just like Rachel was right now.

"Say it again," Ana said with a deep thrust.

Rachel whimpered. "I'm begging you, please don't stop."

That was the last thing Rachel was able to say. Soon she was driving full speed off a cliff, and there was no one in the passenger seat to stop her. She felt her entire body tense briefly before exploding and releasing beneath Ana. Her orgasm rolled across her body like waves crashing on a shore, and Ana didn't stop moving in and out of her until Rachel was twitching with pleasure.

Ana whispered something in Spanish as she collapsed on top of her, the strap-on still fully inside her.

"Yes," Rachel said, unable to move. "Whatever that means. Yes."

CHAPTER THIRTY-NINE

Where the hell have you been, mijo?" Ana hissed into the phone. She looked over her shoulder toward the bedroom, making sure she hadn't woken up Rachel. It had been weeks since she'd heard from her brother, and she'd woken up with the sound of her mother's voice echoing on a voicemail in her ear so loudly she decided if she didn't call him, the anxiety would consume her and she wouldn't be able to enjoy her day with Rachel.

"Ay, chill out, it's not like you've been blowing up my phone lately," her brother protested.

Ana inhaled and rubbed her forehead. He was right, she had been derelict in her sisterly duties lately. In fact, she'd been derelict in a lot of her normal duties lately, but the person sleeping soundly on the other side of the closed door seemed to be worth it.

Elijah meowed loudly and rubbed up against her leg.

"Did you get a cat?" Antonio asked.

"No, it's not mine. I'm not at home right now."

"Is my little sister calling me after a booty call? That's badass even for you. Damn."

Ana shook her head. "One, you're an idiot. Two, she's not a booty call, she's…she's important. I think? Anyway, I don't want to talk about it. I called to talk about you. What the hell have you been doing? Mom thinks you're on drugs, you know."

Antonio laughed. "Of course she does. And even if I was, she'd never say anything about it. We both know she's terrified of me leaving the house."

Ana sighed. "That's true. Well, we both know you aren't on drugs, so spill. What are you hiding?"

Antonio paused. "All right, I was going to make it a surprise, but since you're going all Ally McBride on me—"

"Ally McBeal," Ana interjected.

"Whatever. If I tell you, will you promise not to say anything to the 'rents?"

"Promise. Unless it's illegal."

"Why does everyone assume I'm breaking the law?"

"Oh, I don't know, maybe because the night of your prom you got arrested for drag racing? Papi had to come bail you out in the middle of the night and mami stayed up to light a candle and pray for you."

"That was one time!" Antonio protested.

"Just saying, I never had to get bailed out of jail." Ana paused. "Just tell me, mijo."

Antonio exhaled loudly into the phone. "I'm opening up my own garage. Well, not just a garage. It's going to specialize in antique and vintage cars. Like the one I fixed up with papi."

Ana's jaw dropped. "Shit, Antonio, are you serious?"

"Yup, I took out a small business loan. I've got the lease all lined up. I mean, it's still in the beginning stages, so it's gonna take a while to actually open, but it's happening. And it's only a ten-minute drive from home, so even when I do move out, I'll still be close enough to visit every week."

She couldn't believe what she was hearing. It made sense, of course. Cars were Antonio's passion. Well, cars and pretty girls. But the fact that he had made such an adult decision without consulting the family? Without asking for help? Without asking them for the loan? It was impressive and extremely out of character for Antonio. She couldn't believe she was thinking it, but her little brother was finally growing up. She had never been prouder of him in his entire life. She wished she was home so she could jump into his arms and kiss his cheek.

"Antonio," Ana began.

"I know, it's wild, and I know the market is like so whack right now, but mami and papi came here and started with nothing and look at them now, right? Plus, this is my home. I want to help keep it real around here, and these old muscle cars are dying off. I want to help keep what's left of them in our community, you know?"

Ana smiled. "I am so fucking proud of you."

"Really? Shit, that means a lot to me." He paused and she waited. "Promise you won't say anything?"

Ana wiped a small tear from her eye. "On our abuelita's grave."

"Good." They were both silent for a second. "So," Antonio said, "You want to tell me about her?"

Ana laughed. "Absolutely not. I'll call you later?"

"Word," Antonio said before hanging up.

Ana reached down and petted Elijah, who purred and circled around her legs like a tiny, furry shark. She had never had a cat before, but she could already tell she was going to like this one.

"Are you starving to death, little lady?" Ana asked the chubby cat. "Does your mommy not feed you?"

Elijah purred louder and flopped over on her back, the brown and white fur splaying out all around her wide belly.

"I most certainly do feed her," Ana heard Rachel say from the bedroom door.

Ana jumped a bit and stood up, wiping her hands off on the oversized T-shirt she had snagged from Rachel's drawer after sneaking out of bed that morning.

"Morning," Ana said, unable to hide the excitement in her voice at seeing Rachel.

She looked stunning in the morning light. Her hair was messy and thrown over to one side. She had a large T-shirt on so long it hung below her butt, and she maybe had underwear on, though Ana couldn't fully tell due to the length of the shirt. God, Ana really hoped she wasn't wearing underwear.

Ana waited while Rachel slowly walked over to her. She pulled Rachel close, inhaling the sweet smell of her hair mixed with sweat and sex. Ana could drown in that smell. She began placing gentle kisses on Rachel's neck. Her skin was tangy and salty from the full workout they had put in the night before, but Ana didn't care.

Rachel pressed a soft kiss on Ana's lips.

Ana paused. "How does your breath smell good if you just woke up?"

Rachel shrugged. "I might keep gum in my nightstand. You know, for the many women I pick up in bars."

Ana raised an eyebrow. "Very funny."

Rachel leaned down and placed a kiss on her cheek. "I'm kidding," she whispered. "About the bars. Not the gum." She stuck out a small white piece of gum between her teeth.

"Clever girl," Ana said. "I had to resort to finger brushing with your toothpaste."

Rachel laughed. "Well, you'll have to leave a toothbrush here, then."

Ana paused and smiled. "Yeah?"

Rachel nodded. "Yes."

They kissed again and Ana allowed herself to relax into Rachel's arms. She loved how lean and toned Rachel's body was, and she loved that Rachel was taller than her. She felt so safe wrapped in her strong arms. It was like all the cares in the world faded away when she was in them.

Rachel broke the kiss first and started walking toward the kitchen. Elijah trotted after her, meowing at the top of her lungs.

"Yes, I know you're wasting away," Rachel said to the cat, who now yelled even louder.

Rachel opened a fresh can of wet cat food and placed it in a small pink bowl with the words "Feed Me" written in white on the side. Elijah nearly pushed her hand out of the way before the bowl hit the ground and started eating.

"I'm beginning to think you neglect her, you know. She was telling me a lot of things this morning."

Ana walked over to the couch and lay down, swinging her bare legs over the end.

"Oh yeah? I heard you talking to someone this morning. Have to say I'm surprised to hear it was my cat."

Ana laughed. "Oh, that was just my brother, Antonio. He's opening his own garage for vintage and antique cars. He swore me to secrecy, but I trust you won't call my mom."

Rachel sat down beside Ana's legs at the other end of the couch, taking one in each hand.

"Wow, that's great. Didn't you say he was kinda struggling to find his way for a bit?"

Ana nodded. "Yeah, he's always had some issues. In school he had a hard time because he has really bad dyslexia and ADHD and my parents refused to have him tested. They can be pretty old school about those things. But cars, well, cars he's good at."

Rachel lifted Ana's leg onto her shoulder and began placing kisses down Ana's calf and ankle.

"Do you think you'll go visit them soon? Your family, I mean," she said between kisses.

Ana contemplated the question. "Maybe. I don't know. I mean, going home is complicated for me."

Rachel set Ana's leg down and began massaging her feet one at a time. Ana closed her eyes and relaxed. She could definitely get used to this.

"You should go see them," Rachel said, breaking Ana from her reverie. "Family is important, even if it's complicated."

Ana propped herself up on her arms, not wanting to discuss the topic of her family anymore. She tilted her head sideways to inspect what Rachel had going on beneath her oversized T-shirt and was sad to see a pair of gray bikini cut underwear instead of her bare ass.

"Come here." Ana motioned to Rachel with her finger.

Rachel shook her head. "No way. You were in charge all last night. It's my turn to be alpha for the day." She crossed her arms and jutted out her chin in a way that made Ana laugh.

"Oh yeah?" Ana swung her legs back over the couch and stood up. "You know how alphas are decided in packs, right?"

Rachel bit her lip and stood up herself. "No…"

Ana narrowed her eyes. "They fight for it." With that, Ana took off toward Rachel, and Rachel spun on her heels, laughing and giggling all the way back to the bedroom. She raced across the small room and jumped on the bed, burying herself beneath the covers.

Ana was on her heels the entire time and pounced on top of her in bed.

"Give it up, Cohen," Ana said, grabbing at Rachel from on top of the covers, feeling for her hands to pin her down.

"Never!" Rachel squealed from beneath the sheets.

By the time Ana managed to pin Rachel down, she had completely forgotten why she was chasing her in the first place. The only thing on her mind was taking off that big T-shirt so she could get her hands back on Rachel.

Chapter Forty

Rachel tucked a strand of hair behind her ear and looked over at Ana, who was grinning widely, holding up a disposable camera and trying to get a photo of the Empire State Building.

"So, how does it feel to be a tourist in your own city?" Rachel shouted over the sound of sirens and horns.

They were on the top level of a double decker Hop On, Hop Off bus surrounded by a mob of foreign tourists holding out selfie sticks and giggling as the bus jolted around a corner.

It was Rachel's idea, this little day adventure of theirs. She had read about people playing tourist for a day, especially in places like New York, but she never thought she'd actually get to do it. Now there she was, feeling like a teenager on a field trip with the prettiest girl in class on her arm.

"It's so fun!" Ana shouted back. She turned the disposable camera around and planted a kiss on Rachel's cheek before a bright flash went off.

"Whoops, probably didn't need the flash in the middle of the day." Ana looked down at the camera.

"I still can't believe you hustled that guy into selling us these tickets for ten bucks," Rachel said, holding her blue New York Knicks hat down on her head.

Ana had borrowed Rachel's clothes, and she had to admit, it was definitely a vibe. She had chosen a pair of Rachel's long red and black basketball shorts and kept on her own shoes from the night before. Then she had tucked in a tight plain black tank top of Rachel's and thrown on a snapback hat, which she now wore backward. The outfit would look ridiculous on anyone else, but on Ana it just looked effortless and somehow still adorable.

"Hustled is a strong word," Ana said, shooting her a sideways glance. "I simply reminded him that when the bus left, he could either have two empty seats on it, or ten bucks in his pocket." She shrugged, winding the camera up for another photo. "He chose wisely."

The bus came to a screeching halt at Rockefeller Center, and the group all stood to pile off the bus and see the famed sculpture of Atlas, St. Patrick's Cathedral, and of course Rockefeller Center.

Rachel watched as Ana ran around like a kid, snapping pictures and oohing and aahing over all the attractions. Rachel had grown up there. She'd seen these budlings more times than she could count. She sometimes forgot that Ana had not. She'd come to New York for school and then work. She doubted she had ever taken the time to really sit back and see the clichéd sights.

"So," Rachel said, taking Ana's hand as they entered the gothic cathedral across Fifth Avenue. "You gonna introduce me to your saints?"

Ana laughed and let go of Rachel's hand long enough to dip her fingers in the silver bowl of water and make the sign of the cross. She muttered something in Spanish under her breath, then took Rachel's hand again.

"They're definitely not *my* saints," Ana said quietly as they walked down the long aisle together.

Rachel looked up at the high vaulted ceilings and ornate stained-glass windows. Jewish temples were beautiful, but they abstained from things that could be considered idols. A lot of them had really beautiful works of art and stained-glass windows, but you wouldn't see full biblical stories illuminated and narrated in detail like they were here.

She had to admit, this was one of the most beautiful churches she had ever seen. The high stone ceiling seemed to stretch all the way to the sky before arching over and meeting in the middle. The colored glass on all sides let the light dance on the floor in a playful rainbow. The stories depicted in the windows were recognizable for the most part. Moses holding up the Ten Commandments. Noah and the ark. As they made their way down the aisle, the images got less familiar. A man she assumed to be Jesus seated in a field with a lamb on his lap. Jesus being crucified, a red tear streaming down his forehead from a crown of thorns. Mary holding Baby Jesus surrounded by donkeys and sheep.

"They're definitely more your saints than mine," Rachel said when they reached the end of the aisle where a red rope prevented them from going any further.

Ana nodded. "True, no saints in Judaism, I suppose. Do you still go to temple or…?"

Rachel smiled. "Temple, or shul, or synagogue. They all work really. And yeah, as a family we used to go every Saturday morning. I go when I can now. There's a Reform temple close to my apartment. But with work, I'm not always free. Plus, I like to keep the Sabbath in my own way now. Reading poetry or taking a walk through a park. Visiting a museum or volunteering at one of the shelters. Shabbat is about taking time to pause from the madness of everyday life. Our mitzvot are about doing something that leaves the world a better place. Judaism is more about what we do with the time that is given to us on this earth rather than preparing for what's to come in the next life."

Rachel paused. "Not that there's anything wrong with that…I mean, this." She motioned to the grand room, feeling uneasy. Religion was a delicate topic, and she didn't want to come across as intolerant or offensive.

Ana grabbed Rachel's hand. "I love learning about your religion from you. I wish I had as much reverence for my own as you do yours. But mostly, religion to me was a chore growing up. It was a pain to have to get all dressed up every Sunday morning to go sit on a hard pew with some old man preaching about hell and damnation. I hated it. But I guess, in a way, my religion is like my family. It's part of me, whether I like it or not, and I can limit the time I spend with it, but at the end of the day, it's not going anywhere. It's my culture too, you know?"

Rachel leaned over and pressed a kiss against Ana's lips. "I do."

They looked at each other and Rachel gulped deeply. She had just realized that they were now standing, hand in hand, at the end of a church aisle with Rachel uttering the words "I do."

"I guess I better not say 'I do' back, or we'd be married." Ana let out a nervous laugh and quickly turned to walk back up the aisle.

"Have you thought about it? Marriage? Not to me, of course. I mean, not that I—" Rachel exhaled. "I'm going to stop talking now."

Ana chuckled softly. "Of course. What little girl didn't plan their wedding by the age of ten?"

"This one," Rachel said, pointing to herself. "But go on, tell me all about baby Ana's dream wedding."

She swung their hands in a playful way, trying to keep the topic light.

"Well, it's in a church. Obviously. A lot like this one, actually.

It's Christmastime and my bridesmaids are wearing all black and my flowers are red roses. Real La Llorona vibes, if you know what I mean."

Rachel stared blankly.

"I'll tell you about her later. Anyway, my dress is big and puffy, like something out of a princess movie, and I walk down the aisle to—" Ana paused and looked down.

"What?" Rachel said shaking Ana's hand.

"Well, this is the part where it becomes apparent that I was very young when planning this dream wedding of mine."

Rachel stared at her, waiting for a response.

"I walk down to 'Can You Feel the Love Tonight,' okay?" Crimson spread over Ana's cheeks, and she dropped Rachel's hand to cover her face and laugh.

Rachel burst out into laughter and wrapped her arms around Ana. "Wait, from *The Lion King*? Like, the Disney movie?"

Ana nodded. "Yes! Okay, yes. It was my favorite as a kid!"

Rachel shook her head. "Are we talking the Elton John version or the movie version? They're different lyrics, you know. This is so crucial."

They had reached the entry way now and were almost back outside. "I know they're different lyrics!" Ana replied. "And of course I wanted the movie version. Please. I was a purist, even at the age of six."

The two women laughed as they made their way back to the bus. Rachel chuckled to herself as they took their seats back on the top level. She could see it now: Little six-year-old Ana, full of precociousness and feisty as hell, planning her wedding right down to the song she would walk in to.

She thought about it as the bus pulled away and continued up Fifth Avenue, past the famous storefronts, and around to Columbus Circle. But the more Rachel though about Ana getting married, the more she thought about herself standing at the end of the aisle. And the more Rachel thought about that, the less funny it got.

CHAPTER FORTY-ONE

A na Mendez, so good to see you."
Ana snapped her head up. She had been dozing off waiting for her case to be called for a conference before the judge. They had these things every few months in every case. All of the attorneys would have to show up in court, wait around to meet with the judge or the court attorney, and give them an update on the case. It was a total waste of time, but easy billing for Ana. That's where she was now, zoning out and thinking of Rachel, when Sheryl Peterson interrupted her.

Ana's stomach tensed instinctively. Ana actually really liked Sheryl, but anything that reminded her of that case now gave her an instant ulcer and hives.

"Hey, Sheryl." Ana scooted over in the wooden bench to allow room for Sheryl to sit next to her.

It wasn't uncommon for her to run into attorneys she knew at these conferences, especially since she went to so many of them. The courthouse at 60 Centre Street was essentially a watering hole for Manhattan's litigation attorneys, and Ana was there to get her weekly drink by way of a compliance conference for one of her construction liability cases.

"How are things looking in the *Solomon* case?" Sheryl asked. "I suppose I'll see you next week?"

"Next week?" Ana asked, her mind racing. Was there a conference she had forgotten about? That would be unlike her.

"The deposition of Dr. Cohen. It's on for next Wednesday, right?"

Ana's throat ran dry. She had assumed Micah would tell her when the deposition was scheduled. What's more, she had assumed Rachel would tell her. But as perfect as things had been going between her and Rachel, the pending litigation had become a gaping hole of "we don't talk about that" in their relationship. Maybe Rachel was just trying to ignore it further by not even discussing the logistics with Ana. Still, it made her feel uneasy.

"I, uh…someone is actually covering that for me," Ana said vaguely.

Sheryl raised an eyebrow. "Really, that's not like you. You're always one to wrap up everything with a neat little bow on it." She crossed her arms. "Gearing up for a summary judgment motion I should know about?" A smirk played across her face.

Ana tossed her hands in the air. "Are *you* moving for summary judgment?"

Sheryl shrugged, feigning ignorance. "I guess we'll know once the note of issue is filed in a few weeks, won't we?"

Ana rolled her eyes but smiled. Great, another motion she would have to oppose. She hated motion practice, especially when it was something as silly as this. No court would let any of these doctors out of this case, especially not on Long Island. She knew it, Sheryl knew it, and they both knew that didn't matter. It was all about appearances. Sheryl had to show her doctor clients that she was zealously fighting for them just like Ana had to show Mark Solomon's wife that she was advocating to the fullest extent possible for her. She did not, however, want to mention the part where she was dating, and possibly falling for, one of the doctors involved in her dead husband's surgery.

"One of our junior associates needed some experience, so I decided to let him have this last one. Go easy on him, will you?" Ana said casually. "I figured this doctor doesn't have much useful information anyway. What harm could it serve letting him cut his teeth a little?"

Ana now wondered if she was trying to convince herself or Sheryl of how little Rachel's involvement was in the surgery. But the more she thought about it, the sicker she felt.

Sheryl looked down at her watch. "Well, I better get going," she said, changing the topic entirely. "Sad I won't be seeing you next week." She patted Ana on the shoulder in a friendly way and stood to leave. "Oh, and Ana?" Sheryl looked back at Ana over her shoulder. "You can always dismiss my clients, you know. If you were, say, trying to avoid having to oppose a forty-two-page summary judgment motion." Sheryl winked. "Just a hypothetical."

Ana sighed and dropped her head. Forty-two pages of legal mumbo jumbo to read and analyze and oppose? She'd have to call her experts as soon as she got back to the office so they were ready.

Ana pulled out her phone and made a note in her calendar to do just that. She checked a few more emails and then slid her work phone in her bag. She pulled out her personal cell phone and went to her text thread with Rachel. She shouldn't say anything. She knew she shouldn't say anything. Rachel had just been doing what Ana had asked. She had not talked about the lawsuit. That's what they had agreed to at the start of this whole thing. But it was gnawing at Ana that they had recently spent the entire weekend together and Rachel hadn't mentioned anything about her deposition being next week. Why wouldn't she at least tell her that it was happening? Ana was the one who had told her someone else was covering the thing in the first place. Clearly, they were allowed to talk about it to some small extent. So why would Rachel choose to be secretive now, over something so benign as a confirmed deposition date? Ana turned off her ever-churning brain and pressed send on the text.

Ana: Hi.

Ana tapped her finger and bit her cheek. She wasn't going to be annoyed. She wasn't worried. She would just let it go. Just let it go. *Once this deposition is over, the case can settle and you can forget about this entire thing. You're so close to the finish line, Mendez. Just keep your shit together a little while longer.*

Rachel: Hey you. How's court?

Ana tilted the phone up from where she was seated so that the judge's bench, counsel tables and high wooden ceilings were visible. She sent it. Then she tilted the camera down so that just her leg, one of her heels, and the edge of her pencil skirt were showing. She sent that one too.

Rachel: Stunning.

Rachel added a heart eyes emoji to the end. Ana smiled, feeling good at the direction the conversation was heading. This was what she needed. A nice normal conversation to distract her from the suspicion and insecurity growing inside her.

Ana: Which one? Me or the courthouse?

Rachel: Both, but you're the one I'd like to bend over that pretty wooden table right now.

Ana: Sex in a courtroom on counsel table. Now that's a lawyer's kinky bucket list item.

Rachel: Yeah? How about in an office with floor to ceiling windows at night with the lights on?

Ana: Hmm…Didn't we already cover that I am more of a

voyeur than an exhibitionist during our first hook-up? But it's good to know your preferences.

Rachel: Exhibitionist is a strong term. I think I just like the idea of people seeing me with you. I want them to know that you're mine.

A twinge of pleasure shot through Ana's heart. She liked that idea too. She liked it very much. But seeing Sheryl a few moments ago was causing her to question things. What else was Rachel not telling her?

She knew herself well enough to know that she was not going to be able to just let this topic go. She was going to have to talk about it with Rachel at some point, but she also knew that over text while she was in court and while Rachel was at work wasn't exactly the best timing.

She looked down to another text from Rachel.

Rachel: Speaking of which, I've been thinking…

Ana: Oh Lord, should I be scared?

Rachel: Ha ha no. At least I hope not. I want to invite you to Shabbat dinner with my family this Friday night. I know it's a big step, but it doesn't have to mean anything if you don't want it to.

Ana sat back in her seat. She definitely hadn't been expecting that. Rachel had talked about her family a lot, and she knew they did dinner together every Friday. She also knew how important her family was to her, and that if Rachel was letting her into that selective section of her life, it was a big deal, whether Rachel tried to downplay it or not.

She processed everything that was happening before typing her reply. They had just spent an amazing weekend together. Things had been going remarkably well, probably better than any relationship Ana had ever been in. Then a few moments ago Sheryl had snapped her back to reality with her reminder of the upcoming deposition. Was that why she felt so reluctant to take this next step?

She looked to the empty seat beside her. She knew why. She knew that, yes, it was because Sheryl had just blown through there like a tornado reminding her that she wasn't living in the land of Oz where everything was poppy fields and hot witches in bubbles. She was in New York. And in New York, she had a job to do. She had a case to win. She might have finagled her way out of deposing Rachel, but she hadn't entirely freed herself from this little conflict of interest she was living in.

Without giving herself more time to talk herself out of it, Ana typed out her reply.

Ana: I'd love that.

Four hours later and Ana was sitting in one of her biweekly meetings with Paul contemplating what one actually did at a Shabbat dinner when he interrupted her train of thought.

"Listen, Ana, I've got to talk to you about something."

Ana wrinkled her forehead. This sounded serious.

"You're a good worker, you know that. In fact, you've been one of my top contenders for people to put forward for that open of counsel position. But lately you've seemed distracted from your work."

Ana leaned forward in her chair. "What do you mean?"

Paul frowned. "Frankly, your hours are suffering. Your billable hours are down to under one ninety a month. Some of our junior associates are billing out at two twenty-five. If you're going to be an of counsel, putting in the weekend and weeknight hours is just part of the gig. If we're not billing, we're not making money, and if we're not making money, we're not a law firm. You get what I'm saying?"

Ana nodded but wasn't sure what she could even say.

"See here?" Paul said rotating his screen so she could see it. "Here's your May hours. Two thirty-two. Now your June hours: two thirty. And look at July: one eighty-one. And August: one seventy-two. Then look at September…"

"September isn't even halfway done yet," Ana added.

"True, but right now you're at one forty-five. With the time remaining there's no way you'll bill the hundred hours of difference it would take to get you back to your prior average of two forty. You're slipping, Ana."

Ana felt tears begin to well up behind her eyes. Yes, she had been slipping, the numbers spoke for themselves, but she had also been the happiest she had ever been over the last two months. She hadn't been putting in as many late nights, and she couldn't remember the last time she worked without at least one day off on a weekend. And truth be told, it was fucking wonderful. Not just getting to spend that time with Rachel, but also getting that time back for herself. She had seen Shakespeare in the Park, had a picnic, gone to a bookstore just to browse the travel section, walked the extra ten blocks for her favorite Cuban coffee shop. She was finally starting to enjoy her life here in the city after years and years of selling her soul just to make ends meet.

And now her boss was telling her she might not get the promotion she'd worked so hard for, all because she was living her life at last.

"I don't know what to say, Paul."

"Say you'll kick it back into gear. I'm rooting for you, Ana. I really am. I have every intention of putting your name in as my suggestion to replace Simon as of counsel. And my word goes far with the other managing partners here. But I can't stick my neck out for you if the numbers don't back it."

Ana nodded, fighting back tears of frustration. "I'll buckle down," she said before standing up and leaving his office.

To say this had been a shitty day would be an understatement. She could feel the world she had created for herself beginning to crash down around her. She felt like the Scarlett Witch at the end of *WandaVision* when her spell began to break and everything started glitching back to reality. What had she been thinking? That she could really have everything she wanted? That she could enter a full blown relationship with one of her deponents and still get promoted to the of counsel position? Of course that would never happen. Stuff like that happened in movies or TV shows, but not real life. Real life was hard. Real life meant sacrifices. Real life meant *not* getting everything you wanted all the time. Her parents had taught her that. Why did she think she was somehow an exclusion to that rule now?

Ana bit down on her lip to fight off the rush of tears. She kept her head down as she scurried back to her office and didn't fully exhale until she closed the door behind her. She pressed her hands against the door and dropped her head, finally allowing the tears to come. She had known all along it was a mistake to start this thing with Rachel. She had known she was jeopardizing her career by even talking to her. But she had never been so drawn to another human in her entire life. It was like she was mesmerized from the first time their eyes met, and Ana just hadn't been strong enough to fight against that gravitational pull. And look what it had gotten her. In a huge mess. She was about to meet Rachel's family and lose her shot at a promotion all in the same week. It was too much for her to process all at once.

Slowly, she took long, deep breaths. As she listened to the air move in and out of her lungs, she began to feel her senses coming back to her. She clenched her fist against the door. There was no way she was losing this promotion. She had worked too hard for it. And if that meant making sacrifices in areas she didn't want to, then so be it.

CHAPTER FORTY-TWO

Rachel adjusted the silk scarf around her neck and fidgeted with the collar on her dress. It was one of her favorites, oxford blue with a collar and buttons all the way down the front. It hit just above her knee with a belt that tied around her waist. She had tied a navy blue and gold silk scarf around her neck to add an unnecessary layer of preppy-ness, and had her favorite cream and brown leather purse slung across her arm. Her long hair was half down and half pulled back but it was smooth and freshly washed. She completed the ensemble with a pair of white sandals that she hoped would keep her closer to Ana's height.

She hadn't been this nervous since her high school state playoff games in basketball. And they had lost by two points. She was hoping the nerves would have a better result this time around. She had never introduced anyone to her family before, at least not in a romantic capacity. There was Charlotte, who had been over for more Shabbat dinners than she could count. The woman was a full blown yenta as soon as she walked in their door now, gossiping with Rachel's mother about the neighbors she passed coming in the building. Then there was her girlfriend in college, before Rachel had been out of the closet. She had come to one Shabbat dinner as a "friend" and they had broken up shortly after because the girl had made fun of Rachel for wanting to spend Friday nights with her family instead of partying with her.

Ana would be breaking new ground tonight at the Cohen household, and she was terrified in both the "I'm about to get on a roller coaster" sort of way and also in the "a tornado is heading straight for my town—do I hide in the bathtub or the basement?" sort of way.

She hadn't told Ana about her deposition next week. She had wanted to, she really had. In fact, there were a lot of things about that lawsuit she had meant to tell Ana about by now. She had wanted to tell Ana about what really happened in the operating room during the Mark

Solomon surgery back before they even slept together. She wanted Ana to be the one to know her deepest, darkest secret that she had never told anyone. And under any other circumstance she would be the one Rachel would tell, because Rachel had never felt so seen and so safe by another person. But Ana wasn't just a person. She wasn't even just her girlfriend, if that's what they were calling themselves now. Ana was the attorney who had served her with a subpoena. She was the attorney fighting to prove that something *had* gone wrong in that operating room. What would it even mean if Rachel was honest with her? What ethical conflict would that put Ana in? She'd have to report it to her boss, of course, and how would she explain learning the information? Pillow talk with the witness? There was no scenario that Rachel could envision that allowed her to be honest with Ana and still maintain some sort of professional boundary between them. And so, instead of face any of that, Rachel had remained completely silent on the issue. A small crevasse that was slowly growing into a large chasm in their relationship.

But she didn't have much time to think about all of that now. It was seven o'clock and Ana was getting off the subway, which meant any second she would—

"There she is," Ana said, walking up and sliding her arm around Rachel's waist. Rachel kissed Ana, allowing all of her doubts and insecurities to float away with each second their lips touched.

"Here I am," she said, breaking the kiss. She stepped back and admired Ana's outfit.

She was wearing high waisted jogger style olive-green pants and a pair of black wedges with a little bow tied at the heels. On top she had a slim-fitting black short-sleeved top tucked in and a gold necklace hanging down between her breasts. Her hair was pulled back into a tight, slicked back ponytail that fell in loose waves down the middle of her back. As usual, she was breathtaking.

"Wow," Rachel said, taking her time admiring the beautiful woman standing before her.

"Yeah?" Ana said. "I wasn't sure what to wear, so I googled it, and it was not helpful at all actually."

Rachel took Ana's hand in hers and started walking the half block to her parents' apartment.

"You googled 'what to wear for Shabbat dinner?'"

"False. I googled 'I'm Catholic, my girlfriend is Jewish, what the heck do I wear to meet her family for Shabbat?'"

Rachel slowly smiled. "Girlfriend, huh?"

Ana's cheeks grew red and she looked down. "Sorry, it just slipped."

"Don't be." Rachel squeezed her hand. "I wouldn't be having you meet my family if you weren't at girlfriend status."

Ana grinned while still looking down, and they walked in silence the rest of the way. Soon they were crossing the lobby of her parents' apartment and Rachel was nodding at the doorman she had passed a hundred times before. Ana's hand started to sweat in hers and she let go as they entered the elevator.

"Don't be nervous," Rachel said reassuringly. "I'm the only one in my family who bites, and you seem to like it." She winked.

Ana rubbed her hands together and started bouncing up and down, likely to release her nerves. "If you say so."

Rachel gave Ana a reassuring kiss on the cheek. "They're going to love you."

Ana looked down, avoiding eye contact.

"Everything okay? Besides the nerves, I mean."

Ana shifted her weight a little bit, looking uneasy. "Yup, all good."

Rachel was unconvinced, but there was no time to discuss it further. They were at the fifth floor, and the elevator was opening.

As soon as they entered the apartment, Rachel was met with the familiar sounds of her mother speaking Yiddish in the kitchen, Estie and Benjamin racing around in the living room, Jacob and Noa talking about their schedules for the week, and her father pretending to be a monster, chasing the kids.

"Good Shabbos," Rachel said, stepping into the room.

Suddenly, as if on cue, the entire house went silent for a single second. They stopped to turn and stare at Ana before collectively shouting and coming toward her.

"Good Shabbos! Oh, you must be Ana, we've heard so much about you." Rachel's mother pulled her in to a tight hug.

"My turn, my turn," Noa said, pushing their mother gently out of the way before grabbing Ana and bringing her in close. "So good to meet you," Noa said in Ana's ear.

"All right, all right, let the girl breathe," Jacob said, marching forward and sticking out his hand. "Jacob Rosenblum," he said with an air of formality that made everyone burst into laughter.

"What?" Jake said, looking around the room. "I just said my name!"

Noa stepped forward, sticking out her hand. "Hello, I'm Jacob Rosenblum." The room laughed again.

"Oh, excuse me for not attacking the poor woman with aggressive hugs," Jake said, waving them off.

"It's nice to meet you. All of you," Ana said, smiling brightly.

"Auntie Rachel!" Estie and Benjamin came racing into the room, and Estie threw her body against Rachel's legs. Rachel scooped her up, resting her against her hip.

"Good Shabbos, Estie." Rachel tapped her nose as she always did. "I have someone special for you to meet. Her name is Ana, can you say hello?"

"Hello, Ana," Estie said obediently. "Good Shabbos."

"Good Shabbos." Ana seemed to be taking in the chaos they had just walked into.

Rachel set Estie down on the ground and Estie walked over and grabbed Benjamin's hand.

"This is Benjamin," she said, dragging her brother in front of Ana like a cattle herder parading his best stock. "He doesn't talk much yet, but he will soon. I read to him a lot so he won't be dumb."

"Estie!" Noa stepped forward and took Estie by the hand. "You'll have to excuse them," she said, shaking her head. "They take after their father." She shot a reproachful look at Jake, who held up his hands and hid a laugh.

"Not at all," Ana said. "I'm from Miami. I've heard much worse from kids."

Rachel relaxed and watched as Ana was introduced to her father. He was the quiet one of the family; he certainly wouldn't be one to bombard a guest at the door like her mother and sister.

"Good Shabbos, Tate," Rachel said, kissing her father's cheek.

"Good Shabbos, my daughter," Abraham said, stroking her cheek and smiling widely. "And welcome, Ana. It's a pleasure to meet you. We're so glad you could join us to celebrate the Sabbath this evening."

Ana smiled warmly up at him. At six foot two he was almost a full foot taller than Ana, but her heels offset the difference somewhat and her natural confidence always made her appear taller than she really was.

Rachel watched and listened as Ana rolled naturally into conversation with her father. Jake soon joined them, and Noa dragged Rachel off into the kitchen.

"Okay, wow, you didn't tell me she was a total smoke bomb," Noa said under her breath. "Hashem, she's making me question things over here." Noa fanned her hand in front of her face.

"I told you she was beautiful," Rachel said quietly.

"There's beautiful, and then there's that." Noa motioned into the other room.

Rachel blushed and looked into the living room. Ana made eye contact with her and winked.

"She really is stunning, isn't she?"

Rachel's mom joined them now and began to fawn over how attractive Ana was, how sweet she seemed, how anyone who could carry on a conversation with their father was a blessing, and how nicely she was dressed.

Soon it was time to light the candles and the family all gathered around the table.

"My mother is going to sing a prayer; you don't have to do anything, though."

"Relax, I'm fine," Ana replied.

Rachel's mother lit the candles and waved her hands in front of her face three times. Rachel lifted her hands to cover her face, and out of the corner of her eye she noticed Ana had already beaten her to it.

Soon the prayer was over and they were sitting down to pour wine and eat. Rachel's mother spoke as soon as they were seated.

"Since this is a special night, I think we should all join in and sing 'Shalom Aleichem.'"

"Yay!" Estie squealed. It was one of her favorite blessings to sing.

"Oh wow, bringing out the big guns for Ana, I see?" Noa chided.

Her mother tsked under her breath and waved her hands for everyone to join in.

Ana smiled and swayed in her seat, and Rachel pulled Estie onto her lap so she could bounce her on her knee. She sang loudly, her tiny voice echoing around the room as Benjamin clapped slightly offbeat across the table.

Once the song was over, the wine was poured and the challah was broken. Finally, it was time to eat.

But the first piece of bread had not even touched her mouth before the question Rachel had been hoping to avoid that night was asked— and by her mother, of course.

"So, Ana, how did you and Rachel meet?"

Rachel nearly choked on the piece of bread she was chewing on and took a deep gulp of wine to wash it down.

"We met at a bar," Ana said smoothly, shooting a sideways glance at Rachel. "I just thought she was so beautiful that I'd kick myself if I didn't walk over and say hi. Of course, I had no way of knowing if she was interested in me, or women at all for that matter, but I knew it was worth the risk." Ana reached out and squeezed Rachel's hand.

Rachel had never heard that version of their initial meeting before. She always thought of their meet cute as a night of wild, random sex followed by the most traumatizing in-office experience of her life. But the way Ana described it was actually sweet, romantic even. Maybe this night wouldn't be so bad.

"And what do you do for work?" Rachel's father asked next.

Two for two.

"I'm a lawyer," Ana said simply.

Her mother gasped. "Oh heavens, tell me you don't support what they're doing to our poor Rachel here. The nights she's lost over that cursed lawsuit. It's a crime, I say. Well, I'm sure she's told you all about it, of course. I just can't believe anyone would think she had anything to do with that poor man's death. An accident. A tragic accident and they decide to ruin lives over it? I feel for his family, truly, I do, but how does my daughter being dragged into a deposition fix any of that? The sleep she's lost over this entire ordeal, it's just disgraceful."

"Mamala," Rachel said, pleading. "Please, let's not discuss that?"

Rachel could see Ana tense in the seat beside her.

Rachel looked over to Noa, who sat pale faced and unmoving, a look of terror spread across her face. Estie and Benjamin were being perfect angels, eating their vegetables, or she would have used them to create some form of diversion.

"You're right, you're right, no work talk on Shabbat. Well, Ana, I'm sure whatever you do, it's nothing as heinous as all that. Tell me, what specifically do you do?"

Ana clenched her jaw and took another sip of wine. "I do defense work mostly. Construction liability, premises liability, contract review, stuff like that."

Rachel breathed a sigh of relief. She was good at this. Of course she was good at this. She was a lawyer, after all. Giving the appearance of calmness even in the face of adversity was half of her job.

"Estie, why don't you tell Ana about where your name comes from?" Noa piped in from across the table, and Rachel's shoulders relaxed. This story would take a solid half hour at the pace Estie told it, and there was no chance of revisiting the dreaded topic of Ana's career. God, she loved her sister.

Estie set her fork down and folded her hands. "Well, it all started when the king of Persia, his name was Aha...Ahas...Ahaber..."

"Ahasuerus," Jake leaned down and whispered in her ear.

"Uh-huh, Ahazerees," Estie continued. "He decided he was mad at his wife because she wasn't listening to him..."

Rachel chuckled in silence as Estie carried on and on all about Queen Vashti, Queen Esther, Mordecai, and Haman. Poor King Ahasuerus never did get his name pronounced correctly over the next half hour, but she did her best. More than that, Ana did her best at following a five-year-old's telling of a five-thousand-year-old story. She nodded along and oohed and aahed at all the right plot points. At the end she asked questions to show she was engaged, and Rachel was pretty confident she had competition for the favorite family member award.

"I like her," Estie said as they were clearing their plates later that night. "Can she come every Shabbat?"

Rachel laughed. "I don't even come every Shabbat, silly girl."

"That's okay, you don't have to. Just Ana is good."

Rachel's jaw dropped as the little girl walked out of the room and into the living room.

Ana sidled up beside Rachel and handed her a plate. "Was that a standing invitation I heard?"

"Little traitor," Rachel said. "First my cat likes you more, and now my niece. Keep your paws off my nephew, you hear?"

Ana held up her hands. "What can I say, I'm just cooler than you are."

Rachel whispered in her ear, "I was actually thinking you're much hotter."

"Dr. Cohen, in your mother's kitchen? The scandal."

Rachel took the dish, rinsing before loading it into the dishwasher. Washing dishes would be too much work for Shabbat, so a quick rinse was all the plates and silverware would get. The pots and cooking pans would sit in the sink until tomorrow night.

They soon moved into the living room and played a game of Charades. The couples were split down the middle with Ana, Jake, and Abraham (and Estie) on one side and Rachel, Noa, Hannah (and Benjamin) on the other. Ana shouted a plethora of guesses as Jake hopped around the living room apparently imitating a chicken, which made no sense to anyone except Jake. Rachel sat back and watched as Ana somehow managed to fit right into her family like she had been there for years.

Noa and the kids piled into their car around nine thirty, Benjamin already passed out in his pajamas in Jacob's arms and Estie following sleepily behind them rubbing her eyes. Rachel and Ana followed suit and left soon after.

They walked in silence most of the way, Ana's disposition seeming to change the moment they left.

"So," Rachel said as they walked toward the subway station, "I'm volunteering tomorrow afternoon at the shelter in the village, but maybe you could come stay until then?"

Ana nodded but didn't say anything.

"Everything okay?"

Ana nodded again but still remained silent.

"Okay," Rachel grabbed her by the arm slowing her pace. "What's going on? Did my family upset you? I know they can be a bit much at first, but they mean well. And they really liked you, I mean Estie basically tossed me overboard for you in the end there."

"No, no it's not them at all, trust me. They were wonderful. I loved them."

A wave of relief flooded over Rachel. "What is it, then?"

Ana furrowed her brows and looked up at her. "You didn't tell me that your deposition is scheduled for Wednesday."

Rachel bit her lip and looked down. "No, I didn't. I'm sorry."

What else could she say? She should have told Ana. She knew Ana would find out—it was her case, after all.

"I should have told you, it's just…well, you said not to talk about the lawsuit, and that's not really the reason. That's just the reason I used to convince myself."

Ana waited, staring up at her.

"The truth is, I'm happy with you. Like really, really happy. And this stupid deposition, this lawsuit…I know it's your job, and I know we have to keep things separate, but it's maybe the worst thing happening in my life right now. And you're absolutely the best thing. And sometimes the fact that both of those things exist in the same tiny universe is too much for me. So I compartmentalize. I tell myself you're not the same person I saw in the conference room that day about to rip me to shreds with questions, about to grill me over one of the worst experiences of my life. I tell myself that you're mine, you're just mine. Not Mark Solomon's. Not Byron and Browning's. You're a woman I met in a bar, just like you said. The rest doesn't exist."

"But it does exist, Rachel. You know it exists. That 'stupid deposition' is my entire career right now. Don't you get that? How I perform on this case could be the difference between success and failure for me. The only way I was able to keep what we have going is because I convinced my boss to let a junior associate depose you. But at the end of the day, it's still my case. It's my only shot at a promotion at this job I've been busting my ass at for the last five years, and I can't just walk away from that because—"

"Because what?" Rachel crossed her arms and took a half step back.

"Because of you."

Rachel reeled at the coldness in Ana's voice.

"It's not like I chose this, Ana," Rachel said, ignoring the pain that now shot through her heart. "I mean, God knows this isn't what I want either. But it is what it is. I have to be deposed on Wednesday. I have to tell the truth about what happened to that poor man. I have to tell someone about what happened, for God's sake. It's killing me."

Rachel felt tears beginning to well up in her eyes, and she bit hard on her lip. She hated crying.

"I know," Ana said, crossing her arms. "Maybe it's best if we just—"

"If we just what?" Rachel focused on controlling the pitch of her voice and the tears that now continued to push their way forward.

"If we just push pause. At least until this case is resolved. I've really fallen behind at work, and with you it's…complicated."

Rachel shook her head. "You've got to be kidding me. You just spent the evening with my family. You called yourself my girlfriend. And this is how you want to end the night? Going all Ross Gellar and calling for a fucking break?"

Rachel was shaking now, she was so mad.

"I'm not saying I want to end things, but Jesus Christ, Rachel, I'm so behind on my work hours my boss called me into his office this week just to talk about it. That's never happened to me before. None of this has ever happened to me before. I don't think you understand how hard I've worked to get to where I am. I didn't go to private school; I didn't have things handed to me at every step of the way. I had to claw my way from the bottom for every single scrap I have. I have worked for five years at this firm for this promotion, and I'm sorry but I am not willing to just throw that all away just because you exist!"

A look of regret washed across Ana's face as soon as the words left her mouth, but it was too late. Rachel pushed past her and walked toward the subway. She was not about to be that New York couple that yelled and cried in the middle of the street. No way. She was so much better than that. She deserved so much better than that. She wiped a tear away and felt Ana reach for her.

"Don't," Rachel said sharply, spinning around to lock eyes with Ana. "Don't follow me." She turned and walked down the subway stairs, leaving Ana standing at the top of them.

"Rachel, come on. Stop. I didn't meant that. Let's just talk, please."

She heard Ana's voice echoing from the top of the steps, but she didn't stop to turn around.

Ana was right. Her deposition on Wednesday was a big deal, and she needed to stop pretending it wasn't. She needed to get her mind ready for what was about to happen when she stepped into that conference room. She needed to finally be honest with herself and with whatever attorney was deposing her. She had been lying to herself for a long time about what had happened in that operating room, just like she had been lying to herself about being able to separate Ana from this lawsuit. It was time to come clean. About everything.

Chapter Forty-three

A na had worked from home on Wednesday. She couldn't stand the idea of being in her office while Rachel was down the hall being deposed by Micah fucking Willis. She hated the idea of him with his smug face and stupid ponytailed hair asking Rachel questions. She hated that Rachel would be so close to her office but she wouldn't be able to grab her hand and walk her down the hall and show it to her like every other couple at the firm. No. She didn't get that luxury because she was supposed to be the one seated across the table from Rachel. She was supposed to be the one drilling her with questions about what happened in that operating room. She was the one who was supposed to be putting her career first before anything and anyone. She had done the right thing the other night. They needed a break, a pause, to clear their heads and get things in order. She knew it was the right choice. Maybe that wasn't the way she would have liked it to have gone, and she definitely said things she regretted, but ultimately Ana had done the right thing. Ana rubbed her temples. But if that was true, then why had she sat on her couch surrounded by work but only thinking about Rachel?

She hadn't spoken to Rachel since she had left her standing at the top of the subway steps mumbling like an idiot for her to stop. She should have chased after her. She should have done something. But Ana was never one for dramatics, and she had assumed Rachel would call her the next day.

When she didn't, Ana broke down and called her late that night, assuming she would be done volunteering and ready to talk.

That assumption had also been wrong.

She had texted and called Rachel a dozen times over the last week, and there was nothing but silence on the other end. She knew she wasn't blocked because her messages were being read, but there weren't any dancing bubbles on her screen to give her hope now.

Ana had thought Rachel might call her Wednesday night once the deposition was over. She had hoped that with that behind her, Rachel would be ready to start fresh. To talk about where they went from here. But still, there was silence.

Now it was Friday, an entire week since she had seen or heard from Rachel, and the silence was deafening. Maybe that was her answer. Maybe the place they went from here was nowhere. Maybe it was just too much for them to overcome in the end. But how? How, now that the worst part was over, could things be ending?

She knew she had messed up with the whole "let's take a pause" thing. But she hadn't expected it to be relationship ending. The thought of losing Rachel made Ana sick to her stomach. What the hell had she been thinking?

Over the past week, Ana had kept her promise to Paul. She had worked until midnight almost every night, even on Saturday and Sunday, and her hours were quickly entering the range that the partners liked to see. The of counsel numbers. The numbers that meant no social life whatsoever.

"Hey kiddo," she heard from the entrance to her office.

Ana lifted her sleepy eyes to the door and saw Stella standing there in typical three-piece suit fabulousness.

"Hey."

Stella stepped into the office and sat down across the desk from her.

"Still no word, I take it?"

"Nope, not a peep." She tossed her phone down on the table and rested her head in her hands. She couldn't remember a time she had been this tired. Maybe after taking the bar exam? But even then, she didn't feel like this. This was a hollowness that usually only came after excessive drinking and late nights of dancing and fun. But this was a different kind of hangover. This was a hangover born not from a night of festivities, but from a week of anxiety mixed with overworking and undereating.

"Shit, I'm sorry, Ana," Stella said, reaching across the table and patting her hand. "Any word on how the deposition went?"

Ana shook her head. "No. Every time I try to find that little twat, Micah, he's down in the basement or off shadowing some attorney at court conferences. The kid is a ghost the last two days."

The sound of a phone ringing caused Ana to jump. Alas, it was only her work phone.

"Ana Mendez," she said. "You got it, be right there."

Ana stood and straightened out her pant suit. "Paul wants to see me. Probably firing me for looking like the damn Corpse Bride this week."

"Or," Stella said wiggling her eyebrows, "this could be it, Ana. You've been working around the clock—who knows, maybe it's finally paying off!"

Ana nodded and picked up her personal cell phone one more time to check it before leaving it on the desk. No notifications.

"Sure," she said, walking out of her office.

Ana walked down the long, narrow hall, passing the row of window offices as she did. It was hard to see the allure to them right now when she was this tired, but she was sure it was there in some way. There was once a time when this had been all she wanted: To march into one of these offices that overlooked the city. To finally do something that made her parents proud. To feel like she had achieved something after so many years of grueling work. But right now, these offices felt as empty as she did.

She knocked on Paul's office door and opened it slowly. Inside, she was surprised to see the elusive Micah Willis himself sitting at one of the chairs across from Paul's desk.

"There she is!" Paul said, motioning for Ana to shut the door. "When you said you'd buckle down, wow, did you really mean it. What a stellar week it's been, Ana. I take if you've heard about the deposition Wednesday?"

Ana narrowed her eyes at Micah. "Actually no. I've tried to find Micah several times, but he never seems to be around."

"So busy racing back and forth, I rarely get the luxury of sitting in my office. Hey, maybe once I'm a senior associate, things will get easier, like they are for you." His smug face made her want to punch him in her exhaustion.

"What happened?" Ana asked taking a seat.

"Well, it seems our up-and-coming junior associate here was able to learn some crucial information about the *Solomon* case. Why don't you take a look?"

He slid a deposition transcript across the desk at her.

"You ordered a rush transcript?" Ana asked, turning to Micah. "Did the client approve the extra cost?"

"Never mind that." Paul motioned to the booklet. "Turn to page fifty-seven."

Ana complied and flipped through until she found the page and started reading the transcript in silence.

> **Mr. Willis:** Describe what you observed when Dr. Schumacher entered the operating room on the date in question.
>
> **Dr. Cohen:** I saw that his eyes were bloodshot and he appeared to be intoxicated.

"Holy shit," Ana said, looking up at Paul.

"Keep reading." Paul's eyes were gleaming in a way she had never seen them before. Ana returned her attention to the transcript.

> **Mr. Willis:** What makes you say he appeared to be intoxicated?
>
> **Mr. Blackstone:** Note my objection to this entire line of questioning.
>
> **Dr. Cohen:** He was slurring his speech, and I could smell an odor of alcohol coming from him.
>
> **Mr. Blackstone:** Doctor, do you need to take a break? Why don't we—
>
> **Dr. Cohen:** No, I do not need to take a break.
>
> **Mr. Willis:** What did you do when you observed Dr. Schumacher to be intoxicated prior to the operation?
>
> **Dr. Cohen:** I told him we should stop. I told him that he was not in any condition to operate and that he needed to go home.
>
> **Mr. Willis:** And what did Dr. Schumacher say in response?
>
> **Dr. Cohen:** I believe his exact words were "go fuck yourself."

"Holy shit," Ana said aloud. She kept reading the sentences over and over again to make sure her exhausted eyes were not playing tricks on her.

> **Mr. Willis:** Did you leave the operating room at any point prior to the operation to report Dr. Schumacher's condition to anyone?

Dr. Cohen: I'm ashamed to say I did not. I wish I had. Looking back now—looking at everything that happened, I regret my lack of action every single day. I wish I had done more. I was young and foolish. It's no excuse, I know, but I was scared. I told several people in the operating room that day that he shouldn't be operating, but everyone told me I was just a resident and to be quiet and remember my place. They told me he was fine. But they were wrong. I was wrong. We were all wrong.

Ana closed the transcript and set it on her lap processing everything she had just read. She didn't need to go on. Those few sentences alone were enough to sink the doctors' case. Rachel Cohen had just won Ana her entire lawsuit.

Ana couldn't believe it. She was right. All of her instincts that had told her all along that something more was hiding behind this surgery was right. The canned testimony from the other doctors and OR nurses, the scripted head nods and "I don't recalls," it was all a lie. This changed everything, this—

Her mind went to the woman who had given the damning testimony. Was this what had been weighing down on Rachel for so long? This whole time she had known her, and even long before then, Rachel had been living with this burden. All of her long hours and dedication. All of her personally returning patients' calls in the middle of the night even when she wasn't on call. It all made sense now. She felt responsible for what had happened to Mark Solomon, and she was spending her life trying to atone for it.

Ana's heart broke imagining what Rachel must have been going through these past few years. The guilt that must weigh down on her every single day. It was enough to bring Ana to tears just thinking of it.

"Don't you see what this means?" Micah said. "It means a major settlement coming our way. I just won our entire case. Boy, you should have seen her attorney's face too. He was turning ten shades of red the more she talked. And the attorney for the doctors, Cherry?"

"Sheryl," Ana corrected.

"Yeah, whatever, she was totally tweaking too. Kept clearing her throat like that was going to make the doctor stop spilling the beans."

Paul clapped his hands together loudly. "This is big, Ana. This is exactly what the partners are looking for out of our of counsel attorneys. I am proud to say I put your name in for the position this morning. They're going to make you a formal offer by the end of the week."

"I don't know what to say," Ana said, her mind swirling in a dozen different directions.

"Say yes," Paul said, standing up and reaching over the desk to shake her hand. "You just earned yourself a promotion."

CHAPTER FORTY-FOUR

Rachel staggered up the steps of the subway station. It was past ten thirty, much later than she usually stayed for Shabbat dinners. But the idea of going home to an empty apartment was more depressing than sitting at her parents' house while they peppered her with questions about Ana.

"She's just so lovely," her mother had said.

"And smart," her father had said.

"And hot," Noa had said.

Rachel had just sat there nodding and agreeing for hours on end, taking respite by playing with the kids whenever she could. She knew all of those things about Ana. She had always known all of those things about Ana. Having them tossed in her face while she was being stubborn and ignoring her calls and texts wasn't helping Rachel feel like she was making the right decision. But what choice did she really have? She had to get that stupid deposition out of the way. She had to finally tell the truth. And now, what if Ana didn't want her anymore? What if she had heard the truth from the attorney who had deposed her and decided that Rachel's sins were just too much to forgive? She had let a man die, for heaven's sake. And she had kept it from Ana for months. She wouldn't want to see her either if she was Ana.

Her shoulders slumped as she walked up the steps one by one. It was only a few blocks to her apartment, but each step felt like a mile. She was tired. Truly tired.

This past week had been one of the most exhausting of her entire life. She had introduced Ana to her parents only to turn around and cut her out of her life for an entire week, the same week when she had finally come clean about what had happened during the Mark Solomon surgery. There was still no word from her attorney, but she concluded based on his response during the deposition that her testimony had severely hurt the defense's case.

Good. She was glad she did it. It needed to be said. That man's family needed to know the truth. She hoped that by being honest, some good might yet come of this mess she had helped create. She knew no amount of money could ever really make Mark Solomon's family whole again. Not after a loss like that. She hadn't done enough to stop Dr. Schumacher back then, but she sure as hell did everything she could on Wednesday.

Thinking back to the testimony gave her a sense of lightness. She could finally let it all go now. She would always feel partially responsible for what had happened to Mark Solomon that day, but she had told the truth, and the truth, it seemed, really could set someone free. Unfortunately, telling the truth the same weekend you were breaking up with your girlfriend could also make you feel like you just ran a marathon.

As she rounded the corner, she had to blink twice and convince herself that she wasn't imagining things. Sitting on the steps in front of her building was Ana. She looked gaunt and worn, like she hadn't slept in days. Dark circles pooled under her brown eyes.

"Hi," Ana said, standing up.

"Hi," Rachel replied in shock. "What are you doing here?"

"You weren't answering any of my calls or texts."

"So naturally that means you show up at my apartment?"

There was a pause, and Ana looked as if she was contemplating what to say next.

Ana clenched and unclenched her jaw. "I know about the deposition."

Rachel nodded. "So, what, you came here to break up with me in person, then?"

"That's your problem, you know that?" Ana crossed her arms.

Rachel took a step closer. "What's my problem? Please, tell me, Counselor."

"You always assume the worst. It's your way of trying to control the outcome. You assume the worst so that way when it happens, you can say that you already knew it was going to happen. Like that somehow makes it less painful or something."

Rachel let out a loud huff. "Please, like you know me so well after a few months?"

The words stung; she could see that from a flicker in Ana's eyes. But the woman wasn't backing down. Instead, she was moving closer to Rachel.

"I know you better than you realize," Ana said defiantly. "I know you care about what happened in that operating room." She took another step. "I know you feel guilty for not doing more to stop the surgeon."

Rachel swallowed hard, trying to maintain her composure as Ana continued to close the space between them.

"I know you're a really good fucking doctor who cares about her patients."

"Well, that's—"

"And I know you missed me just as much as I missed you this past week."

Ana stopped, but she was close enough to touch. Close enough for Rachel to reach out to her if she wanted. Instead, she bit down on her lip until it was almost bleeding instead.

"I know you have feelings for me, Rachel." Ana looked up at her, her eyes now warm and soft. "And that's really good news, because I am absolutely fucking crazy about you."

Ana took the final few steps and grabbed Rachel's face, pulling her down into a kiss. Rachel didn't fight it. She didn't want to fight it. All she wanted was to pull Ana so close she couldn't feel the difference between their bodies anymore. She never wanted to let this woman go. Not tonight, not tomorrow, not ever.

She had never felt stronger and more at peace with herself than she had since she met Ana. Everyone could see the change in Rachel, and everyone could see that it had been for the better. There was no going back now.

"I missed you," Rachel finally managed to say between breathless kisses.

"I'm so sorry," Ana said, stopping long enough to look Rachel fully in the eyes. "For what I said. For not coming after you. And for waiting so long to show up here."

"I'm sorry too," Rachel said, holding back tears. "Come upstairs?" she said hopefully.

"I thought you'd never ask."

There was a difference in the way they moved together that night. As if nothing between them was rushed anymore. Rachel took her time caressing Ana's nipples, tracing kisses down her neck, her stomach, and eventually her clit. And the way Ana moved in response felt different. Like she had been holding back this entire time and now she was free to fully relax into Rachel's touch. She moaned louder, whimpered softer, and came harder than she ever had with Rachel. And when they drifted off to sleep, naked and wrapped in each other's arms, Rachel slept better than she had since the Mark Solomon surgery.

CHAPTER FORTY-FIVE

The next day Ana decided to take Rachel to a matinee of *Wicked*. For a woman who had spent her entire life in the city, Rachel had seen an alarmingly small number of Broadway shows, a situation which Ana sought to remedy immediately. There was an ease between them now. The deposition was done, the truth was out, and they could finally stop being so secretive about their relationship. Well, once the case settled. Of course, with Rachel's testimony it was a sure thing. But as the partner, Paul would handle the settlement negotiations, not Ana. Ana's work on the case was done. It was now just a question of how much Mrs. Solomon would be getting from the insurance companies.

"You know what I can't stop thinking about?" Ana said as they waited in line at will call. "What your mom said to me at dinner. About how much just being subpoenaed to testify affected you."

Rachel tucked a strand of hair behind her ear. "Why?"

"I don't know. I guess I never thought about how it would impact doctors—good doctors like you."

Rachel sighed. "We're not all Dr. Schumacher. In fact, most of us aren't like him at all. Most of us became doctors because we wanted to be the change we want to see in the world. We wanted to leave a positive impact and help people in a big way. It's not fun to be the one to answer the phone at three a.m. when your patient is having chest pains. It's not fun to work so many weekends and be off random Thursdays. But it's worth it in the end, you know?"

Ana nodded. "I wonder how I would feel, defending good doctors like you."

Rachel raised her eyebrows. "Yeah? Thinking about switching to medical malpractice, Counselor?"

Ana shrugged. "No. I mean, that would be ridiculous. I just got this promotion, after all."

Rachel grabbed Ana's shoulder and squeezed. "Mazel tov again, by the way. I'm so proud of you." She kissed Ana's cheek.

Ana whispered "Thank you" in Hebrew.

"Someone's been practicing." Rachel smiled.

"Well, I can't exactly keep losing in our little bedroom lessons, can I?"

Rachel shrugged. "I wouldn't complain if you did."

They stepped up to the counter and gave Ana's name, collecting their tickets. Orchestra center for sixty bucks? Yes, please. Rachel laughed as Ana swiped her card.

"You really are a wizard at these deals. Too bad hustling isn't a field of law—you could open your own practice."

"What can I say, I know how to get what I want." Ana laughed as they made their way into the Gershwin Theater. "But really, think about all of the good doctors who get wrongfully named in these malpractice suits. And their insurance companies don't feel like fighting it so they just pay, even if they did nothing wrong. That's gotta be so frustrating."

"You're really stuck on this, aren't you?"

"It's just been bothering me ever since I talked to your mom."

Rachel sighed. "Welcome to Judaism 101, my dear. If your parents aren't guilting you about your life choices, they aren't doing it right."

Ana laughed. "Well, in that case, may I introduce you to my friend, Catholicism? You should meet my mother. She'll have you convinced you're either a saint or a sinner damned to hell in five minutes."

"I'd love to," Rachel said, smiling at her as they took their seats. "Meet her, that is."

Ana kissed Rachel's hand and browsed the Playbill. She hadn't technically accepted the promotion yet. She'd asked Paul for a week to think it over. She wasn't sure why. This was everything she had been working for for the last five years. She should jump at the chance now that it was presented to her on a silver platter. But she hadn't jumped. Instead, she had paused. *Pause*. That simple word that Rachel had taught her over the last few months. The word that went against everything she had ever been taught her entire life.

The pause. It was everything Ana was not, and yet, when she was with Rachel, it felt natural. Rachel made Ana feel still, calm, assured. She didn't need to constantly be striving for validation when she was with her. Rachel was proud of her no matter what she did. Heck, she was proud when she got them cheap theater seats. She didn't need to try to prove anything with Rachel. She could simply exist, and Rachel was content to exist right alongside her.

Soon, the lights were going down and the overture played. They were so close she could see the paint on Elphaba's ears.

Ana looked over at Rachel halfway through the performance. The stage lights bounced off of her porcelain face, making her bright eyes dance and sparkle. Ana wasn't lying when she told Rachel she was crazy about her last night. But that was only a silly substitute for the word she really felt. The word that society told her it was too soon to admit out loud. The word that she would keep in her back pocket until the time felt right.

She looked back to the stage and watched as Elphaba and Glinda held hands, staring into each other's eyes.

As the lyrics to "For Good" echoed softly through the room, Ana looked back at Rachel, grabbed her hand, and smiled.

EPILOGUE

The sea breeze swirled around Rachel's neck, tickling her hairline. It was May, but in Miami that meant it was only less hot than really hot and sometimes it was cloudy in the afternoons.

They had spent last Christmas here in Miami, at Rachel's insistence, and still been back in time to celebrate some of Chanukah with her family.

"Thank you for bringing her home, mija," Ana's mom had whispered in her ear when she hugged her for the first time.

The palm trees covered in Christmas lights had made Rachel laugh at first, but soon she settled in to the routine of south Florida. She had gotten to know Ana's family in such a special way that trip. That's why, now, she felt comfortable asking them for help with the little surprise she had planned for later that evening.

"Thank you, everyone, for coming," said Ana's brother, Antonio, into a microphone.

About twenty or so people clapped and hooted, Ana loudest of all. They were all Ana and Antonio's childhood friends and family who had showed up to support him. Then they were having a big cookout back at Ana's parents' house to celebrate.

"This shop is a dream I've had for a long time. I want to thank my papi for teaching me everything he knows about cars."

"Almost everything!" Ana's father shouted from the crowd. There was an eruption of laughter as Antonio nodded.

"Guess I'll have to get you on payroll soon, then!"

More laughter. Ana clapped beside Rachel, her grin reaching all the way up to her ears.

Ana had not accepted the promotion at Bryon & Browning. Instead, she had taken a job with Sheryl Peterson's firm. She was now defending good doctors in medical malpractice lawsuits. It fit naturally with dating a doctor. Plus it came with a pay raise, easier hours, and a better sense of fulfillment. At least, that's how Ana had put it when she came running into Rachel's apartment to tell her about it.

That was six months ago. In June, it would be Ana and Rachel's anniversary. Well, anniversary of meeting each other, anyway, and that was enough. Because for Rachel, once she laid eyes on Ana, there had never been anyone else.

Antonio finished his speech and cut a red ribbon in front of the garage. Everyone clapped and cheered and lined up to hug and congratulate him. Rachel stayed a few people behind Ana as she stood in line to see him.

"Mazel tov," Rachel said, hugging his wide shoulders. "Still set for later?" she whispered in his ear.

He let her go and gave her a firm nod. "You got it, sis."

Rachel smiled and tucked a strand of hair behind her ear.

They all went back to Ana's parents' house and the cookout officially began. Ana's mom had special dishes catered and set to the side with little Stars of David over them indicating that they were kosher. "For Raquel only" the sign said, with ten exclamation points. Rachel had laughed when she saw it, and it warmed her heart that Ana's mother had made such an effort to make her feel included. She still didn't have the heart to tell her that she wasn't kosher. She also secretly loved that Ana's mother called her Raquel instead of Rachel, no matter how many times Ana corrected her.

A few hours later, Rachel grabbed Ana and pulled her aside. "Let's go for a walk on the beach to see the sunset."

"It's a half hour walk to the beach, my love," Ana replied.

Rachel shrugged. "Maybe Antonio can give us a ride in his sweet Mustang convertible?"

Ana looked over at her brother. "And take him away from his party? Yeah right, he lives for these glory moments."

Rachel shot Antonio a beckoning look and he was at her side within seconds. "What's up, little sis?"

"Antonio, I'm older than you."

He shrugged. "Yeah, but physically you're my little sis."

Ana rolled her eyes. "Whatever. Feel like blowing this Popsicle stand and giving two gals a ride to the beach?"

"You got it, boss," he said before pulling his keys out of his pocket.

A look of shock spread over Ana's face. "Well, that was easy."

Rachel shrugged. "Must be riding the high of the event."

Ana looked around. "I do feel bad leaving everyone here. I mean, they came to see me too, not just Antonio."

Rachel grabbed Ana's hand. "I promise to have you back before you turn into a pumpkin. Thirty minutes won't kill you, right?"

Ana laughed. "Deal."

Soon they were racing down the side streets, passing rows of tiny houses with even smaller yards. The candy apple red machine roared down the road like a lion on the prowl. The deep rumble of the old car mixed with the wind blowing in their hair gave Rachel a sense of excitement and freedom. For a moment, she let herself forget what she was about to do. Antonio pulled up to the sand and stayed in the driver's seat. The parking lot was empty except for them. It was a local beach, and locals didn't really care about sunsets on the East Coast.

"You two go, I gotta make a few calls."

Ana smirked. "Oh yes, important businessman now, I get it."

Rachel gave him a knowing nod and winked as they got out of the car. She took Ana's hand as they walked, the sun just beginning its final descent behind them. They walked down by the water, staying close to Antonio. After about ten minutes, she looked back to the car and took a few more steps before stopping and dropping to one knee.

"Ana," Rachel said. "From the moment I met you, I knew you were different than anyone else. I've loved every second I've spent with you this last year, and even some of the not so great seconds." Rachel laughed nervously. "I never want to wake up and not see your face. Ana Mendez, will you...will you..."

She couldn't get the last words out before crying, and Ana dropped to her knees in the sand in front of her.

"Yes," Ana said, grabbing Rachel's face. "Yes, yes."

They stayed that way on their knees in the sand for a second, embracing each other and kissing. Suddenly, from the parking lot, a song began to play loudly.

"Oh my God," Ana said, laughing through her tears.

They both looked back at the parking lot to see it was now full of cars. Ana's parents and friends had all piled into as few cars as possible and were now lining the parking lot cheering and waving and honking their horns while Antonio blared music from his Mustang and grinned from ear to ear. He was holding his phone up, and Ana could see two tiny faces from where she sat in the sand. Charlotte and Stella were smiling back at her, their heads pressed close together.

"Can you hear the song?" Rachel asked, before kissing Ana's cheek.

"Of course I can." Ana burst into laughter and started to cry. "It's the freaking *Lion King*."

You Are Invited

to the Wedding of

Rachel Talia Cohen

and

Ana Sofía Mendez

5:00 P.M.
July 26, 2026
The Riverside Church
New York, New York

About the Author

Morgan lives in Boston, Massachusetts, with her beautiful wife and their three fur babies. She was raised in Orlando, Florida, and moved to New York City shortly after attending law school in Virginia. A product of the many places she has lived, Morgan enjoys a wide array of hobbies, including exploring historical homes, hiking, scuba diving, traveling, and volunteering in her local community.

Morgan loves connecting with her readers and she can be reached at AuthorMorganAdams@gmail.com. Follow her on Instagram to find out about her upcoming works.

Books Available From Bold Strokes Books

A Conflict of Interest by Morgan Adams. Tensions rise when a one-night stand becomes a major conflict of interest between an up-and-coming senior associate and a dedicated cardiac surgeon. (978-1-63679-870-7)

A Magnificent Disturbance by Lee Lynch. These everyday dykes and their friends will stop at nothing to see the women's clinic thrive and, in the process, their ideals, their wounds, and a steadfast allegiance to one another make them heroes. (978-1-63679-031-2)

Big Corpse on Campus by Karis Walsh. When University Police Officer Cappy Flannery investigates what looks like a clear-cut suicide, she discovers that the case—and her feelings for librarian Jazz—are more complicated than she expected. (978-1-63679-852-3)

Charity Case by Jean Copeland. Bad girl Lindsay Chase came home to Connecticut for a fresh start, but an old, risky habit provides the chance to save the day for her new love, Ellie. (978-1-63679-593-5)

Moments to Treasure by Ali Vali. Levi Montbard and Yasmine Hassani have found a vast Templar treasure, but there is much more to the story—and what is left to be found. (978-1-63679-473-0)

The Stolen Girl by Cari Hunter. Detective Inspector Jo Shaw is determined to prove she's fit for work after an injury that almost killed her, but a new case brings her up against people who will do anything to preserve their own interests, putting Jo—and those closest to her—directly in the line of fire. (978-1-63679-822-6)

Discovering Gold by Sam Ledel. In 1920s Colorado, a single mother and a rowdy cowgirl must set aside their fears and initial reservations about one another if they want to find love in the mining town each of them calls home. (978-1-63679-786-1)

Dream a Little Dream by Melissa Brayden. Savanna can't believe it when Dr. Kyle Remington, the woman who left her feeling like a fool, shows up in Dreamer's Bay. Life is too complicated for second chances. Or is it? (978-1-63679-839-4)

Goodbye Hello by Heather K O'Malley. With so much time apart and the challenges of a long-distance relationship, Kelly and Teresa's second chance at love may end just as awkwardly as the first. (978-1-63679-790-8)

Emma by the Sea by Sarah G. Levine. A delightful modern-day romance inspired by *Emma*, one of Jane Austen's most beloved novels. (978-1-63679-879-0)

One Measure of Love by Annie McDonald. Vancouver's hit competitive cooking show *Recipe for Success* has begun filming its second season, and two talented young chefs are desperate for more than a winning dish. (978-1-63679-827-1)

The Smallest Day by J.M. Redmann. The first bullet missed—can Micky Knight stop the second bullet from finding its target? (978-1-63679-854-7)

To Please Her by Elena Abbott. A spilled coffee leads Sabrina into a world of erotic BDSM that may just land her the love of her life. (978-1-63679-849-3)

Two Weddings and a Funeral by Claudia Parr. Stella and Theo have spent the last thirteen years pretending they can be just friends, but surely "just friends" don't make out every chance they get. (978-1-63679-820-2)

Firecamp by Jaycie Morrison. Going their separate ways seemed inevitable for two people as different as Fallon and Nora, while meeting up again is strictly coincidental. (978-1-63679-753-3)

Coming Up Clutch by Anna Gram. College softball star Kelly "Razor" Mitchell hung up her cleats early, but when former crush, now coach Ashton Sharpe shows up on her doorstep seven years later, beautiful as ever, Razor hopes the longing in her gaze has nothing to do with softball. (978-1-63679-817-2)

Fixed Up by Aurora Rey. When electrician Jack Barrow and artist Ellie Lancaster get stuck on a job site during a blizzard, close quarters send all sorts of sparks flying. (978-1-63679-788-5)

Stranded by Ronica Black. Can Abigail and Whitley overcome their personal hang-ups and stubbornness to survive not only Alaska but a dangerous stalker as well? (978-1-63679-761-8)

BOLDSTROKESBOOKS.COM

Looking for your next great read?

Visit BOLDSTROKESBOOKS.COM
to browse our entire catalog of paperbacks, ebooks,
and audiobooks.

Want the first word on what's new?
Visit our website for event info,
author interviews, and blogs.

Subscribe to our free newsletter for sneak peeks,
new releases, plus first notice of promos
and daily bargains.

SIGN UP AT
BOLDSTROKESBOOKS.COM/signup

Bold Strokes Books
Quality and Diversity in LGBTQ Literature

*Bold Strokes Books is an award-winning publisher
committed to quality and diversity in LGBTQ fiction.*

www.ingramcontent.com/pod-product-compliance
Lightning Source LLC
Chambersburg PA
CBHW022014010726
47494CB00003B/1035